# Shopgirls

**Also by Jessica Anya Blau**

*Mary Jane*

*The Summer of Naked Swim Parties*

*Drinking Closer to Home*

*The Wonder Bread Summer*

*The Trouble with Lexie*

# Shopgirls

A Novel

Jessica Anya Blau

MARINER BOOKS
*New York Boston*

HarperCollins books may be purchased for educational, business, or sales promotional use. For information, please email the Special Markets Department at SPsales@harpercollins.com.

The Mariner flag design is a registered trademark of HarperCollins Publishers LLC.

FIRST EDITION

*Designed by Renata DiBiase*

Library of Congress Cataloging-in-Publication Data has been applied for.

ISBN 978-0-06-305235-2

25 26 27 28 29 LBC 5 4 3 2 1

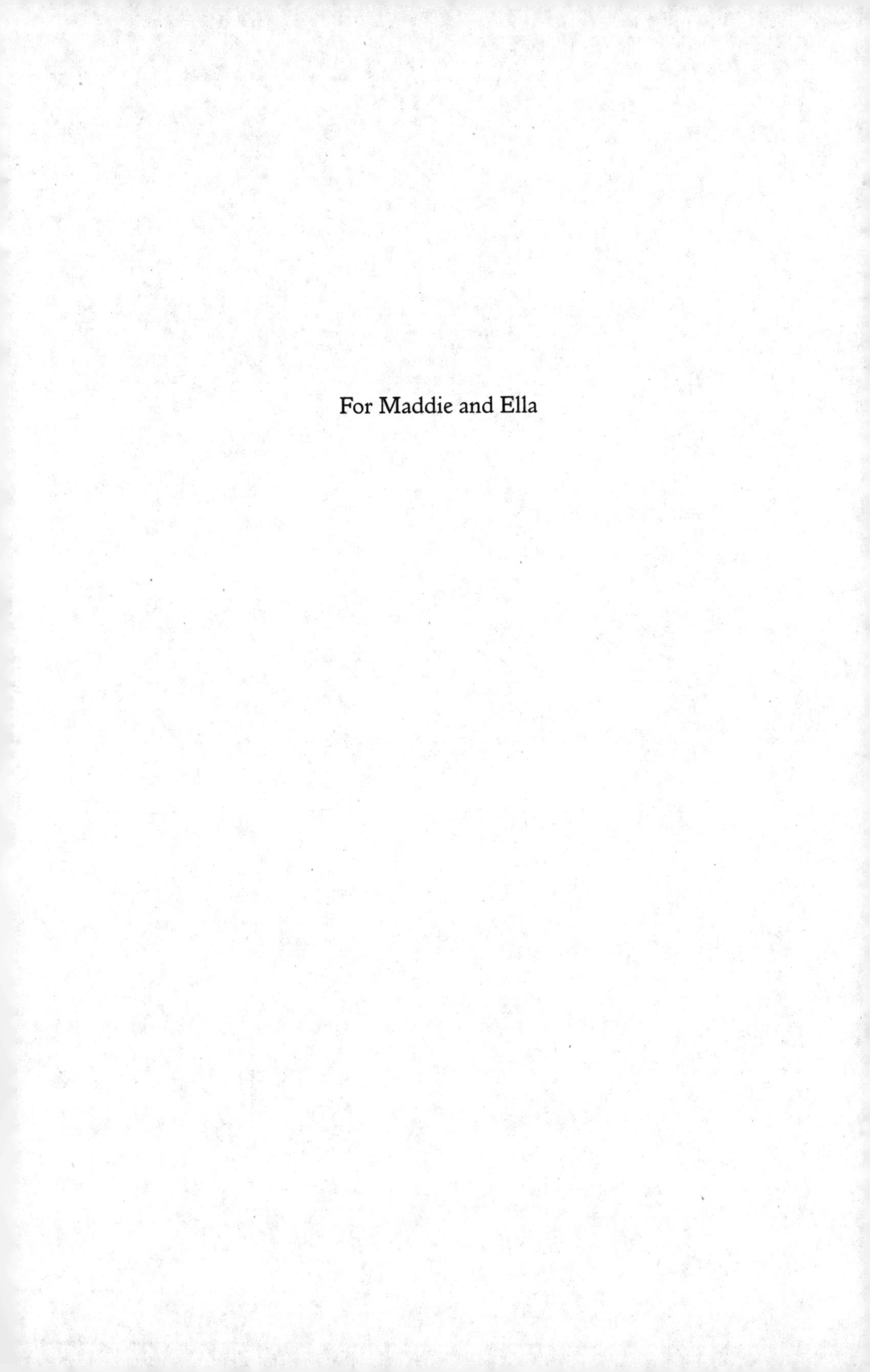

For Maddie and Ella

# Shopgirls

# Chapter 1

**I had been** working as a salesgirl at I. Magnin, "San Francisco's Finest Department Store," for one month when the guy from the shoe department leaned in to my ear and whispered, "See me when you can." He was beside me in line at the employee entrance and exit where we clocked in each morning and had our bags checked at the end of each day.

"Huh?" I smiled nervously. Each shift, I showed up expecting to be fired for any or all of the following reasons: (1.) I'd never bought anything from I. Magnin (money was something other people had); (2.) I was rotating three cobbled-together Salvation Army outfits (two pencil skirts on which I'd replaced the zippers and buttons; two bleached and starch-ironed blouses, either of which went with both skirts; and one slate-blue shift dress, shortened, spot-cleaned, and ironed to look as sleek as a slab of steel); (3.) I wore the same Salvation Army pumps every shift, which I tried to make new by regularly coloring in the scuff marks with eyeliner and then blending and buffing the eyeliner with Vaseline.

"Your pumps. They could use some sprucing up. Come see me at Second-Floor Shoes and I'll take them to the back and make them look like new." He stamped his time card, dropped it in the wall slot, and stepped into the employee elevator.

I wasn't sure if I should be embarrassed or grateful. I quickly stamped my time card and then fumbled with it and watched it sail, like a leaf, to the dank, flat carpet. When I picked it up, I glanced at the line of people behind me. Every one of them was wearing flawless, pristine shoes.

"See you on your break!" the shoe guy said as the elevator doors closed.

I. Magnin's back halls and employee stairs reminded me of the shadowy, cluttered wings of my high school theater. Each time I walked out onto the sales floor, it felt like I was making a curtain call. That day, I paused for a breath. I needed to regain my composure, and, in a way, I needed to find the character I was playing before I walked onstage. On the other side of that door were professionals, life-timers who dressed like they'd floated directly off the pages of *Vogue*. I was a girl who had shopped by cruising I. Magnin, and places like it, to see what was in fashion and then sifting through the dirty-sweat-sock-smelling racks at the Salvation Army to buy pieces that resembled what I'd seen in the luxury boutiques.

After a few breaths, I opened the heavy beige door, pulled up my spine, and stepped onto the gleaming marble of the first floor: cosmetics and accessories. When I shut the door behind me, it disappeared into the pink velvet wallpaper. By now I'd talked to enough of the women at the glass-case counters to know that no matter how glamorous they looked, at the end of each day they went home, kicked off their high heels, rubbed their sore stockinged feet, and turned on the lineup of the night. That year, 1985, Thursday was the best night for TV: it started with *The Cosby Show* and then went to *Family Ties*, *Cheers*, and *Night Court*. I wondered what these women ate while they watched TV. Most of the salesgirls were so skinny, I couldn't imagine them scarfing down a burrito the size of a preemie baby. Or eating a plate of nachos washed down with a Coke. How did they do it?

The woman at the Estée Lauder counter wasn't one of the skinny ones. She was the size of a large man, always draped in black, with a glittery face and short hair that looked like an oil spill covering her head. Her name was Mimi. When I recited the cosmetic women's names to Raquel Martinez, my roommate, she said, "It sounds like the Playmate of the Month lineup." It did. Misty, Mimi, Camilla, Sulinda, Vivi, Kat, Analise . . . there were no Debbies or Kathys in cosmetics. Next to theirs, my name was like a bee sting. Or a sound. Or maybe a feeling more than a name.

"ZIPPY!" Mimi said, and I went right to her. She was my first friend at I. Magnin. We'd met in the lunchroom my second day; both of us were shoveling in the baked mac 'n' cheese. That was an eating day for me: I'd recently started a new diet Raquel had invented in which we only ate every other day. Raquel swore it worked and I had no reason not to believe her. She was skinny. In those years there didn't seem to be a girl or woman alive who didn't want to be skinny.

"Heya!" I rushed to Mimi and stood on the customer side of the counter as she went back to opening her register. I ran my hand along the eye shadow testers. "May I?"

"Be my guest, girlie. You know I got you covered."

While Mimi opened the cash bag and counted out bills into her register, I examined my face in the mirror. Eyes: brown. Hair: honey colored. Nose: straight with nostrils tucked flat so it was impossible to see up them without a lifted chin. Skin: freckled. Mouth: wide, each lip the width of a pencil.

Mimi whispered, "Five, ten, fifteen . . ."

As far as I could tell, I was a blank canvas. A clean slate. A line drawing or a Charlie Brown cartoon. And after nineteen years of being the girl no one noticed (okay, wait, there was one guy who noticed me once. A man. He stopped me on the street and said, "Girl! You know, you'd be *totally* cute if you lost ten pounds!" I didn't know how to respond, so I said nothing and rushed past him, my back feeling like it was a billboard about to be egged), I'd decided that I wanted to be like Raquel. Pretty. Thin. And stylish. The thin and stylish part, I knew how to achieve. Prettiness, though? I wasn't sure how that would ever come to me.

Mimi stopped counting bills, reached under the counter, and handed me a tube of foundation. "Use this first. Put it on your ring finger and tap it on. Tap. Tap. Tap." She tapped herself with the finger I'd always called Lazy Man and then counted out her ones.

I opened the tube, squeezed some onto my fingertip, and applied it exactly as Mimi had said. Instantly my skin looked like suede: smooth but with the faintest shimmer. Mimi pulled the coin tubes out of her money bag, set them on the counter, and then reached her long, thick arm around to the testers and pulled out eyeliner and mascara.

"Line the outer edges of your eyes. And use this mascara. I'll put the shadow on you when I'm done with the coins."

Mimi poured each roll of coins into its proper tray, making a winning-slot-machine sound. I'd only finished with the eyeliner when she reached over the counter, opened the mascara wand, and held it level with my pupil.

"Blink," she said. I did and the mascara wiped onto my top lashes. "Blink. Blink. Blink. Blink. Blink. Blink. Blink. Other eye."

I remained as I was as Mimi moved her hand to the other eye.

"Blink. Blink. Blink. Blink. Blink. Blink. Blink."

When she was done, she pulled out powder shadow and did some strange magic on my upper and lower lids so that my eyes looked like Beverly Johnson's: smoldering and doe-like.

"Perfect," Mimi said. "Come down before your lunch break so we can powder away any shine."

"Do I have shine?"

"You were shining at the end of your shift last Tuesday."

"Why didn't you tell me?!"

"It was the end of the day. I figured you were about to go home and wash it all off anyway."

She was right. I had washed it off. It was an eating day, which meant my post-work schedule was to put on sweatpants, pull my hair into a ponytail, and scarf down the kung pao chicken and pot stickers Raquel and I often picked up from our favorite place in Chinatown, Ka Ka Lucky Seafood Barbecue Restaurant. I loved the place so much that I tried to never disrespect them by shortening the name. I always said every single word: *Ka. Ka. Lucky. Seafood. Barbecue. Restaurant.* This drove Raquel crazy. She usually called it *Ka Ka Lucky* or, worse, *Ka Ka*.

"What perfume do you want to wear today?" Mimi asked.

"Poison gave me a headache yesterday."

"I put on Fendi today. Here—" Mimi held her wrist to my nose and I inhaled. It smelled woodsy and soft, like fresh water running over clean rocks and moss.

"Yum," I said.

"The Fendi girl has fake blue eyes," Mimi said. "Check them out when you take a spritz."

"How do you have fake eyes? Can she see?"

"She wears colored contacts."

"Does everything look blue to her?"

"No. There's a hole in the center for the pupil. Though sometimes there's a colored halo."

"How do you know? Do you have them?"

"I know a bunch of people who have them. Don't get them, because they can ruin your vision. That halo can stay for the rest of your life—it's like your eyes get used to it and then re-create it when you're not wearing the contacts."

"Okay, so no colored contacts. If I ever need contacts or glasses."

"Yup," Mimi said, and I left her to go to the Fendi counter. Sure enough, the woman's eyes were like blue spin art with lines radiating toward the pupil. She was on the phone and gave me a thumbs-up as I lifted the display bottle and sprayed my wrists and neck. Without breaking the pace in her conversation, she reached under the counter and pulled out a pile of glass vial samples that she released into my hand.

I mouthed *thanks*, dropped them into my sack purse, and waved goodbye. In the elevator going up, I restated what Mimi had told me about colored contacts so I could remember it clearly. There was so much daily advice coming toward me each shift that I'd started writing it down on hold tags and then taking the tags home and copying them into my Day-Timer. Just yesterday, the lady at La Mer told me to exclusively date men who wear a Rolex watch because those were the only ones with taste and class. Five minutes later the woman at Clinique asked me what I used to remove my makeup at night. I told her I used Vaseline on my eyes and Dove soap for my face. She said, "Oh, don't use Vaseline. Ever. It gets stuck in your eyes. I had a customer who used so much Vaseline, she had to go to the hospital and they removed her eyeball so they could scrape out the Vaseline." Raquel laughed so hard when I repeated that story to her. And then she laughed even more when she saw that I'd stopped using Vaseline. I knew I'd never have to get my eyeball removed. But what if there was some buildup? Maybe a small slice of that story was true?

I don't know if I was given advice because I was the youngest salesgirl in the store or if there was something on my face that conveyed my naivety to the other salesgirls. Could they see at first glance that I had little experience with boys and that I'd only recently moved out of the third-floor walk-up I'd shared with my mother and her husband, Howard? In some ways, this pod of in-person advice columnists replaced my mother, who had never held back anything. For as long as she'd been with him, my mother gave detailed reports on how she dealt with Howard's snoring, or how she got him to break his habit of clacking his spoon against his cereal bowl in a way that made her want to leap over the table and strangle him. Right before I'd moved out, she'd offered this piece of advice: "Don't sleep with a man if he doesn't cut his toenails. If I'd seen Howard's toenails *before* we'd had sex, there wouldn't have been any sex and he wouldn't be here now."

I'd slept with no one. And I'd only kissed one boy once: the guy who had the lead in my high school's production of *Bye Bye Birdie*. He broke up with me the day after our spit-filled kiss, citing a need to be free: "Like, we're never going to be seniors in high school again, and this is, like, the greatest year of our lives, right?" It certainly wasn't the greatest year of my life, but I didn't question his reasoning; all I felt was relief that I'd never have to endure that lip wrestling again.

Employees weren't allowed to use the customer elevators during store hours. We could use them before the store opened, though, so I got in the marble box, pushed five, and then tried to see myself in the reflection on the walls. If I put my face between the gold-and-brown veins in the white marble, I could see that I was truly there: a woman in the I. Magnin elevator.

I went to the bathrooms on the fifth floor before heading to my station. Most women in the city knew that I. Magnin had the best public toilets in San Francisco. Each door was solid wood and completely framed in so you didn't have to look at anyone's feet or hear their sounds. I had a hard time using public bathrooms in general—I was self-conscious and hated knowing what was going on beside me. But these bathrooms made everything okay. I could drink coffee or Diet Coke all day long and not worry about how many times I had to run in. Of course, employees were supposed to go to the ninth-floor lunchroom and use the bathrooms up there—regular ones with short metal doors the color of tobacco-stained teeth. But no one ever did. Not with private bathrooms like these around.

Miss Yolanda, whose station was Work Dresses and Suits, was washing her hands at the sink when I walked in. She was French, wore fitted skirt suits, and kept her hair cut close to her head like a brown velvet cap. She sucked hard candy all day and usually had a perfectly round ball sticking out of one cheek. She'd move that ball from side to side—sometimes in the middle of a sentence. I imagined it like a little animal that lived there and scurried from one cozy nook to another. Miss Yolanda seemed to hate everyone, even customers. But she sold the most on the floor because when she told people what to do, they obeyed. Women bought what she said they should buy and rarely did they bring anything back. I think it was because they were too afraid to face her on the sales floor if they dared walk in with a return.

She looked at me from her reflection in the mirror. "You're not allowed in this bathroom." She'd been in America so long, her French accent didn't sound sexy or alluring. It sounded *off.* Like she had phlegm stuck in her throat and a problem opening her mouth too wide.

"Neither are you."

"Seniority." She dried her hands on the thick hand towels that were arranged like a fan on the counter and then walked out.

When I came out of the bathroom, I spotted Miss Liaskis frantically punching keys on her register. She worked in Formal Dresses, had a frilly Greek accent, and wore frilly clothes—all lace, flouncy sleeves, and necklines with roller-coaster ribbons of fabric. Even her red hair was a frilly mop of dyed ringlets. I felt bad for Miss Liaskis because she couldn't do more than one thing at once and she could barely do the one thing she was doing. If she was ringing up someone, she couldn't answer a question or pick up the phone. And if she had one customer in a fitting room, that was all she could manage. It was as if her entire brain had to sit on hold and wait for that person to decide if they were going to buy anything or not. Recently, the cash registers had been updated and Miss Liaskis couldn't figure out how to open her register in the morning or close it at the end of the day. I helped her every time we worked together.

"Miss Zippy! I am waiting for you!" Miss Liaskis shouted. At I. Magnin, you were called *Miss*, followed by your first or last name, in every department but Cosmetics. Those women went by their first name unless they wanted to be called *Miss*. It was also only there that you might find a *Mrs.* Married or not, no one who sold clothes was ever a *Mrs.*

Miss Liaskis hugged me; she smelled like perfume and coffee. I came out of the hug and looked down at the hold tag, taped to the register, on which she'd written her sales number in a frilly script. I punched in her number and, when the drawer slid open, sorted the cash and counted out the bills so quickly, I felt like a blackjack dealer in Tahoe.

When I was done with Miss Liaskis, I moved on, passing Cocktail and Party Dresses, where Miss Braughn and Miss Braughn stood side by side at their register like *The Shining* twins. I waved at them. Only one waved back. The Braughn sisters were tall blond Canadians who acted like they were better than everyone else because they were Canadian. If you said anything about anything—like how much a slice of pizza cost or how crowded the BART train was or how long you had to wait at the dentist, they pointed out how it was better in Canada. Miss Yolanda often said to them, "Oh, go back to Canada and freeze your arse off if you think it's so much better."

The Braughn sisters didn't speak to me, nor did Miss Lee and

Miss Karen, who worked in Knit Dresses. They, along with Miss Yolanda (who spoke to me as if I were a small dog pooping on her lawn) appeared to hate me. Even Miss Lena, who worked in Petite Dresses with me, agreed with my assessment. And she didn't agree with me in the way mean girls in high school were happy to confirm any little self-loathing comment—she agreed in a comforting way. What she said was this: "Do not take it to heart, and forgive them if you can. It is very hard to work somewhere for twenty or thirty years and then to have a young person like you come in and sell more in their first week." Miss Lena herself wasn't jealous of my sales; her brain didn't appear to operate in the low places of jealousy or self-loathing or shame and embarrassment, even. And when I thought about it (which I did often when I worked with her), I couldn't even think of something she'd be able to dislike about herself or feel shameful about. Nothing! Miss Lena was all good. She loved Jesus more than anything, and she could see the better side of every person—like the salesgirls who were mean to me; the customers who dropped clothes inside out on the floor and then waited for you to pick them up; or the customers who bought dresses and then wore them with the tags hidden so they could return them the next day. (It was usually obvious—the armpits smelled like old bread, sometimes there were red wine spots, and always the dress had a softness to it from having been sheathed over a warm human body for so many hours.) And if being good wasn't enough, Miss Lena was also as pretty as Grace Kelly in that old jewel-thief movie with Cary Grant. It wasn't a showy pretty; in fact, it took a few days for me to notice. Every day, she wore a straight, starched sack dress that tied at the waist with a sash. She pulled her blond hair back into a tidy bun or a small ponytail, and she never wore a drop of makeup. Miss Lena claimed her face was typical of Yugoslavia, where she grew up and which she called Yugo. Yugo was one of her favorite subjects, along with Jesus, and Tito, the now-dead former leader of her home country.

"Zippy, you are here!" Miss Lena said when I arrived. Miss Lena enjoyed opening our cash drawer and had already done so. She was standing at the counter, straightening the hold tags, sales tickets, and pens.

"Here I am!" I did jazz hands, and Miss Lena applauded.

"You were in my dream last night and I can't remember what happened, but I remembered you were eating dinner and I was very happy."

"Was I eating a burrito? Raquel and I ordered burritos last night," I said. "I also ate rice and beans, even though I don't like rice and beans."

Miss Lena looked concerned. "Why do you eat the rice and beans if you don't like them?"

"Because they came free with the burrito. And it was an eating day, so I thought I shouldn't waste them."

"I am very confused by this diet Raquel has put you on. If you are hungry, eat!"

"Do you think Jesus or Mary or anyone from back then ever went on a diet?" I was asking this sincerely. To think of Jesus dieting, or Mary eating every other day, made dieting sound absurd. But it was hard to shut my eyes to the *get thin* message that was broadcast through the skinny people I saw on TV and in magazines (where there was *always* at least one article with dieting tips) and shopping the beautifully and sparsely displayed clothes at I. Magnin.

Miss Lena clapped her hands. "Jesus thinks each person is perfect exactly as he or she is born!"

Until Miss Lena, the only time I thought about Jesus was when I watched Jim Bakker on *The PTL Club*. *The PTL Club* was one of Howard's favorite shows. He shushed me when we watched because

I couldn't stop talking about *the way* Jim Bakker talked or his side-by-side-TV-shaped glasses or his wife who looked like Phyllis Diller but with more in-control hair and more out-of-control makeup. Howard never sent any money to *The PTL Club*, even though they asked for it several times every show. And he never talked about Jesus the way Miss Lena did. Once, I asked Howard *why* he liked *The PTL Club*. He shrugged and said, "Why do I like Ruffles ridged potato chips? I just do. No idea why." I sort of understood that answer, as I, too, felt almost hypnotized when *The PTL Club* was on.

I said to Miss Lena, "Well, Jesus definitely gave you perfection when you were born. I mean, come on! How many people have a face that doesn't even need mascara?"

Miss Lena laughed as if that were funny, even though I was entirely serious. I laughed too, only because she laughed.

Miss Yolanda approached us. She moved the mouth ball from one cheek to the other and said, "What are you jackals laughing about?"

"Jesus has blessed us today!" Miss Lena said.

"We'll see how much he's blessed us in ten minutes when the rats arrive."

Rats were what Miss Yolanda called customers, though not to their faces. I hadn't been there long enough for a big sale day, but Miss Dani, the manager of Fifth-Floor Dresses, once said that when there were big markdowns, the women poured in "like rats from a sewer." I wondered then if she had originated the term or if Miss Yolanda had. Also, did she mean the sheer number of customers was like rats from a sewer: a giant, snaking river of bodies? Or was she saying that sale days drew a less desirable crowd? I was too new and unsure of myself to ask Miss Dani to elaborate, and now that we were so many days past that statement, I couldn't bring it up again.

As usual, ten minutes before the store opened, Miss Dani came out of her office and walked the floor. Other than when she rolled out racks of clothes, or if I went into her office to ask a question, this was the only time I saw Miss Dani. I'd rarely even seen her in the lunchroom. The first time I entered her office, I was so surprised that I almost burst out laughing. The space was like the school broom closet. The floor was cement and the only light came from a bare bulb that hung so low, you couldn't help but lift your hand and give it a push to watch it swing. Even the beautiful clothes were crammed together on rolling racks that filled all the non-desk space. Still, doing what Miss Dani did seemed like one of the coolest jobs in the world. She got to *be* with the beautiful clothes, in the beautiful store, but she didn't have to act like she was one of the beautiful people the way we salesgirls did. It was like she was involved in the fun of the production, but never onstage.

Miss Dani waddled to Miss Lena and me, and then ran her hands down her body to show us the emerald knit dress she was wearing. "Andrea Jovine. The buying offices are loving it." Her voice was deep and clangy, like she was speaking from a metal bucket in her chest.

"Does it come in petite *and* regular?" I asked.

"Of course." Miss Dani was about Miss Lena's height but a lot thicker, so it looked like she'd been crocheted into that frock the way women at the Academy Awards were often sewn into their gowns.

Miss Yolanda came back over. Whenever more than two people gathered, she'd join, as if she worried we were planning a coup to overthrow Fifth-Floor Dresses' number one salesgirl (maybe number two since I'd arrived).

"That the new Andrea Jovine?" Miss Yolanda moved her cheek ball from the left to the right.

"Yup. I've got them all in the office. Whaddya think?" Miss Dani's sapphire earrings were as big as her eyeballs. She wore so many rings on her short fingers that you lost sight of the fingers. She reminded me of those sea creatures in tide pools who cover themselves with shells so they can't be seen.

"Looks terrible on you," Miss Yolanda said.

"Oh, come on!" Miss Dani smiled and turned in a circle. Her bottom was as flat as a cookie sheet.

Miss Lena said, "You look wonderful! Jesus has blessed you with a petite dress for your petite body."

"She's short. Not petite," Miss Yolanda said. "And she's as wide as she is tall." I still hadn't acclimated to the shocking things Miss Yolanda said. On TV shows people made comments like that—they insulted each other with what was supposed to be a joke. With Miss Yolanda, I was finding that there actually *were* people (well, at least one person) who said mean things aloud. It often made me so uncomfortable that, whenever my mind was idle, I worried about whoever had been insulted, even when the "victim" herself didn't seem hurt by what had been flung at her.

That day, Miss Dani laughed in her deep, raspy honk. It sounded like she was trying to clear something from her throat. "Yeah, yeah. At least I got legs. I can walk. And hell, these legs ain't bad." She scooched up the hem of her dress and kicked out her tiny leg. Compared to the rest of her, it was slim, muscled. She was right. They weren't bad legs.

Miss Lee and Miss Karen came over. The Braughn sisters were still standing side by side at their register. If they were talking to each other, they were doing it like ventriloquists, because I couldn't see their mouths moving. Miss Liaskis was on the phone. She frequently looked over at us, a desperate panic on her face—it seemed she wanted to be with us but couldn't get off the phone. There was a pencil in her hand and she was writing things down, but her arm movements were jerky. Nervous. A customer was probably asking for more than she could handle.

"It's the new Andrea Jovine," Miss Yolanda told the newcomers. "In stumpy and regular."

Miss Karen rolled her eyes. That was as expressive as she ever got. She leaned over, took the hem in her fingertips, and rubbed as if she were making the *gimme money* sign.

I listened as the women asked questions about the dress. They knew to ask things I didn't know I *should* know. My first week on the job I felt like I was trying to sell cars when I didn't even have a driver's license. By week three, I was memorizing facts: price, fabric, fit, care. There were the broader, more trend-based associations to keep track of too: the dominant color of the season, the newest hemline, what type of person identified with each designer (younger people liked Jessica McClintock, working women liked Anne Klein, funkier women liked Betsey Johnson), what each designer him- or herself was like, which dress would be right for which function, and, of course, which shoes and undergarments one should wear with it. When a dress came in that needed a T-back or strapless bra, I went down to lingerie, found the right items, and took note of where they were on the floor so I could send my customers there if I didn't have time to fetch them myself. Selling, it turned out, wasn't only selling. It was understanding an entire social structure surrounding the dress, as well as understanding who the customer wanted people to think she was. (Who she was in reality was insignificant. Putting on a dress was, like many other things, an effort to create the ideal self; it was aspirational. That was one thing, if not the only thing, I already knew and understood when I started the job.)

Miss Dani reached her short arm toward her back, trying to find the tag. She reminded me of a turtle—all body, small flippers. Miss Lena went to Miss Dani and pulled the tag out of her neck.

"One eighty-nine."

Miss Karen shrugged, like maybe that was a little high for what it was. I'd never spent a $189 on anything other than half a month's rent. It amazed me how big numbers like that meant nothing to the women who shopped at I. Magnin.

"It comes in emerald and ruby, and there's a skirt and top and a long cardigan to wear over the skirt or the dress. I'll put it all out this morning."

Miss Dani looked at her watch. It was ten o'clock, time to open. Like an exploding firework, the salesgirls in the huddle burst apart to retreat to their stations and Miss Dani waddled off.

Miss Lena clapped her hands and smiled at me. "Zippy, I have a very good feeling about today."

"You do?"

"Yes! Today Jesus will bless us with lots of customers!"

Jesus did. Or it could have been that full-page ad in the *Chronicle* for made-to-measure Ferragamo shoes. The thing about being on the fifth floor was that anyone taking the escalators to the higher floors (Designer Shoes, Designer Dresses, Designer Sportswear) had to walk a half circle to keep going up. If there was something catchy on the front racks, they paused. And when you're about to spend $2,300 on a Chanel dress, or $800 dollars on a pair of Ferragamo mules, $180 dollars for an Andrea Jovine dress is like dropping quarters into a slot machine on your way to the baccarat table.

It was so busy that day, I never made it down to Second-Floor Shoes to get my pumps polished. And when the floater came to cover me for my lunch break, I was in the middle of such a huge sale that when the customer left, I only had ten minutes remaining in my break. This was barely enough time to get up to the lunchroom, where I bought a can of Diet Coke for my no-eating day meal.

At six p.m., Miss Lena closed out our register and I closed out Miss Liaskis's while she separated her sales from her returns. Every transaction was punched into either a pink or green duplicate. Green was for sales, pink was for returns. At the end of each shift, each girl (we were all called girls no matter our age) added her sales and then subtracted her returns to find her dollar number for the day.

Miss Yolanda came by with a hold tag and a pencil. "Totals," she barked. Miss Yolanda turned our sales numbers in to Miss Dani at the end of each shift. Everyone played along as if this was protocol and Miss Dani was waiting for the numbers. But I had a feeling it was actually something Miss Yolanda invented to prove her dominance. No one added up the totals on the days Miss Yolanda was off.

"Miss Lena's doing ours." I finished closing out Miss Liaskis's register and then headed toward my station. I could hear Miss Liaskis behind me adding numbers aloud and then re-adding them as she messed up her totals. Miss Yolanda lost patience with her and met up with me again at the Petite Dresses register.

"Jesus blessed us today!" Miss Lena said.

"How much?" Miss Yolanda asked.

"Zippy did $2,800—"

"You took out returns?!" Miss Yolanda leaned over to see the hold tag where Miss Lena had done the math. She moved the candy ball to the other cheek.

"Yes! She was blessed today. And I did $1,600."

"Well, goody-gumdrops for you two."

"What did *you* do today?" I leaned over and tried to, but couldn't, read the hold tag in her hands.

"None of your damn business." Miss Yolanda swiftly tucked her arm behind her back.

"Did I beat you?!"

"Smarty-pants," she grumbled, and then walked over to the Braughn sisters to collect their totals. I couldn't hear them, but I watched closely, as I was determined to find some way to differentiate the Braughns. So far, all I'd come up with was the moles on their faces. One had one above her right eyebrow, so in my head I called her R. The other had a mole above her left eyebrow, so she was L. These monikers were only good for telling stories to Raquel, since neither R nor L ever spoke to me or looked my way.

Miss Lena said, "It is very likely that you beat Miss Yolanda today. She would have told you if you hadn't."

You'd think this would have made me feel good, but it only made me feel bad. I had known I was killing it—there wasn't a minute where I wasn't ringing up, fetching a new size, or checking on someone in a fitting room. But I didn't really care if I beat Miss Yolanda. If it was so important to her to be number one, couldn't I let her have that joy? If I had thrown a sale Miss Lena's way, I'd have made less, Miss Yolanda would have been number one, and Miss Lena would have been better off. We *did* earn commission, but how much smaller would my paycheck be if I had given my Petite Dresses partner one more sale?

I shut my eyes and made a promise to myself right then and there. *Tomorrow I will not compete with Miss Yolanda! Also, if Miss Lena is more than 30 percent behind me, I'll ring up a dress for her. If I don't follow through on this, then may God give me herpes or scabies or some other disgusting skin condition that makes me so gross and unappealing that I'll never kiss a real man and I'll never lose my virginity like Raquel wants me to. Amen.*

# Chapter 2

**When I got** home, Raquel was on the living room floor in the shape of the letter X. Her dark brown hair splayed around her head like a mermaid's in water. The phone was on the floor beneath the counter that separated the kitchen from the living room; the coiled cord was pulled taut as Raquel had the receiver pressed against her ear. I sat on the couch.

"Yeah, I know . . . I know . . ." She looked up and waved at me. "Okay, Dad . . . I love you too. Talk tomorrow!" Raquel let go of the receiver and it retracted across the carpet toward the kitchen, bouncing and stumbling.

"How's your dad?" Like the fact that I'd never yearned for a Chanel dress until I started working at I. Magnin, I'd never yearned for a father until I'd listened to Raquel talking to hers. He was like a giant soft waterbed that was always there to catch Raquel so that she could climb as high as she wanted without fear of crashing against the pavement.

I did have my mother to rely on, but her lifestyle provided very little security or cushioning. And my father was so unknown to me, I'd never even heard his name. My mother claimed to have forgotten it following their single night together.

Raquel didn't seem to think it was *that* big a deal that I was raised by a single mom, didn't know any grandparents, grew up in an apartment above a liquor store, and wasn't in college. Still, I hadn't yet gathered the courage to introduce her to the unconventional world of my mother and Howard, whose marriage had been revealed to me by their best friends in the building, Toby and Jo, when they'd dropped off a wedding present a year after the event. Toby's eyes had shot up into clown-brow arches when I asked why they were delivering a wedding present to a couple that wasn't married. *Didn't they tell you?* he asked, and then I heard about a drunken night in Lake Tahoe, Nevada. When I questioned my mother about it, she waved her hands around and said something like, "Eh, who cares. We're not going to spend money on rings, and the only thing that changed is we can do family health insurance at work, which is a lot less expensive."

"My dad's great. As always," Raquel said, and then she rolled from side to side and said, "Oh my Gaaaaaawd!"

"Oh-my-God good?" I kicked off my pumps, lay down beside her, and made an X with my body so we filled the whole space between the coffee table and the two chairs. Raquel grabbed my first two fingers and wrapped her fingers around them. I scooted up closer to her and knocked the top of my head against the turned-out leg of a chair. The furniture had been given to Raquel by her mother: a burgundy-and-blue chintz couch, matching blue-and-pink chintz armchairs, and a pink-stained wooden coffee table. These were decorator-coordinated pieces that reminded me of the floral puff-sleeved Jessica McClintock dresses sold at I. Magnin and worn by women all around town. It was furniture entirely unlike the funky one-beat stuff my mom bought at thrift stores and antique stores. The one thing Raquel and I had bought together was a dhurrie rug, but there was no pad beneath it, so it was not only super scratchy but also hard as wood against my back.

"This guy. Jason. Oh my God. I'm in love."

"Is he a lawyer?" Raquel, who was a lawyer herself, had told me she was going to marry a lawyer. If they both worked in law, they wouldn't get sick of each other; there'd always be new cases to discuss. *We'd speak the same language,* she'd said. I admired and envied her confidence and sense of direction. Raquel knew *exactly* where she was headed and had no fear of going there.

"HELL YEAH!" Raquel lifted our two hands and then let them drop.

"How old is he?" Raquel was twenty-five, six years older than me. I saw her as both a grown-up—and as an equal. She was half girl, half woman.

"Mmm, maybe thirty? He graduated from Boalt and was working at his dad's firm in Palo Alto. Now he's left the family business and works with a firm that's co— OH MAH GAWD, I'm in love. Oh, also, he passed the California bar on the first try."

Raquel, too, had passed the bar on her first try. It was from her that I knew that the California bar was the hardest in the country. Though maybe that was the thing lawyers in California said.

"Dang," I said.

"Hell yeah!" Raquel said.

A little over a month ago I'd answered a classified ad Raquel had placed and then moved into the small bedroom in her apartment near Coit Tower. I liked her instantly. We watched the same TV shows, liked the same movies, read the same magazines, and we both loved clothes (she had loads of cute clothes; I had very few and continually yearned for more). She didn't care for musical theater the way I did, but once we started talking, my backstage stories about the theater arts kids in high school were her favorites. Until Raquel, I'd had no interest in law, but Raquel's law stories were mostly stories about the people at the firm where she worked. There was the sixty-year-old partner who joined an orgy club; the lawyer who hit on every receptionist so hard, they were quitting one after another; the group of men she found snorting lines of coke off the conference table; and the partner who was so straight and conservative, he didn't have the imagination to ever guess what the others were up to. There were six times as many men as women who worked at the firm, and none of the partners were women. Raquel felt confident that she would change that soon enough.

Within a week of living with Raquel, she was a close friend. By the time we hit the three-week mark, she was the person to whom I was closest in my life, beside my mother. The couple friends I'd had in high school had gone on to college, but I hadn't even applied, as my mother had never gone to college and there was no money to pay for it anyway.

"So, do you have a date with him?"

"Not yet, grasshopper, not yet. But wait and watch, wait and watch." Since Raquel and I had seen *The Karate Kid,* she'd been calling me grasshopper.

"Was he flirting with you?"

"Oooooooh, yeah." Raquel grinned and rolled around a bit. Then she bolted upright. "Oh my God! I have an idea."

I sat up and watched as she went into her bedroom first, and then mine.

"I'M HUNGRY!" I shouted at her. "CAN WE START EATING AT MIDNIGHT?!"

Raquel popped her face out of my bedroom. "No." She returned and handed me my Day-Timer. We moved to the couch and sat side by side. Raquel let a stack of Day-Glo pens fall onto the coffee table in front of us. "If you follow the rules, you'll lose weight."

"Fine. What are we doing?"

"I'm going to write Jason on my list as if it's already happened." Raquel logged the name and pertinent details about everyone she fooled around with in her Day-Timer. They had to at least kiss with tongues to make it onto the log. If they went all the way, she put a star next to their name. There were twenty-seven stars on the log. That number astounded me the first time I read it, but Raquel assured me that in the world beyond high school, it was low, low, low. Her pal Garry had had sex with over one hundred men. Her best friend from law school, Stacy, had been with over fifty men and seven women. Even Raquel's Christian friend who wore a cross and didn't believe in premarital sex had slept with three people.

"But that's premarital sex," I had said.

"She claims she thought each one was going to be her husband."

"It's still premarital."

"Yeah, but according to the other Christians in her Christian lawyers group, if the guy ends up being your husband, it isn't a sin to have sex before the ceremony."

"Funny rule," I'd said, and Raquel had shrugged.

"So, you're going to write down what you imagine Jason will be like and look like *if* you have sex with him?" I clarified.

"Yeah. I'm going to focus on what *might* happen, how he *might* look naked, what he might say, and how the night *might* go down. Then, once I do have sex with him, I'll amend the entry."

"Fine," I said. "What am I supposed to write?"

"You're going to start your starred list. Write down your dream man and all the pertinent details *AS IF* you'd had sex with him."

"I don't have a dream man."

"START DREAMING!" Raquel hugged me and then turned to her Day-Timer and began writing. I stared at my blank page.

One night, after we'd drunk a bottle of wine, I did a dramatic reading from Raquel's man-log. She had been a good single-member audience, roaring with laughter as I put on English, Irish, and French accents. I even put on a Russian accent when I read the entry about the guy whose penis was so lumpy, it looked like a miniature sack of kittens. I tried to do a Dutch accent when I read the entry for the guy who smelled like Edam cheese, but a Dutch accent is both round-edged and choppy, so hard to pull off. Raquel had thought a close examination of her list would make me *want* to start dating, but instead it repelled me.

The only kiss I'd ever had—from the senior-year boyfriend who'd lasted for five whole days—also didn't help inspire desire in me. What happened was this: We were sitting on a rock in Golden Gate Park when he pushed his face against mine and then did tongue gymnastics in my mouth. For over an hour. Nonstop. So much spit built up that it pooled over my lips and ran down my chin. The next day, when I woke up to swollen lips, I was convinced he'd given me herpes. My mother and Howard were on the couch watching TV. I showed them my mouth, told them about the face-breaking kiss, and then, with tears in my eyes, asked if I had herpes. My mother looked up and put her finger on my lips; she leaned in close and examined my mouth. "Nope," she'd said. "Only a horrible kiss."

**"Why aren't you** writing?" Raquel asked.

"It's hard to imagine the right guy," I said.

"Well, since he's going to take your virginity, start with a medium to smallish dick," she said.

"Why do we say *take* when it comes to virginity? It's not like he walks away with anything. Unless I have a disease."

"How could you have a VD if you're a virgin?" Raquel was filling her page. She had a lot to say about her imaginary sex with Jason.

"Maybe I got something from one of the toilets at work."

"You don't have a venereal disease! And I don't know why people say *take*."

"Do they say it for boys, too? Does a girl 'take' his virginity?"

"Yeah, I think so. Yeah, definitely."

"Okay, so it's not sexist."

"Maybe it is. We have to think about that later. For now: imagine!"

"Let's watch TV, too."

Raquel picked up the clicker and put on the news. Immediately it went to the Berber Coffee ad that only played at night: *Berber Coffee, the perfect end to a perfect evening!* I preferred the Berber Coffee ads that played in the day—they had a narrative, a conflict, a resolution, even!

"Yum," Raquel said. She, like most people I knew, loved the Berber Coffee guy. I could see how handsome he was, but I'd never had a crush on him. He was too grown-up, too old, too hot, and he'd never like me back. The idea that he was an impossible mate diminished all desire.

"What if you actually met him"—I nodded at the TV—"and he asked you out? Would you go out with him even though he's not a lawyer?"

"I'd quit my job and move to Berber Coffee Land for him."

"I think the Berbers were from Morocco."

"I'd move to Morocco for him." The next commercial came on: Mutual of Omaha life insurance. "Go," Raquel said, and she turned the page of her Day-Timer and continued writing. When she was done, she'd filled three pages, which she read aloud to me. The imaginary sex with Jason had been mind-blowing. His body looked like it was sculpted from stone. He was madly in love with her and professed that love while their mouths were only a millimeter apart. He greatly appreciated her flat stomach and supported her Day On/Day Off diet. Etcetera.

I read my entry aloud: "*His hands don't smell, his thing is neither too big nor too small, when we kiss there is no extra slobber, he doesn't think*

*I'm fat. He can look like anything and come from any country, an accent is a plus (I'll learn to imitate it!). He needs to be kind. And funny. And not have AIDS or any other VD."* The world had only recently learned that AIDS was not an unfair terror for *only* gay men but could be passed between any two people. Could you get it from kissing? I had yet to find the answer to that one.

"I don't know if I should laugh or cry," Raquel said. She was smiling in a tense way that made me slightly anxious. "Why are you worried about his hands smelling?"

"Mimi in cosmetics said she was with a guy once whose hands smelled and that I should never date a guy with smelly hands."

"Where is Mimi meeting men? The horse stables? The chicken farm?"

"The limburger cheese shop?" I added, and then I said, "Can we please, please, please have a snack? I'm not asking for a meal!"

"Shh," Raquel said. "It's time for Roz." Roz Abrams was reporting the news. We both lifted our heads and watched closely. She was our favorite anchor and we had a shared fantasy about becoming her friend.

Once Roz was no longer speaking, Raquel said, "We can have drinks, but only out of the house." I knew this rule already. Raquel was so convinced of the brilliance of her Day On/Day Off diet that, with my help, she was writing a book about it. "Partying on an Empty Stomach" was chapter two. We had a yellow legal pad on which I wrote chapter titles and then bullet points of what would be in the chapter. The bullet points for chapter two said: *Drinking is preferable on no eating days. You need less alcohol to get wasted on no eating days. Money is saved, as you spend fewer dollars at the bars.*

Before Raquel, I had never tried alcohol. The theater kids in high school snuck it into cast parties a couple of times, but I declined. My mother, Howard, and their best friends, Toby and Jo, had been sliding drinks my way since I was thirteen. *We're like the French,* one of them often said, and then my mother and Toby would speak French, a language my mother knew from her French Canadian mother, who cut her off after I was born out of wedlock. Even knowing that French kids learned to drink wine early on, I wasn't tempted. The day I met Raquel, she declared she was going to teach me to drink in a reasonable way that would allow me to hold on to my senses.

"Let's go to Blue Light," I said. This was my favorite of the few bars Raquel had taken me to. It was owned by Boz Scaggs. Raquel said she'd seen him there twice and everyone she knew had seen him there at least once. I'd been twice so far and hadn't yet seen him. In my recurring fantasy, I was standing at the bar, singing along with the music. He was standing next to me, listening closely, and then he asked me to sing backup for him.

"Maybe I could lose my virginity to Boz Scaggs," I said.

"Too old."

"But he's BOZ SCAGGS! I should have written *him* down in the Day-Timer."

"Fine. Let's go and try to pawn off your virginity to Boz Scaggs."

My stomach dropped. "Wait. Do you think he sleeps with all kinds of women? Do you think he has, like, a load of venereal diseases?"

"Probably. But antibiotics can take care of anything. Come on. Let's go." Raquel stood, grabbed my hand, and pulled me to standing. Then we went to her room to look through her closet. We didn't wear the same size, but some of her tops fit me and, as Raquel frequently pointed out, they were all way sexier than anything I owned. Nothing I owned was sexy. Sexiness had never been something I'd thought about until I met Raquel.

Once we were dressed, we went downstairs and outside to fetch the blue Volvo Raquel's parents had given her when she graduated from law school. "I feel the parking juju happening already," Raquel said as we teetered in our high heels up the steep sidewalk to where the car had been parked last. The spot was so good that we had skipped the regular grocery shop two days earlier so as not to lose it. Like the fact that every lawyer who passed the California bar exam the first time let you know that it was the hardest test in the nation, everyone who owned a car in San Francisco told you that there were more registered vehicles in the city than parking spots to hold them. If this were true, there was continuously a great hunk of vehicled people who simply couldn't park. I thought of those people more than I should have, always wishing they weren't cruising the hilly streets and were, instead, en route to visit a town where they *could* park their car.

Once we were in the Volvo, we each did a gentle tap on Air Freshener Jesus, who hung from the rearview mirror. Raquel claimed He brought her parking spaces, but we had to tap Him once before the ignition was started and then pray to it to make it work.

It didn't take long to get to Union Street, where the bar was, but as anticipated, there were no parking spots. We circled the block three times. "I think we have to chant the prayer louder," Raquel said.

"I'll sing it," I said. "And you chant in the background so it's like an a cappella song."

Raquel glanced up to Air Freshener Jesus. "He says that will work."

I started singing loud and clear, pushing my voice out through my nose, the way Barbra Streisand does. "*Dear Jesus, Air Freshener Jesus, help us find a spot, a spot, a spot, big ENOOOOOOUGH, for this CAAAAR, because you ARRRRE, Dear Jesus, Air Freshener Jesus, help us find a spot, a spot, a spot, big ENOOOOUGH, for this CAAAR, because you ARREE, Dear Jesus . . .*"

Raquel did an excellent job thumping out a low beat in the background and chanting, "*Dear Jesus, Air FRESHener Jesus, Dear Jesus, Air FRESHener Jesus . . .*" The song filled all the space in the car. I closed my eyes and was belting it when Raquel screamed, "HOSANNA!"

I opened my eyes. She was pulling into a spot directly on Union Street, right in front of Blue Light.

In the darkness of Blue Light, Raquel flashed her driver's license to the bartender. I flashed the Alaska driver's license I'd bought from a woman in Chinatown for fifty dollars, the same price as a one-way ticket on People's Express to fly from San Francisco to LA. I had to bring her the photo and pay ahead of time. A week later she gave me the ID and threw in a small blue fabric box that held two silver balls she told me to roll in my hand to relax. This was shortly after I'd moved in with Raquel, my first week at I. Magnin. I guess she could see on my face how terrified and *not* relaxed I was during this headfirst dive into being a grown woman.

The band was wailing and loud. They were at the other end of the bar and I couldn't see them through the crowd, but it sounded like there were at least three horns. The lights were dim, so everyone was a blur of contours. Raquel shouted to me, "We're doing zombies. It will feel like food. Okay?" I gave a thumbs-up and she leaned over the bar, slapped down her green American Express, and ordered for us. Raquel insisted on paying for drinks when we went out since she made more money, I didn't drink much, and men usually bought her drinks, so it was like she was only paying for one person.

Before the zombies arrived, there was a glass of champagne in Raquel's hand and a Tom Selleck–looking guy whispering in her ear. I could tell by the way she was throwing her hair around from shoulder to shoulder that she was enjoying him. I moved my head to the music a little, not too much. There was something embarrassing about standing alone at a bar while my friend had her back to me with Tom Selleck's hand on her waist.

The bartender placed two zombies in front of me as Raquel was being led away to the dance floor. She turned back and I pointed at the drink.

"YOU HAVE IT," she shouted over the music.

I picked up one drink, pulled out the cherry, and ate it. It was exquisite. Then I removed the straw and started chugging the drink. It was the texture of a Slurpee and the swirling color of the sand candles we made in grade school. I felt a wonderful sliding sensation—cold and heavy—as it dropped down my throat and filled my empty stomach. Raquel was right. It felt like a meal.

"IS THAT GOOD?" a guy in a white Izod Lacoste shirt shouted over the music. He was leaning across the bar holding out a credit card and trying to get the bartender's attention. His hair and eyes were black, his skin was dark and creamy. He smiled and his teeth looked as white as an X-ray.

"So good," I said. "It tastes like a Slurpee. But sweeter."

"WHAT?" He leaned his ear toward my face. I could smell the tanginess of his aftershave.

I spoke a little louder. "Like a Slurpee."

He put his mouth near my ear and I felt a shiver run across my head. "What's it called?" He had an accent, but it was unidentifiable. Subtle.

"Here." I slid the other one over to him. He looked at me. I leaned in toward his ear and said, louder, "YOU CAN HAVE THIS ONE."

He held the glass aloft until I picked up mine. Then we clinked them together and he shouted, "CHEERS!"

"CHEERS!" I shouted, smiling so hard, I couldn't yet take a sip. "I'M ZIPPY."

"WHAT?"

"I'M—" I started, and then he turned his head and motioned to a tall blond guy who was giving him *What's taking you so long?* up-palms.

"THANKS AGAIN!" he said, and he was off.

When Raquel returned (without Tom Selleck), I bubble-sucked up the last half inch of zombie in my glass. I had finished the rest of it long ago, but had kept that bit there so it looked like I was doing something—drinking a zombie—when in fact I was blowing in the straw while waiting for time to pass.

"FUN?" I shout-asked.

"HE WAS TOO MUSTACHY AND NOT A LAWYER," Raquel shouted back as the Izod Lacoste guy returned holding an empty glass.

Raquel jolted back in surprise as Lacoste leaned into my ear and shouted, "THANKS FOR TURNING ME ON TO THIS!" He shook the glass and then moved his face so it was right in front of mine. I backed up an inch as he moved forward two inches and kissed me. Lip to lip with a micro hold.

The feeling of his mouth against mine was startling. New. Astonishing.

Lacoste pulled his head away, leaned over the bar, and slammed down the empty glass. Raquel and I locked bugged-out eyes. Neither of us spoke. Her keys were in her hand, but it was clear she was going to stand right there until this—being kissed by someone who was as good-looking as the Berber Coffee guy—played out. Our eyes stayed locked save a couple glances to see what Lacoste was doing at the bar. After securing another zombie, Lacoste turned around, lifted his drink, and shouted, "LOVE THIS STUFF!" I hadn't yet formed a response when he rushed off and was swallowed into the crowd like a penny tossed into a laundry pile.

"A very quick relationship," I said into Raquel's ear, and she laughed.

We made our way out to the car. "Oh my God!" Raquel said as she started the ignition.

"Shh," I said. "Wait till we've pulled away in case he comes out and can hear us."

Raquel rolled her eyes, but she did remain silent until we hit the first red light on Union Street. Then she looked at me and said, "Oh my God, he was so hot! Did you give him our phone number?"

"I gave him your drink, but I didn't give him our phone number. I guess that was a thank-you kiss?"

"Even if you didn't give him our number, it was a good start, grasshopper! A very good start!"

"You think so? He took the drink, ignored me, then returned and unignored me for one kiss's time before ignoring me again."

"Don't take everything so personally. You have no idea what's going on in his head. You have no idea what's going on in his life. All you know is what you think and feel and if that one brief kiss felt great, then dang! Enjoy it!"

"If it had been you, he would have asked for a phone number."

"He didn't even glance my way."

"Do you think I got AIDS from that kiss?" It had given me the shivers in the best way. But would I regret it for the rest of my now shortened life?

"If you got AIDS from that peck," Raquel said, "then my mouth is like the entire ward at the AIDS clinic after the saliva exchange I did with mustache man on the dance floor."

I knew she was kidding, still I surreptitiously tapped Air Freshener Jesus to remind Him to *please* look out for both of us.

# Chapter 3

**The next night,** Raquel and I were watching *60 Minutes* when the phone rang. I answered to my mother squalling like a deranged woman. She was making so much noise, Raquel got off the couch, came to the counter where I stood, and watched to make sure I was okay. It took a full two minutes before my mother could choke out a word. All I got was *hospital.*

My heart started beating in my stomach. Was she in the hospital? Had she been run over by a bus? Hit by a cable car? Robbed and stabbed by street thugs?

"MOM! What hospital?! I'll be right there!"

"HOW-ARD!" Mom screeched out, followed by a short silence, which I soon realized was her gathering her breath before she began wailing again.

I held in the urge to vomit, steadied myself, and asked, "Is he alive?"

"YESSSSSSSSS!"

Raquel and I looked at each other, relieved. Mom's wails turned into normal, tumbling crying.

"Did he have a heart attack?"

"He"—sob, sob, sob—"cut"—sob, sob, sob—"off"—sob, sob, sob—"his fingers!"

Raquel cupped her hand over her open mouth.

"Did he cut off his fingers on purpose?" I would not have asked that question about anyone else. But Howard spoke in a kooky Elizabethan accent whenever he was drunk; he wore socks that had a tennis-shoe print on them so he could take off his shoes at work (did he actually fool people? They were obviously socks); he had once lived on a commune in Santa Cruz where he was in charge of growing root vegetables and fixing bikes; the last time his car was towed, he failed to pick it up and hadn't had a car since; and he had been fired from three different jobs before he landed at Hardware Depot, and in each case he'd been fired for not wearing shoes (at the Depot, he wore shoes; my mother claimed he *finally* understood the importance of them). Cutting off his own fingers felt almost normal within the range of Howard's life.

"No, not on purpose!" Now my mother was crying in a more contained way. My heart throbbed for her.

"How did it happen?"

Raquel leaned her head against mine. I held the phone at an open angle so we both could hear.

My mother's grief switched instantly to sobbing rage. "HOW?! HOW?! IT HAPPENED BECAUSE HE'S A DUMBASS WHO WORKS ALL DAY CUTTING LUMBER BUT SOMEHOW FAILED TO PROPERLY USE A TABLE SAW!"

"I'm confused, Mom. Please tell me how *exactly* this happened and how many fingers."

My mother cried some more and then she panted into the phone. "He decided he'd build a skateboard. A SKATEBOARD! In a city where no one could possibly roll up a hill and anyone who rolled down one would probably die!" The crying bubbled now, percolating like brewing coffee.

"Yeah, a skateboard here doesn't quite make sense . . . Can we clarify how many fingers?"

"ALL OF THEM!"

"On both hands?"

"Of course not!" The crying slowed; I could hear my mother taking deep, gulping breaths. "Once one hand was missing the fingers, he couldn't hold the saw to cut the others off."

"So four? Five? Are you talking thumb, too?"

"No." My mother sniffed. "His thumb's still there. At least he can hitchhike!" My mother cried and laughed at once.

"Oh, Mom, I'm so sorry. Listen, I'll be right there—"

"I'll drive you," Raquel said.

"Raquel will drive me—"

"No, sweetie," my mother said, "don't worry about it—"

"I'll even wait outside the hospital and then drive you back!" Raquel said.

"Raquel will—"

"You're good girls," my mom said. "But they only let one person in the room anyway. I'll stay with Howard and hold his remaining hand. You come see him once he's safe at home."

**The next day** at work there were so few customers, I had too much time to think. All I could think about was my mother and Howard. After I'd finally completed a single sale, I called my mother's apartment. No one answered, so I tried the Hardware Depot.

"Hi, honey." My mother sighed. "It's been a horrible twenty-four hours."

"Is Howard still at the hospital?"

"Oh yeah. Every time he wakes up, he waves around the white ball of his bandaged hand and laughs at *thumbkin* sticking out."

"He's laughing at his fingerless hand?"

"Well, he's doped up on painkillers and it is kind of funny-looking."

"I can't believe the Depot didn't give you the day off! Should I visit him there after work?" My stomach pinged. My mother had worked so hard my whole life. She loved her job; still, it didn't seem right that today would be like any other.

"Only visit if you feel like it. He's happy now—the TV's on in the room and I dropped off some Gatorade and a box of Cap'n Crunch this morning."

I cringed a little. Minutes ago I'd sold two three-hundred-dollar dresses to a woman around my mother's age who told me the only job she'd ever had in her life was that of trying to make her husband happy. I'd asked if she made him dinner each night and she'd waved her hand and shook her head.

"Someone else takes care of that," she'd said, and I imagined elegant meals set out on a long table set with folded cloth napkins and silver candlesticks. Not a box of Cap'n Crunch in sight.

"So you, uh, you keep your husband company?" I'd asked.

"I wear nice dresses and never complain," the woman had said, and then she shrugged before walking off toward the up escalator, en route to the designer floors.

"Will the Depot give Howard disability?" I asked.

"Nope," my mom said. "If he'd done it on the job, sure. But he did this on his own damn time, so . . . I have no idea how we're going to pay these medical bills."

"You have insurance, right?"

"Yeah, but that will barely cover what we'll be facing. I guess we'll economise."

"Economise," I repeated. "Funny word."

"Canadian," my mother said. "As my mother always said, 'We need to economise, *ma chérie*!'"

I repeated the words in my head—more to catch my mother's French Canadian accent than anything. And then I said, "Maybe I can help out." Though I knew I couldn't. Even as a top salesgirl on the floor, I barely made enough to live in San Francisco. It seemed like the more glamorous a job was, the less you earned. My mother gasped when I told her what my latest paycheck was. She and Howard each made about twice as much as I.

"Oh, sweetheart, you don't have to take this on. I'll figure it out—we'll stop picking up Chinese food or something."

"You hardly ever eat Chinese food." Since I'd been living with Raquel, I'd eaten out more than I had in my entire life. In Raquel's world, eating in restaurants was as normal as buying a pack of gum. I always tried to order the least expensive thing; still, with that, rent, and half the utilities, I was down to zero at the end of each two-week pay period.

"We do a couple times a month—it's an easy one to give up."

My mother's life, when I looked at it from a distance, seemed like a series of give-ups: she gave up high school and her country to get out of her mother's crowded house; she gave up her family, who rejected her when she ended up pregnant with me after a one-night stand; and then, once I was born, she gave up court-reporting school because she could no longer afford to work part-time and send me to the illegal day care down the road. That's when she took the job at the Hardware Depot.

A customer came off the escalator. I looked toward her and she looked away and walked faster: the universal *Don't ask me if I want help* signal. She paused at the Donna Karan rack, pulled out a dress, and held it against her chest.

"Hold on, Mom." I put the phone on the counter, took a couple steps toward the customer, flashed a smile, and said, "How are you doing today?"

"Just looking!" she said sharply. Angrily! I wanted to say, *I didn't ask if you wanted help; I asked how you are.* Instead I returned to the phone.

"Mom, I need to get going here. I'll come by and visit soon."

"All righty then. Don't worry about us, honey."

"Okay," I said, but of course I was worried about them. Or, more specifically, about my mother. We'd been a tiny unit of two until I was fourteen and Howard joined us. Alone, my mother and I functioned quite well in the one-bedroom apartment on her Hardware Depot salary. When Howard moved in, I dragged my bed out of the room I shared with my mother and into the unlit hallway, where one or the other of them would stumble past me in the night on the way to the bathroom. There wasn't any extra spending money with Howard pitching in because he created far greater expenses. Food, for one—Howard was a man who ate endlessly and still his jeans hung so loosely, they appeared to be draped over piping rather than a human form. And then there was alcohol, which my mother didn't drink much of until she fell in love with Howard.

I hung up the phone and stared out at the sales floor. Light poured in through the windows. The clothes looked like hanging jewels—so still and perfect. Even though I was terrified of getting fired, even though I wasn't making enough money to buy the clothes sold in the store, even though it appeared that none of the salesgirls except Miss Lena and Miss Liaskis liked me, I was excited to work at I. Magnin. For the first time in my life, I was happy to be exactly where I was: in that store, in my apartment, enjoying the emerging-adult lifestyle I had with Raquel. So what was I supposed to do when Howard had no family and my mother had only me to help them out?

**It was an** eating day, but instead of going to the lunchroom, I walked over to Blondie's Pizza, which consisted of a window where you ordered, paid, and were given your food in a single transaction. Each slice was the size of a triangular dustpan and cost only a dollar. If I was going to save money, this was one way to do it. The line snaked down the sidewalk—I barely noticed it moving as I was going through finances in my head: how much I needed to sell each day to pay rent and utilities; how much I needed to sell to bolster that paycheck enough to help out my mother and Howard. I tried to pause a number in my head when my turn approached. I stepped up to the window and said, almost robotically, "One slice of cheese, please." A crumpled soft dollar was already in my hand. I laid it on the counter, looked up, and realized I was facing *the* Blondie's Guy whom all the I. Magnin girls discussed, even the Fifth-Floor Dresses ladies, who usually didn't talk about men.

"Do you want a Coke with that?" He leaned his elbows on the window counter and smiled, revealing a swath of white teeth.

"No." I returned the smile and almost laughed. There was no doubt that this was the man about whom I'd heard numerous stories. There was the Sportswear girl who was once so taken by him that she couldn't speak. The impatient woman behind her had shouted, "Oh, sweet Jesus, just give her a slice of pepperoni and a Coke!" There was the Clinique girl who didn't eat dairy but regularly bought slices only to see him. And Mimi told me she once, with his permission, reached through the order window and touched his James Dean swoop of honey-colored hair.

I wasn't speechless and I didn't want to touch his hair, but I did lose the number I'd been holding in my head. More thrilling than meeting him was the simple fact that I could finally report to Miss Lena and Mimi that I'd encountered the Blondie's Guy.

"Thanks so much!" I said, when he handed me the shiny slice with cheese dripping off the sides of the paper plate like a melting Dali clock.

"You come back and see me *any* time," the Blondie's Guy said, and then he shouted, "NEXT!"

Sometime after my pizza break, I was standing outside the fitting room door of a customer who was a size twelve but insisted she was a six. (She blamed the dresses until I cut the size tag out of an Adrienne Vittadini and told her it was six.)

"You doing okay in there?" I asked.

She opened the door and dropped the inside-out dress into my hands. "The pattern's too busy."

I righted the dress, put it on a hanger, and returned it to the four-way rack where it belonged. I was feeling desperate in a way I hadn't before; I had to try to make more sales.

If I could rearrange Petite Dresses—organize it so it would pull in more people—I might be able to sell more. I'd worked out which dresses made people stop and look and which dresses they actually wanted to try on. My imagined floor design started with *lookers* but pulled the customer toward *tryers*. Miss Dani was the only one allowed to stage the floor, and it seemed impossible that she'd say yes to Fifth-Floor Dresses' newest salesgirl's staging ideas. But maybe soon, if I proved my competence, I could ask?

Since I couldn't act out my floor design fantasies, and I couldn't stand in front of the store and beg people to come in and shop, I started cleaning and organizing the supply drawer. Miss Lena, who had been helping a woman who ended up buying nothing, came to stand beside me. Her compact body took up as much room as an upright vacuum cleaner. She started talking about Tito and the beaches of Dubrovnik. It was one story that combined the two: her childhood on the beach with Tito's ambitions to build a seaside tourist industry in Yugoslavia. I drifted off to Yugo with her and stopped thinking about my mother needing money and Howard sawing off his own fingers.

Miss Yolanda scurried over to us. She must have just stuffed the candy in her mouth because her cheek ball was as big as it ever got. "What have you done today?" she snapped.

"Nothing!" Miss Lena quickly clapped her hands. "But Jesus has blessed us with good conversation."

"If Jesus had blessed us, we'd have customers and not this goddamned bowling alley," Miss Yolanda said. I'd heard many employees say that, or some version of it, on slow days. I loved imagining rolling a bowling ball down the aisle, past the racks of dresses. Miss Lena would likely be the only one to laugh, though she'd be scared that customers getting off the elevator might get hit by the ball.

Miss Yolanda turned away and headed toward Miss Lee and Miss Karen's section, shouting, "How much have you two sold today?!"

Miss Lena turned and took my hands into hers. She shook them once, as if she were shaking out a sheet to fold, and then said, "Let's go pray for customers! Follow me." She turned and walked toward the dressing rooms.

I followed. "Raquel and I prayed to Air Freshener Jesus the other night and we got a parking spot right in front of Blue Light."

"See!" Miss Lena turned around and smiled. "Jesus loves us. All we have to do is ask."

We were standing outside the first of five fitting rooms. The door was made of tilted slats; from the outside, you couldn't see in, and from the inside you could see if someone was standing on the other side. Miss Lena used the key she wore on an elastic phone cord wristband and opened the door. It was a big room with a chair in the corner and a three-way mirror. Miss Lena closed the mirrors, got down on her knees, and put her hands in a prayer position below her chin.

I stood in the open doorway, frozen. "Wait. You're praying right here?"

Miss Lena nodded and then dropped her head. I took a deep breath and held myself still, as if I were also praying. In fact, I was studying Miss Lena. Her narrow feet in brown ballet flats looked like two dead squirrels. She wore flesh-colored hose that were so thick, her tiny calves looked like they were made of injection-mold plastic. Her naturally blond hair was pulled back into a shiny bun. She was mumbling and whispering; the only word I could make out was *Jesus*.

As the praying continued, I started to get nervous. What if Miss Yolanda came back here? Or a customer? I took a few steps toward the sales floor and looked out to make sure all was clear. Then I went back to my post in the doorway. The longer Miss Lena prayed, the more I believed in the power of her prayers, the power to bring forth the things we both needed (customers, sales, enough money to hand some over to my mother and Howard). I had the strangest idea that if Miss Lena opened the mirrors, they would be transformed into a triptych and Jesus and Mary would be painted there. Or maybe Mary alone, a different stage of existence on each panel: sitting beside Joseph while tending to baby Jesus in the manger, holding grown Jesus's dead body, and then assumed into the sky on her death. Everything I knew about Jesus and Mary, I knew from Miss Lena. My mother was an atheist; I had no idea what the *PTL*-watching Howard was; and none of my friends from high school had ever talked about God. Raquel had gone to church every week as a kid, believed in God, and loved to pray. But she didn't know anything about the Bible.

"Zippy. Join me." Miss Lena kept one hand where it was and waved the blade of the other toward me without opening her eyes.

"Okay, lemme check the sales floor first." I rushed out and looked again. Miss Yolanda was standing at a rack showing a suit to a tall woman with Linda Evans shoulders. I couldn't hear the words she was saying but could tell from her shrill patter that she was dictating what this woman should buy. Everyone else was hanging around, chatting. Except Miss Liaskis, who was on the phone.

It seemed safe enough to start praying, so I went back to the fitting room, stepped inside, and closed the door. When I knelt, my stomach folded over the waistband of my wool pencil skirt and my white blouse puffed out. The blouse was as stiff as cardboard because I'd starch-ironed it last Thursday, which was "Must See TV" night. Raquel and I liked to save our ironing for the week, pile it up, and then take turns at the board while we watched our favorite shows. Raquel had lots of shirts to iron because she never repeated the same outfit twice in a month. I ironed everything I owned, which was only a fraction of what Raquel had. When my ironing was done, I worked on hers so we were at the board for the same amount of time. We tried to finish by the time *Cheers* came on, as we both wanted to relax on the couch for that one.

Before I got to the praying, I reached back and took off my pumps. I was worried that my feet smelled, so I leaned backward like a lawn chair clicking back and sniffed. Nope. All good. My stockings, like Miss Lena's, were so dense (control-top L'eggs), they probably wouldn't let out a stink anyway.

"Okay," I whispered. I wanted Miss Lena to know I was about to do it. Dive in and pray. My prayers so far in life had been one-sentence asks for things that . . . well, selfish things that were for me alone. Of course there were the regular prayers to Air Freshener Jesus, but those were all for parking spots. Also, because the car was only used when we were going out at night, and Raquel usually (and I less frequently) had exposed cleavage during the Air Freshener Jesus prayers, it all seemed more playful than serious. But this, being on my knees, with my hands positioned just so—this felt like the real thing: actual communication with God.

*Dear God,* I said (in my head), and my stomach went all whirly-twirly. It could have been from the control-top pantyhose, or it could have been from the massive breakfast I'd scarfed down that morning (four Eggo frozen waffles with butter and syrup) plus the wedge of pizza. *Dear God,* I started again, and then I lifted my finned hands from my heart to my forehead and back again. I looked over at Miss Lena. She had a little smile on her face, like God was whispering something sweet into her ear. I shut my eyes and tried to continue, but I wasn't sure what to say. I wanted this prayer to be right and true and proper. Was it wrong to pray for customers even though I absolutely needed to make more sales to help out my frazzled mother? Shouldn't I pray for bigger things than myself? Maybe if I *started* with praying for other people, it wouldn't seem so awful if I prayed for myself in the end.

I started again: *Dear God, please bless Miss Lena's family in Yugo and give them whatever they need. Stuff I can't remember now, but Miss Lena knows, so maybe you can dip into her brain and find it. Please, God, may Howard find a way to live happily without four of his fingers and may he and Mom be able to pay their medical bills and have money left over to eat and all that. (Oh, and thank you, God, for letting Howard keep that thumb. It seems like one thumb/no fingers is much better than no fingers/no thumb.) Hey, God, I bet everyone prays for world peace, but I'm going to add my voice to that chorus.*

I smiled as I remembered a bumper sticker I saw that read *Pray for Whirled Peas.* I shot a glance at Miss Lena, who was as still and holy-looking as Mina Bliss, who had played Mary every year in the high school Christmas pageant. Closing my eyes again, I carried on: *God, I'm sorry I was thinking of that world peace joke. I truly, honestly, do want world peace and I swear I don't even know what whirled peas are. Do people eat them? Not your place to answer that one, God . . .* I looked at Miss Lena and then looked toward the door as if that might help me hear if anyone was out there. *Okay, God, I can't stop myself from being a little selfish now. Let me start by telling you, I love being part of I. Magnin. I love this store even though I can't afford anything in it. So please, God, help me be so good at this job that I can stay here forever. Oh, God, I'm sorry I'm asking for so much for me, but there's one more thing I want. Well, after hearing Raquel talk to her father on the phone, I think I really, or kind of, I mean, I guess . . . I want to find my dad. I mean, I know that sounds nuts since I don't even know his name, but gosh, I'd love to meet the guy who helped create me. I mean, I guess you created me, but you know what I'm saying.* I looked around again. Miss Lena was still at it. I wondered if she had loads and loads of prayers or if she was reciting the same few over and over again. I closed my eyes again and thought that I better add more selfless prayers to dilute the abundance of selfish ones: *God, please bless all the girls on the fifth floor, even Miss Yolanda, who is downright mean to me, and even the bitchy-as-heck Braughn sisters who think they're better than everyone else, and even Miss Lee and Miss Karen, who look past me as if I'm invisible. And, God, please help Miss Liaskis figure out how to use the register, and . . . Oh, and God bless Miss Dani in whatever she does in that dingy little office all day. Wait! One more. God bless Miss Lena in particular. Because, I mean, come on! Is there anyone more prayer-worthy than Miss Lena? Oh, last thing, again, I seem to be dipping into the me-me-me stuff a lot here, but can you help one-handed Howard figure out a way to fix the bathroom door in their apartment? It's swollen and won't shut all the way and I can never relax when I'm in there. It's like being in a stall at a Greyhound station where the lock never works and the door swings open the moment you're grabbing the toilet paper . . . Oh, God, I'm sorry I brought that up! So . . . uh . . . to summarize: world peace, Miss Lena's family, Howard's denuded hand, the fifth-floor salesgirls, the bathroom door, and, if you don't mind, me doing well at this job and, maybe, if I haven't already asked for too much, meeting my father. Thank you, God. For everything.*

*Amen*. And then I said it again, aloud. Firmly. As if it were the period at the end of a very powerful sentence. "Amen."

Miss Lena looked over at me with a sweet closed-mouth smile. A second later a voice floated down the fitting room hall. "Hello? Can someone help me?"

I jumped up and put on my shoes. Miss Lena looked at me and whispered, "You go, dear, I'll keep praying for more."

I opened the door a crack and slipped out so that Miss Lena wouldn't be seen. A woman was standing there holding the new Andrea Jovine knit dress. Her brown hair was slicked back like the women who worked in designer dresses. She was wearing a red pantsuit that hid her shape. My guess was she was about my mother's age, but she seemed powerful and grown-up in ways my mother never seemed. "Can I try this on?" she asked, as if it were an accusation.

I smiled big and took the dress from her hands. "Of course! What are you looking for exactly?" I walked her to the fitting room at the end, as far as I could get from Miss Lena. The room key was in my skirt pocket. The skirt was so tight that putting my hand in the pocket was like trying to stick my fingers under the crack of a door. I wedged in my pointer finger, wiggled out the loose key (had a flash thought that Howard wouldn't be able to do something like that with his left hand), and then unlocked the door.

The woman walked into the room and removed her suit jacket. "Divorce." I could see she was small on top and a lot bigger on the bottom. Like one of those books where you flip the half pages and mismatch the animals: a giraffe head on a hedgehog body.

"You're looking for a divorce? Do you need something to wear to court?"

"Nope. That part's done. I'm divorced now. I've lost sixty-seven pounds. And I want a whole new wardrobe."

"Excellent," I said. "Size four?" I could see she was a six in dresses, probably an eight in pants, and a four in tops.

"Four or six. Or eight." She flicked her right wrist as if to say *la-di-da*.

"Do you want work dresses or weekend dresses?"

"Everything! I love the color of this." She stroked the Andrea Jovine I'd hung on the hook in the room. It was peacock blue. If she liked that, she'd probably like emerald green and ruby red, too. After only a few shifts at I. Magnin, I'd discovered that people who liked rich colors seemed to like all rich colors. People who liked white seemed to like beige and straw and sometimes black, too, but rarely the jewel colors. People who liked yellow were in their own category, predominantly old women.

"Okay," I said. "I'm going to bring you some rich colors and sexy dresses too. If you lost the weight, you should show off, right?"

"Exactly!" She unbuttoned her pants and let them drop. I closed the door and went out to the floor. I was used to people getting undressed in front of me. Some women seemed to do it deliberately—they'd call me in for another size and I'd find them standing there, entirely nude. Others wouldn't even take off their coat until I'd firmly shut the dressing room door behind me. The more they undressed in front of me, the more they talked. The women who leaned against the open fitting room door frame with their bare breasts out would say anything. One woman told me about her sex life. It was like talking to Raquel, only I gave absolutely nothing in return.

I quickly grabbed a few things from petites and hung them outside Miss Divorce's door. I needed to keep her stocked with enough dresses that she wouldn't put on her own clothes and give up before I had time to search the entire sales floor for outfits that would work. My heart thrummed like a revving engine.

Even though she was bossy and mean, I had already learned

things by watching Miss Yolanda. She was never wrong about what would look good on whom. In most cases, she knew more than the women themselves. At least once a day I heard her say to someone, "I don't care that you don't like it. When you try it on, you'll love it." She matched the dress to the body and found the style and cut that complemented, accentuated, or hid a woman's shape depending on . . . well, on what the woman herself wanted. A couple days ago a woman came in with breasts so large that my mind immediately scanned the mental inventory in search of something to conceal them. It only took one tried-on dress to discover that the customer wanted to cantilever those breasts and show them off instead. With Miss Divorce that afternoon, I thought I had no time for failed attempts. Finding the perfect dress felt as urgent as matching the right organ donor to a patient already on the operating table.

As I walked the floor, customers started pouring off the escalator like foam from a waterfall. Was this the result of praying with Miss Lena? Was God going to help me make more money so I could help out my mother and Howard? I said hello to two women wearing Chanel flats. Before they could say hello back, Miss Yolanda scurried over and stood directly in front of me.

"I've helped you both before," she screeched. "I have all your info in my Blue Book. Come!" She waved her hand and they followed.

I, too, had a Blue Book, which had been given to me the day I started. The pages were as clean and white as bleached bedsheets. I had been instructed to record my customers' names, address, phone number, credit card number, age, size, and other pertinent information, like her birthday and the names of her children. I had also been told to write down what my customer bought and when. According to Miss Deborah, who trained me, true professionals sent their customers birthday cards and always asked after their husband and children (by name!). "Nothing will ensure future sales better than saying, 'And how is little Tommy enjoying third grade?'" Miss Deborah had said, and she'd clapped her hands together and over-opened her eyes in a way that looked so eager, it was almost scary.

So far, I had been too timid to ask anyone for the details required for a Blue Book entry. But as I watched Miss Yolanda trot off with the Chanel-shod ladies, I made a vow to start using the book.

A middle-aged woman in a cowboy hat asked for help finding a formal dress. I didn't speak for a minute, as I had an internal battle between doing the gracious and correct thing, which was taking her to Miss Liaskis in formal dresses or stealing the sale Miss Yolanda–style.

"Hello?" the woman said, waving her hand at me. "I'm looking for a formal dress?"

"Yes! Sorry, I was . . . Well, come this way." I walked her over to Miss Liaskis. If God was bringing me these customers, then I'd better do the right thing and not cheat others out of their proper sales.

As I was leaving Miss Liaskis's section, a girl about my age stopped me. "Oh my God," she said. "You can help me find dresses, right?"

"Of course!" I said. "Walk with me."

The girl was blond with black eyebrows and eyelashes that outlined her big eyes. She was skinny in that big-calved-slender-thighs way that only girls who can eat and eat and eat and never gain a pound are. She explained that she needed dresses for sorority mixers at her school, USC, and that everyone in her sorority (Delta Gamma) was cool and fun, but the girls in the other houses were so judgmental about clothes (Delta Delta Delta, in particular) that she wanted to feel like everything she wore was exactly right.

"We can do this," I told her, and I wondered about the world of sororities. I couldn't imagine any sorority, even the nice-girls one, ever letting me in with my Salvation Army clothes and Vaseline-buffed shoes. The more this girl talked, the more I envied her life in Delta Gamma. After growing up in the tiny sorority of two with my mother, the idea of having forty built-in friends sounded fabulous—a no-abuse version of *Little Orphan Annie* where you hung out with a troupe of people you could count on, sing with, laugh with.

Sorority Girl was pulling out a dress to look more carefully at it when I noticed that she was wearing a Rolex. It effortlessly hung off her wrist, like she'd found it on the windowsill as she was walking out the door and simply threw it on. Voilà. No biggie.

"That one's very expensive," I said, about the dress. "Do we need to stick within a budget?"

"Oh my God," she said, "like, no budget?" She let go of the dress, smiled, and patted her chain-strap purse. "Like, my dad wants me and my sister to have whatever we want so, like, there's, like, no limit."

"Cool." What would it be like to have a father who wanted you to have whatever you wanted? I wondered if this girl spoke to her dad on the phone the way Raquel did with hers: laughing, telling stories, making fun of distant relatives who did ridiculous things like buying time-shares less than a mile from their hometown and then vacationing in them two weeks a year. My mother never told family stories—once her family dropped her, it was like they had disappeared. All I'd heard about my father was that my mother had met him in a San Francisco nightclub and they'd had sex in the empty stairwell. She was eighteen and she thinks he, a student at Stanford, was about the same age. She never saw him again, though a check from his parents arrived after my birth. That check allowed her to buy the apartment where I was raised. But tell me this: Who gets a check big enough to buy an apartment and can't remember the surname on the check? (Answer: my mother.)

"Are your parents married?" I pulled the four and the eight of a Bill Blass that would look great on both Sorority Girl and Miss Divorce.

"Yeah, like, totally. My mom's, like, one of the daughters. My dad spoils all three of us."

What world was this? And could I ever be part of it? The thing I was most jealous of was the fact that she got to go to college. In my last year of high school, no one asked what I'd do next—not my mom or Howard and not even the teachers or counselors at school. According to my mother, no one in her family had ever gone past high school; it seemed logical that I wouldn't either. If I could have figured out *how* to go to college, I would have tried. But *how* was never apparent. I even went to the library and looked for books about paying for school when you had no money. (The librarian sent me to a section of study books that helped you take tests to get into college.) The path from a walk-up apartment two floors above a liquor store to any school in America is invisible when you've never seen a person take that walk before you.

Jealousy was one of the things I hated most about myself—it felt like a character flaw, a failure of generosity. Why couldn't I simply be happy that this or that person didn't have to endure some of the stuff I did? The more Sorority Girl talked (about rushing sororities, about life at USC, about her father flying her up for the weekend specifically to shop but also to have dinner with her aunt who was turning sixty, about how much fun she has with her family), the more I committed myself to *not* being jealous. I even blinked my eyes shut once and did a quick prayer, *Please, God, help me not be jealous; help me be happy for this happy girl.*

When Sorority Girl was in her fitting room next to Miss Divorce, I knocked on the door where Miss Lena was still praying and then opened it with my key. I kept my body blocking the doorway in case someone came out of a room or down the hall.

"Your prayers are working," I whispered. "There are loads of people on the floor."

"Oh goody!" Miss Lena fluttered her fingertips and then stilled them again. "I'll ask for even more!"

"I've got two people in fitting rooms." I lowered my whisper. "You take one and I'll take the other." Of course I needed both of the sales. But stealing sales from Miss Lena, the only person who was kind to me, was downright wrong.

"Oh, you take them both, dear. I'll get someone soon enough."

I took a step inside the fitting room and shut the door behind me. "Miss Lena. These are going to be big sales; the girl is wearing a Rolex, and each wants many, many, dresses."

"Jesus has blessed us today!" Miss Lena said. "You've done the work—you take them! I'll get the next one."

I looked at Miss Lena, trying to decide what to do. Taking every possible sale would allow me to help my mother. But could I stand myself if I did?

"I'll ring up one of them for you," I said quickly, and then I left the room before Miss Lena could object.

Two women were handling the burnt-orange Vittadini dress when I came out. They both had broad, thick-skinned faces and were about six inches and forty pounds apart. The shorter one was the heavier one. The tall one wore orange painter pants and an orange silk blouse that looked ridiculous with the pants. The shorter one was in an orange knit tunic over thick orange tights. She also wore Day-Glo orange tennis shoes and a floppy pinkish-orange hat that reminded me of Stevie Nicks. Both were in desperate need of fashion advice.

"Let me know if you need help," I said.

"We'll take them," the hat lady said. "I'm a twelve and she's a six."

"Oh, and that one there, too." The taller one pointed to the orangey-red wrap dress that was I. Magnin's own knockoff brand called Huntington Bridges.

"These are petites, so I'll grab the regular-sized one for you. It's the same dress."

"Fine. Do you have anything else that's orange?" the shorter one asked.

"Yeah. Deep orange is happening now. There are a lot of rich jewel tones—"

The tall one interrupted. "Bring us a twelve and six in everything orange. Nothing but orange."

"Do you want to try them on?"

"Nope." She shook her head and her short friend shook her head too.

"We hate shopping," the shorter one said. She took a seat in the chintz armchair in the corner. So far I'd only seen men sit there when they waited for their wives, girlfriends, or, once, daughters.

"I'll shop for you! Hang out here and give me a few minutes." I remembered a collared orange dress in Miss Karen and Miss Lee's section, so I rushed straight across the marble floor to get it. They both halted their conversation as if I'd interrupted them. As I pulled two dresses from a four-way rack in the back, Miss Karen and Miss Lee silently watched. I started to walk away, then returned to the rack and grabbed one more for Miss Divorce. Next I took a fitted, knee-length ribbed knit dress for Sorority Girl. It looked like something Jackie Kennedy might have worn. Miss Lee and Miss Karen did not turn their silent heads away from me until my feet were back in Petite Dresses.

I hung the dresses for the Orange Ladies on a hook by the register. "I'm not done searching yet," I said to them as I hustled down the fitting room corridor. Miss Divorce opened the door wearing only her panties, no bra. I held out the orange dress I'd picked up for her and she took it from my hand. The way her breasts were hanging reminded me of an unfurled skein of yarn. If I gathered them up in my hand, they would make a nice plump ball.

"I need new bras, too," she said. "And underwear. And I'll take all these." She pointed to the dresses hanging on one wall.

"Okay." I shot a second look at her breasts to try to get an idea of her bra size. "38C?"

"I think. I used to be 44F. But 38C sounds good. I haven't worn a bra since I lost the weight. My bras are all too baggy."

"That's funny," I said. "You're the first person I've heard describe a bra as baggy. Most people describe them as handcuffs."

"Mine became the opposite of handcuffs."

"Like empty nylon bags strapped to your chest?"

She tilted her head as if she were considering that. "Yeah," she said. "Sort of."

"I'll be back in a second."

I left her to check on Sorority Girl, who opened the door in one of the dresses I had picked for her. Andrea Jovine would have wanted her to model it.

"You look perfect," I said.

"You think so?" She tilted her head and turned toward the mirror.

"Yeah, I think so." I felt the snake of jealousy writhing in my gut and accidentally bit my tongue. The taste of dirty pennies filled my mouth—I'd drawn blood. I hoped it wouldn't show on my teeth. I swallowed it down and then hung the ribbed knit dress on a wall hook. "This will be as perfect on you as that one."

"You're so sweet!"

"If I were you," I said, "I'd go to LA and audition for movies."

"Why don't you go as you?" She was still looking at herself in the mirror, turning from back to front.

"Well . . ." I shrugged and stared at the two of us together in the mirror. How much chance did a girl like me have in Los Angeles when girls like her were flooding the place? Also, after participating in all the shows at school, I realized I liked being backstage more than being onstage. The process of creating a show was way more gratifying than the performance. Maybe that's why Miss Dani's job seemed cool to me. She was like the stage manager.

"Can you get me shoes to match this one. And these?" Sorority Girl pointed behind her to four more dresses. There was only one in the reject pile.

"What size?"

"Six and a half."

"Do you need to be able to dance in them?"

"I can dance in anything!" She danced to music in her head. It was actually good dancing. Another thing she had going for her. She could go to New York and do musicals. I smiled and then quickly licked the blood off my teeth.

"Can you repeat shoes or do you want one pair for each dress?"

"Like, how much fun would a pair for each dress be?"

"Very?"

"Totally." She danced again and snapped her fingers in quick little pops. I rushed out and passed the Orange Ladies again. The tall one was now sitting on the arm of the chair next to the short one, who filled the chair.

"Give me five minutes!" I said.

I was about to get on the down escalator when a black-haired woman with a giant mole in the center of her forehead, like a target for an arrow, stopped me. "Oh, I need your help!" she said. Her nails looked like they'd been dipped in blood. They matched her lipstick. "I have an engagement party tonight and I need the perfect dress."

"Is it your engagement?"

"My cousin's. It's formal."

"Okay, I'm going to take you to Miss Liaskis in formal dresses—"

"Is that the Greek lady?"

"Yes."

"No, she's too slow. I want you to help me."

"Okay, follow me." I rushed with her to Miss Liaskis's area. Miss Liaskis was in a fitting room with a customer; I could hear the musical lilt of her voice. The fact that she was helping someone and—as I'd seen—was unable to help more than one person at once, relieved me of the guilt of taking a sale from Formal Dresses. "Size eight?"

"Yeah. Or ten."

Finally someone with a realistic view of herself. I pulled eights in the dresses that I knew ran large and tens in the others. Then I led her to Miss Liaskis's fitting rooms and let her in one.

I did a near-jogging sweep of the floor, pulling every orange dress I could find. Miss Yolanda yelled at me as I passed her, "What are you rushing about for? How many people do you have in rooms?!" I ignored her and kept going.

Back at my register, I hung all the orange dresses I'd gathered. I waved over the ladies who were still overtaking the chair with their bodies. Only the tall one came over.

"Why don't you look through these and lay the ones you want on the counter? I'll be back in five minutes."

She made a pouty face but nodded and started fingering the dresses.

I quickly trotted down the escalator stairs to lingerie and shoes.

The shoe guy lifted both arms and said, "Hey, hey! Finally you've come! Gimme the shoes." He made twinkle movements with his fingers. "Also, what's your name?"

"Zippy. You?"

"Pablo. I'm going to make your shoes look brand-new!"

"You're so great!" I said. "But I actually need to pull shoes for a customer who wants a pair for every dress she's buying."

Pablo let out a low whistle and shook his head. "Good sale! Gimme your shoes to fix while you're picking out stuff for her."

"Can I walk around in my stockings?" I looked around as if Miss Dani, or worse, the store manager, Miss Kitty, would suddenly appear in the shoe department.

"Here." Pablo picked up a pair of ballet flats from the cushioned bench seat and laid them before my feet. I stepped out of my shoes, handed them over, slipped on the flats, and did a fast sweep of the inventory.

While Pablo pulled the shoe selections, I went to lingerie and found bras with matching panties for Miss Divorce. I wasn't trying to make it more expensive for her, but the Lejaby bras were the prettiest: delicate lace on the cups and tiny bows on the straps. They were expensive in a way I couldn't understand (there wasn't more fabric! They weren't spun from gold!). Was it that they were so damned pretty? I had planned to buy one for myself once I'd saved enough money for two months' rent.

When I returned to shoes, Pablo dropped to one knee as if he were going to propose. "Mademoiselle," he said, and he slipped off the ballet flats and slid my foot into one pump and then the other.

I looked down at my beautifully polished shoes and thought, *I love this job!*

Pablo carried the shoeboxes to the customer elevator and waited with me. I told him about Sorority Girl and that she was going to dance in each pair of these shoes.

"You ever been to I-Beam?" he asked.

"No, is it a dance club?" I only knew the places where Raquel took me.

“Yeah, I was there last night dancing my brains out. Everyone was so joyous that it felt like the end of something. I couldn’t help but wonder: Is this going to be *the last party* for one of the men here?”

“You mean, because of AIDS?” It had never occurred to me that Pablo was gay, but it seemed that this was his discreet way of telling me he was.

“Yeah, yeah.” He smiled in a sad way. “It’s everywhere now. I mean, it’s like a domino-death-topple that runs from France to LA to San Francisco . . . If there’s one way to prove that all the people of the world really are connected, one species netted together on the planet, it’s by following the trail of a deadly virus.”

“It’s scary,” I said. “I’m afraid to go to the dentist because I read about a woman who got it from a dental tool.”

“Oh, Zippy! Go to the dentist! And use protection with every guy you meet.” Pablo winked at me, and then the doors opened. He placed the shoeboxes in my arms.

“Okay. I’ll go to the dentist,” I said, and glanced at the other women in the car. “And, if the circumstances ever arise, I’ll do that other thing too.”

“Wait!” Pablo shouted. He stuck his arm out to stop the doors from closing. “Take these.” He opened one of the shoeboxes in my arms and dropped in a hamster-sized wad of stockings. Pablo blew me a kiss goodbye as the doors closed.

Miss Divorce was waiting in her underpants. I put the shoeboxes on the ground and handed her the lingerie. She reached her hands to the waistband of her panties and was about to strip totally naked when I lifted a hand to stop her. “You have to keep your underpants on when you try on underpants.”

“Are you serious?”

“Yeah. It’s the law.” I had no idea if it was a law, but who would want to try on panties that other people had tried on without their underwear? I mean, what about crotch sweat and crabs and herpes and anything else you could get? AIDS!

"Fine. Whatever," Miss Divorce said, and started to put on a pair of panties over the ones she had on when I picked up the shoeboxes and moved on.

I knocked on Sorority Girl's door with my foot. She opened it to reveal herself in another fabulous dress.

"It's like there's no limit to how great it would be to be you," I said sincerely.

She grinned. "Does that mean you like this one?"

"Amazing. Try on all the shoes. I'll check back in a second." I dumped the shoeboxes on the ground, started to leave, then remembered the little stockings in one box.

"Stockings," I said, and I opened the box and pointed down. She shrugged and shut the door.

The Orange Ladies were standing by the register. "These," the short one said.

"Check? Charge?"

"Charge," the short one said. "One card."

It was eight dresses. Four each. I paused in front of the register. I should ring this sale up for Miss Lena. But my other two sales hadn't been completed yet. What if Sorority Girl was a lunatic with a fake Rolex, no money, and a good fictional story of her life? What if Miss Divorce got a sudden rush of depression and wanted nothing but to walk away and weep? The only way I could be sure I made a single sale today would be to ring up this one under my number.

"So," I said as I punched in the numbers on the register. "Are you in some orange club?"

"Sort of."

"Are you sisters?"

"Sort of."

"Sort of?"

"We consider ourselves sisters. We're part of the Rajneesh movement."

"Huh." I kept ringing up, my fingers clicking fast against the keys. "I don't know what that is."

"We follow this guru named Osho—" the tall one started.

"We lived in a commune in Oregon and in one in India—"

"So we're not blood sisters, but—"

"We're truly sisters." The short one hugged the tall one.

The tall one said, "Things are kind of falling apart in Oregon, so we're opening a center here in order to continue the good spiritual work."

"So a bunch of orange dresses from I. Magnin is part of the good spiritual work?" I asked.

"Well, members of the Rajneesh movement only wear orange. And since we're starting the center here, we figured we needed to look a little authoritative, you know? Nice dresses instead of the usual." The tall one shrugged and ran her hands down the sides of her orange overalls.

"Sex is a spiritual, beautiful thing," the short one said.

I stopped typing in numbers and looked at her. So far this conversation had had nothing to do with sex. *Was* sex a spiritual, beautiful thing? Neither Raquel nor Mimi in cosmetics had ever mentioned that. From what they'd said, sex was either a true love thing or a sexy-sexing thing.

"Huh. Cool." I hit *total* and then took the card from the short one. While I was running it through, she and the tall one stared at each other in the eyes.

"Okay." I handed over the sales receipt. She broke her eyes away and signed: $2,578. A huge sale. As I was bagging the purchases, the woman I'd put in Miss Liaskis's fitting room approached with one of the dresses I'd chosen for her. Miss Yolanda ran to her, tried to take the dress from her hands, and shouted, "I'll ring you up." The woman pulled the dress into her chest and said, "No! She helped me!" She walked fast away from Miss Yolanda, who moved the candy ball to the other cheek and squint-glared in my direction.

I handed the bundled dresses to the Orange Ladies and took the dress from the forehead mole lady. The Orange Ladies floated away, deep in conversation with each other.

"This is perfect," Mole Lady said. It was a sapphire-blue Oleg Cassini with a turned-up collar and a built-in cummerbund, $575.

"I'm so glad." I punched in Miss Lena's number, relieved that I had already made a big enough sale for myself that it didn't harm me to give one away. "Pablo downstairs can help you find the perfect pair of shoes. Should I call him and tell him you're coming?"

"That would be so nice," she said. I was glad to be able to throw a sale Pablo's way. I needed to thank him for making my thrift store pumps look brand-new.

Miss Divorce came out of the fitting room as I was saying goodbye to Mole Lady. She had a heap of dresses in her hand, the bras and panties piled on top. Half the bundle tumbled to the ground as she approached the register.

I rushed to get what remained in her hands, but before I got there, she released them all and sighed. "You know what?"

I glanced at the clothes on the ground. "What?" What kind of a person didn't take care of elegant, expensive clothes—especially if they didn't own them? I looked at the woman and could feel my face sagging, melting toward my neck. My guess: she'd claim she needed lunch and that she'd come back and buy everything afterward, though she wouldn't. It had happened to me before. People fled the bigger sales. No one walked away from an eighty-nine-dollar Hunt Club foulard-print dress.

"I'm going to go get lunch and then I'll come back and get all this."

"No problem," I lied in response to her lie. "I'll have it waiting by the register for you."

"But can you ring it up and bag it while I'm gone?" She reached into her handbag, pulled out an I. Magnin credit card, and handed it to me.

"Absolutely." Hurrah! If she signed that charge slip, I'd enter her as my first customer in my Blue Book.

"Okay then. Ta-ta." She trotted off toward the escalator.

Miss Lena emerged from the fitting room. Her hair was falling out of the bun as if she'd been making out with someone rather than praying.

"Everything okay?" I asked.

"Jesus has blessed us today!" Miss Lena bent down and started picking up the dropped clothes. I joined her.

"This is the lady who was in the far room," I said. "She left her credit card so it can all be rung up." And then I wanted to say, *You take this sale*. But if Sorority Girl didn't buy her load, it would be a huge loss to me. I hated myself for thinking about it too much, for being so stingy and selfish. But the medical bills for one-handed Howard were waiting on the other side of this problem.

Sorority Girl called from the fitting room, "Hey, girlfriend!"

"Coming!" I assumed she meant me, and started down the hall. Then I turned around, came back, handed the credit card to Miss Lena and forced myself to say: "Ring this up under your number and I'll take the girl who's calling me." Before I could change my mind, I ran off.

Sorority Girl was leaning against the doorway of her dressing room, wearing her own clothes. "So, like, I want to talk through all this with you and maybe try some on for you before I decide."

"Sure." I took her place at the open door while she stepped into the room. As I tuned in and out, Sorority Girl sorted through the dresses with a monologue about themed parties, dates, what each date looked like, and what her best friends were wearing. I hoped that all this chatter wasn't leading to the selection of a single dress. If so, I'd cheated myself by giving Miss Lena what might end up being the biggest sale on the floor this month. As soon as I had that thought, I felt guilty about it. Why not give Miss Lena the biggest sale?

Sorority Girl kicked a shoebox with the toe of her white Capezio jazz shoes and I jolted back in. "So," I improvised, "if all your friends are wearing white to the—"

"Winter formal."

"Right. That one. Then this dress is an absolute."

"Yes." She moved the white dress from a hook on one side of the dressing room to the other.

We continued on in this way until she had selected four dresses and four pairs of shoes. Two of the four dresses were expensive and each of the shoes cost almost as much as the dresses. I didn't even know shoes could cost that much until I'd started working at I. Magnin.

By the time I hauled her clothes to the register, Miss Lena had rung up and bagged Miss Divorce's sale.

"What was her total?" I whispered.

"$4,200," Miss Lena whispered.

"Holy moly," I whispered, and I simultaneously felt regret that it wasn't my sale and joy that it was Miss Lena's sale.

The sorority girl pulled out a credit card and laid it on the counter.

"She goes to USC," I said to Miss Lena, "and is getting these dresses for Greek system mixers."

"Oh, wonderful!" Miss Lena clapped her hands. "Tell me, dear, What is a Greek system mixer? Does it happen in Greece?"

They talked as I typed in numbers (*department: 365, class: 81, item: 8725*) and then removed the security sensors. Miss Lena pulled out hanger bags and wrapped the dresses after I hung them on the hook beside the register. She placed the shoeboxes in a handle bag.

I hit *total.* It was a little more than half the total of Miss Divorce's sale. Regret panged in my heart. I felt guilty for that pang, so I blinked my eyes and tried to reset my brain. I had already made enough today with the orange-dress ladies. Why couldn't I be straight up generous?

"Before you go," I said, and I pulled out my pristine Blue Book from the supply drawer, "can I write down your info? This way you could call me from Los Angeles and I could have dresses sent to you."

"Oh my God! You'd, like, do that for me?"

That she saw my wanting her in my Blue Book as a gift *to her* made me want to laugh. Not only was I doing my job better, but I'd—hopefully—be able to follow Sorority Girl's life. Would the dresses she bought that day be a hit at the mixers? Would her family throw a party on, say, Memorial Day or Labor Day and would she need dresses for those parties? Would she ever come in and shop *with* her dad? Knowing these details about her life seemed possible once I had her information (including the numbers on the I. Magnin card her father paid off every month) safely recorded in my book.

Miss Divorce returned seconds after Sorority Girl left. She wasn't as excited to be entered into my Blue Book, but she didn't seem to mind, either. Once Miss Divorce was gone, I dropped my head on the register counter for a couple seconds. When I stood again, Miss Lena was staring at me, her face as smooth and pure as a bowl of plain yogurt.

"I feel like I ran a marathon," I said.

"And you won! Such big sales! Jesus is smiling at you today!"

The rest of the day was more like any other. Customers here and there, far more people looking than trying on dresses, and far more people trying on dresses than buying them. Those who bought only bought one.

Near the end of the day, the floater who covered us on breaks wandered down to chat. She was a fat-cheeked, skinny woman with thick hair cut short to her head. She wore a long mustard-brown skirt with a matching jacket and old-fashioned lace-up heeled boots. She looked like a fancy lady from *Little House on the Prairie*.

"You were busy down here today," she said.

"Yes, dear." Miss Lena patted her forearm. "And how did you do?"

"That nasty French lady kept stealing my sales."

"All of them?!" I asked.

"Pretty much. Every time I started to help someone, she swooped in, took the clothes from my hands or theirs, and took them to the fitting rooms."

"You earn commission, too, don't you?"

"Yeah, but at least I don't live off this paycheck. We're in Marin and it is dead as heck out there, so I basically work to get out of the house." She shrugged.

"Oh dear! Is it hard to make friends out there?" Miss Lena asked.

"Everyone my age has babies. It's a drag. And my husband works late hours. He's in finance. I've got a cleaning lady, and you can only spend so much time making dinner or going to Jazzercise." She was fingering through the dresses on the racks by the register as she talked. Then she pulled off the new pale-blue Vittadini. "This is cute."

"It would look great on you," I said, but I wasn't really thinking that. Instead I was wondering what it would be like to take a job at I. Magnin only so you could get out of the house. And what did she do with the paychecks that were entirely unnecessary as far as paying for rent, utilities, or food? Did she use her employee discount and buy clothes and makeup?

"I'll take it." She laid the Vittadini on the counter and Miss Lena started ringing her up. I looked over her shoulder and watched her punch in my sales number. This made me feel even worse for regretting giving her the Divorce Lady instead of Sorority Girl.

"No, no, no—" I hit *void* and started the sale all over again, under Miss Lena's number.

"Oh my God," the woman said. "You're exactly like the French woman!"

Miss Lena and I laughed. "No, dear," she said. "It's the opposite. She rang it up for me."

"Are you serious? I mean, I don't need money, but I don't give it away on purpose." The floater signed the receipt. When she put down the pen, she looked up at us and asked, "Rich husbands?"

Miss Lena and I both burst into laughter again. "No husbands!" Miss Lena said, and she stomped her little foot.

"Okay, then, you two are weird." The floater picked up the dress and marched away.

"The sensor, dear!" Miss Lena shouted, but she didn't seem to hear.

Once the store was closed, Miss Dani came out. Sometimes she reminded me of a zoo animal hiding in the shelter until none of the paying visitors were around to observe her. As usual she was decorated from her ears to her fingers. Today it was all orange, everything big and shiny. Her earrings looked like teacup saucers in a kid's playhouse.

"You know, I had two women today who were wearing orange. They bought only orange dresses."

"Did they now?" Miss Dani stuck out what should have been a hip. In my head I heard the voice of the cartoon rooster Foghorn Leghorn: *She's like the road from Dallas to Fort Worth . . . no curves.*

Miss Yolanda zoomed over to us, as usual. "What are you hyenas talking about?" she asked.

I looked toward Miss Liaskis, who was fretting over her register. I waved my arm that she should come join us and then shouted, "I'll close you out in a second." She looked up and rushed over. Miss Braughn L had already closed out her register and gone home. And Miss Lee and Miss Karen simply stayed in their area, as if the rest of us existed inside a bubble and they were allowed to float around outside it.

"Jesus blessed us with enormous sales today!" Miss Lena said.

"There were two ladies here who *only* wanted orange dresses," I explained. "They were from some spiritual group."

"Oh, those crazy yoga people!" Miss Yolanda said. "It's a bunch of hocus-pocus bull-malarkey. They have lots of sex. Orgies."

Miss Lena said something that sounded like *OOOOO* and clapped her hands once. Miss Liaskis gasped.

Miss Dani said, "Hold on. Hang fire. Yoga women from a sex-orgy cult bought all the orange dresses on the floor?"

"They follow a guru," Miss Yolanda said.

"How do you know this?" Miss Dani asked.

"My cousin left Paris to be with these dopeheads in India. They have sex and give all their money to this bearded man who doesn't say anything. They're complete lunatics. He doesn't speak, so everyone assigns great intelligence to him."

"Maybe he is intelligent," Miss Lena said.

"He damn well is!" Miss Yolanda said. "But not in the way they think. He's getting their money, he's having sex with them, he has lots of Rolls-Royces."

"Where does he keep the Rolls-Royces?" Miss Liaskis asked, and we all looked at her but no one answered.

Miss Yolanda's response was to pull a pen and hold tag from her skirt pocket. She said, "What did everyone do today?"

"We haven't totaled yet," Miss Lena said. "But Miss Zippy had three huge sales. The orange ladies and then one for over four thousand and one for around two thousand."

"Jesus!" Miss Yolanda said. "You're joking, right?"

Miss Liaskis actually hooted and then she hugged me, but I couldn't concentrate on the hug. I pulled out of it and said to Miss Lena, "Didn't you ring up that divorced woman for yourself?"

"Why would she do that?" Miss Yolanda was scowling so hard, her candy ball lowered almost to her jawline.

Miss Lena ignored Miss Yolanda. "No, dear. You did the work. I rang it up for you."

"But—" My head felt like it was full of fizzing milk. I was at once happy that I got all the huge sales and ashamed of my happiness. I felt greedy and grabby. "But you were helping me. We needed to share those sales!"

"What is wrong with you two donkeys?" Miss Yolanda said. "We earn commission! This isn't Russia!"

"But we work together, so it only seems fair . . ." I could never tell anyone that Miss Lena had been praying in the fitting room and that *that* may have been the reason the big sales came our way.

"You're a good egg," Miss Dani said, and she pinched my cheek like I was a kid.

"A very good egg! You help me with my register!" Miss Liaskis said, which only made me feel more embarrassed and ashamed.

"Can we get back to business here?" Miss Yolanda turned toward Miss Liaskis, her pencil poised on the hold tag.

"We don't need totals today!" Miss Dani said. "Everyone's doing fine and I'm proud of all of you." Miss Dani turned to me and winked as if she were secretly only proud of me. All I could think right then was that I needed to try harder to make more sales *and* give more to Miss Lena.

I needed to atone.

# Chapter 4

**Almost a week** later, Pablo was in front of me again as I entered the line to clock in.

"Zippy!" He hugged me. "I sold six pairs of shoes to the twins you sent down! Thanks so much!" He gave me another hug and then went off to the elevator.

The twins to whom he was referring appeared to be from a different era. I'd only ever seen them in the exact same outfit, including hats and gloves. The day Pablo sold them the shoes, I'd sold them two dresses each, size eight. I would have sold them three dresses each, but I didn't have two of the same size left in one that they liked. I had suggested that I order the second one from another I. Magnin or that they buy the single one and take turns with it. They declined both offers. Impatience against the former, and the fact that they dressed alike every day against the latter.

I'd had about five hundred questions for them, but these two were efficient shoppers and spoke mostly between themselves. The only thing I got out of them was that they had exactly the same taste and never disagreed about what to buy. After they'd left, I took some hold tags and made a list of things I wanted to find out about them. I figured if I showed my list to the other salesgirls and each person found out one thing each time they came in, my curiosity could be satisfied. The questions were: *Have they ever lived apart? Has either had a romantic relationship? Do they wear matching underwear and matching nightclothes? If one was going somewhere, but the other was home, did they still wear the same clothes? Do they order the same thing in restaurants? Do they like the same books and movies? Do they get into fights?*

Miss Lena read over my list and crossed out *Do they get into fights?* She said, "We don't want to bring up the bad stuff." When the sales team met with Miss Dani after the store closed that day, I read the questions aloud and asked everyone to help out. They all looked at me with dead or slitted eyes, except Miss Lena.

Miss Yolanda said, "You're a total nutcase."

Miss Lena said, "Zippy has a wonderful mind!"

**I punched my** time card and headed to the cosmetics floor. The girl with spin-art eyes had changed from blue-eyed to green-eyed. I waved at her and went straight to Mimi, who was organizing her stock drawers.

"I'm seeing a younger man!" she whispered.

"Cool! How much younger?" The cosmetics ladies were always direct and open when it came to sex and their love lives. When I sat at their table in the lunchroom, I never said a word, as the talk was too compelling to interrupt.

"Five years," she said. I thought about the fact that if a man were seeing a woman who was five years younger, he wouldn't even call her a *younger woman*. But for a woman to see a guy who was even a year younger was to see a *younger man*. "And it's, like, totally fun. He smells like flowery perfume."

"Wow. What parts of him smell flowery? Are you talking about his hair or his skin or—"

"Both, everything! My best friend in college smelled flowery like him. We used to shower together and then get in bed and nap all afternoon. The usual stuff all girls do."

Nothing about that sounded usual to me. Until Raquel, I'd never even had a best friend. Well, I suppose my mom had been my best friend; maybe that's why I'd never had one. "So you found the college best-friend replacement," I said.

"Totally. He's kind of like a woman too, now that I think about it. But it's weird. I mean, it's great—total blindness every time he touches me."

"Blindness?"

"Yes, have you ever had that with a guy? The blindness thing?"

"I've never been with a guy. Kissed one once and it was horrible."

"Oh, are you into women?"

"No, I like boys. They don't like me."

"They do, or they will." Mimi flapped her hand at me like *Don't worry.* "Blindness is when the sex is so amazing, some of your senses go on the blink. Like you can't hear or you can only hear him breathing. And you can't see. It's like there's a blackish-red sheet hanging over your face. It's all feeling."

"Does everyone have that?"

"I hope so! Sex isn't worth it if you're not going blind when you do it."

"It's not?"

"No, it's gross if it's not fabulous. I mean, who wants to be near other people's skin, holes, fluids, smells . . . like, yuck."

"Huh." If you went by TV, movies, and teenaged chatter at school, sex was the single greatest thing there was. "Okay, so don't do it unless it makes you blind." Hold tag advice.

"Exactly."

"How can you know before you embark on it?"

"Hmmm, usually there's an unrelenting urge. And if there's no unrelenting urge, it probably won't make you blind."

"And then it's just holes and smells."

"Exactly!" Mimi slapped her hands on the counter like we'd solved some chalkboard-sized math problem. "Let me do your eyes." She picked up an eye pencil. I leaned in toward her. "Look up," she said.

I looked up. The liner below each eye felt cool and soothing.

"Look down."

I looked down. The top lid wasn't as sensitive.

"Mascara now." Mimi held the wand below my top lashes. "Blink. Blink. Blink. Blink. Blink. Other eye. Blink. Blink. Blink. Blink. Blink. Blink."

"Are my lashes even?"

"Yeah. Why?"

"I counted more *blinks* on my right eye."

Mimi moved the wand to my left eye. "Blink. Blink. Blink." She went to my right eye. "Blink. Blink. Blink." They were still uneven as far as brush counts went, but I let it go.

Mimi dabbed some blush on my cheeks and then she pulled out a lipstick, wiped the tip with a tissue, and then applied the lipstick to my lips.

"You're so pretty, but you don't realize it," she said.

I was silent as I tried to take in the compliment. It was hard to believe, and I wondered what she saw. Finally I said, "People have never told me I'm pretty."

"That's because you're not flashing it. It's like there's a world of peacocks around you and you're this gorgeous little chickadee hiding behind a fallen branch."

"Definitely not a *little* chickadee."

"You think you're large?" Mimi ran her hands down her middle again, and I felt bad for having made the joke. However overweight I was, she was double. "The weight-obsessed world can kiss my grits!

There's more of me to love. And right now I got myself a hot young lover!"

"And I got myself a no-eating day," I said. "Hey, can I sit with you at lunch? Your stories are the best distraction."

"Hell yeah. I'll call you." She pointed at the phone on the counter. Beside it was a stack of cards in a plexiglass holder.

"What are these?" I pulled one out. On the top it said, *Tell Us About Your Magnin Day!* Below that it asked for the name of the salesperson who helped you, if they were helpful or not, and why.

"Miss Dani didn't tell you about them?"

"Nope."

"Well, then your department is the only one that doesn't know. Each week, the salesperson who gets the most praise gets a gift card to a spa."

"Cool."

"And the person with the most complaints gets fired!" Mimi said.

"Really?"

"No, they didn't say that. But if there's space to complain, there's always someone who will, right? And if anyone gets enough complaints . . ." Mimi shrugged.

**I took the** usual route. Customer elevators to the fifth floor. Customer bathrooms for a final pee before my shift started. Then I crossed the floor; nodded at the Braughn sisters, who didn't nod back; and went straight to Miss Liaskis's register to open it for her. Her eyes were glossy with grateful tears.

I was standing beside Miss Lena before the store opened when Miss Dani hustled out of her office and then stopped by each register.

I watched her place the praise/complaint cards on each counter. She got to Petite Dresses last; her bowed chest rose and fell.

"Forgot about these," she said. "Complaint cards."

Miss Lena picked one up and read it. "Or praise!"

"Yeah, yeah. Tell the others when you see them. The person with the most praise gets a gift card to a spa. Jesus, I'm late!" Miss Dani rushed off, jerky and fast, like a cartoon character in motion.

Soon after the store opened, Miss Dani emerged again. This time she was with an elegant blond woman who was probably around my mother's age. She was wearing a black dress that looked like it had been handmade for her body. Everything about her looked smooth, buffed. I glanced at the other salesgirls. No one else took note of her. Was she a manager from another department? A manager from another store?

They stopped near Petite Dresses. The elegant woman turned in circles, her eyes roving as if she were taking a 360-degree photo with her face.

"Who is that?" I whispered to Miss Lena.

"She's—" The phone rang and Miss Lena answered it without finishing her sentence.

I walked closer, pretending to adjust a four-way rack, trying to hear what the woman and Miss Dani were discussing.

"Zippy!" Miss Dani said. "Come here." She waved a jewel-weighted arm.

Up close the elegant lady looked more interesting than beautiful. There was something about the way she was taking everything in, moving her head, looking at me, even, that made her seem smart.

"Hey!" I said.

"This is Virginia Summers. She's one of the buyers. This is Miss Zippy. She's with Miss Lena in Petites."

Virginia smiled with her mouth closed. "How are you doing with the new Vittadini?"

"Great!"

"Great?"

"Well." I hesitated a minute, but Virginia's face seemed too wise to be after flattery. "It doesn't fit women who are long waisted. It puffs out at the wrong place and looks misshapen. So, when those women look at it on the rack, I direct them toward the Donna Karan wrap that is flattering no matter your size or shape."

"And they'll buy the Donna Karan?"

"Yeah, because we have the Donna Karan in the red, too. So if they're looking for red, they'll look fabulous in the Donna Karan."

"Zippy is selling the heck outta everything," Miss Dani said. "If it can be sold, she'll sell it."

"And what do you think is the hardest sell on the floor?" Virginia asked.

"Uh." I looked toward Miss Dani to make sure it was okay to tell her she'd bought a clunker of a dress. Miss Dani nodded. "The gold Anne Klein, it . . ." Could I say it? "It looks like stiff wrapping paper on each body that puts it on."

Virginia nodded heavily, slowly. "We'll mark it down and move it off your floor soon. What do you think is the best buy on the floor?"

"That gray knit skirt suit, the Calvin Klein. There's only one left."

"And you sold one of those?" She was asking because it wasn't in Petite Dresses; it was across the floor in Miss Lee and Miss Karen's area.

"Yeah, I sold three or four of them. Hipper people can wear it with a camisole or a white tank and it's sexy. Conservative people can wear it with a blouse. It's long enough for everyone, but can be shortened. And the jacket cuts in at the waist in a nice way that makes every body look curvy and sensuous." The words came out so fast that I blushed. Had I said too much?

"Thanks, Zippy. Great work." She nodded again and I was dismissed. Miss Dani was smiling as if I'd made her proud.

"Okay, wow. Okay, then. Uh, bye!" I lifted my hand, awkward and embarrassed, but also thrilled that she was interested in my opinion. Was she actually going to mark down a dress simply because I said I couldn't sell it?! I rushed to my station and then stood there and watched Miss Dani and Virginia as they continued circling the floor. How lucky was this woman who got to pick out the dresses that ended up here? Had she been a rich girl who had grown up with clothes like these and knew her way around a store? Why did she have such good taste, and where did taste come from anyway? My mother had been wearing the same patched and repatched clothes since I was in kindergarten. To her, the sole purpose of clothes was to allow her to go out in public, shop at Safeway, and put on her Hardware Depot apron. But to me, clothes were magic. Like fresh white snow on a gritty dirt road, they transformed the mundane into the spectacular. Did believing that make my taste any better than my mother's?

Lunch with Mimi was fun. She was popular, so what started out as a twosome ended up as a passel of women. Most of the women had been working at I. Magnin for at least ten years (if not twenty or thirty)—they knew each other well. I sucked down a Diet Coke, listened, and observed. All these women were beautiful. I studied their faces and tried to figure out *why* they were beautiful. Was it what they were born with, or how they did their makeup and hair, or what they radiated through their voice, movement, and expressions? When I focused on particular parts of individual women, I found things that weren't considered "beautiful" in any magazine: a nose too big, eyes as wide as a lizard's, a mouth with no lips. But beauty was conveyed, nonetheless. If I could figure out *how* it was conveyed, maybe I'd feel beautiful too.

When I returned to Petite Dresses, Miss Lena clapped her hands and did a little jump. "Zippy! You got two phone calls."

"I did?" My mother and Raquel were the only people who had ever phoned me at work.

"Your father called and Raquel called. They both said you should get back to them as soon as possible."

It was so odd to hear the words *your father.* For a second I felt like Miss Lena was magic and being with her had created an alternate reality. One where I had a dad. Finally I reentered reality and said, "I don't have a father."

"Well, I know your mother's husband who cut off his fingers is not your real father, but I thought maybe he referred to himself that way."

Would Howard do that? Maybe in his painkiller-drugged state he might. "Well, he wouldn't usually say he was my father. He never fathered me. But who knows, right?"

"This gentleman had a very nice voice. He said he was your father and that he was phoning from Los Angeles. I was confused about the Los Angeles part because I thought it was the fingerless man."

"Okay, now I have *no idea* who this could be! I don't even know anyone in Los Angeles."

"So it's not your biological father?"

"My mother claims she doesn't remember his name. And he lived in the Bay Area at the time of their one meeting. So—" I shrugged and then watched as Miss Lena rapidly blinked while her mouth formed the letter O. I was so taken aback by a *father* having called that I didn't think before I spoke. Of course Miss Lena could never have imagined that someone might have sex with a person whose name they didn't remember after the act. I hoped she wouldn't think less of me. Or my mother!

"Goodness," Miss Lena finally said, and then she smiled at me in a way that let me know she'd never judge me. "Here. He left this number." She reached into her dress pocket and pulled out a hold tag with a 213 phone number on it.

I stared at the hold tag as if it could provide the answer to my questions. "This is so strange."

Miss Lena put her hand on mine and said, "He said, very clearly, 'Tell her that her father called.'" Just then Miss Lena's customer yoo-hooed from a fitting room. It was almost a yodel. Miss Lena shook her head and hurried off.

I picked up the phone and dialed the number for Raquel's office. My brain felt like it was filling with swirling brackish water.

The receptionist at Raquel's office answered, rattling off the five partner names like "I Am the Very Model of a Modern Major-General."

A few rings after being transferred, Raquel picked up and said her name in a breathy way.

"Why do you sound like that?" I asked.

"Like what?" Raquel asked in her normal, middle-C voice.

"Like Marilyn Monroe singing to Jack Kennedy on his birthday."

Raquel said, "It's my phone voice. You never noticed before. How's work?"

"Okay. Slow."

"Send Miss Lena into the fitting room to pray."

"She's helping a customer. Maybe she'll pray after."

"Can you ask her to pray for me, too? I need help enlisting Jason into the position of Mr. Martinez." Raquel, who loved her last name, claimed she would convince her husband to change his last name to hers.

"Have you seen or heard from Jason yet?" I asked.

"Nope. Hence the demand for prayers!"

"On it. Hey, did some guy who said he was my father call our house?" Raquel compulsively checked our answering machine from her phone at work and then erased the messages.

"Yeah! How'd you know?"

"He called here, too." I paused, as I wasn't sure if I should admit to Raquel that I had actually prayed for my father to show up. Something about it seemed childish. Embarrassing! But I blurted it out before I could think it through much further. "And the weird thing is, when Miss Lena and I were praying the other day, I actually prayed my dad would show up."

"No way!" Raquel said.

"Way," I said.

"But you don't even know his name!"

"I know. I can't explain it! I prayed for a dad and a dad called. Who knows if it's really mine."

"I dunno, Zippy. I've been praying my whole life and it seems like everything I got came to me because I worked my ass off and not because God decided it was time for me to have it."

"You just asked me to ask Miss Lena to pray for Jason!"

"Habit," Raquel said. "Anyway, now that you prayed for him, you *have* to phone back and see if the strange dad-man caller is in fact your no-name dad."

I hesitated. Did I? "I guess, I mean—"

Raquel started talking to someone else in the room, a man. The conversation sped up and then wound and turned; now they were talking over each other. I hung up.

Miss Yolanda was pacing the floor. She reminded me of a hawk circling for carrion. In a reversal of the usual, Miss Liaskis and Miss Lena were helping customers while the other salesgirls chatted or stood around. The Braughn sisters were at their register, facing each other. I couldn't tell if they were talking or not because their bodies weren't moving and the one Braughn had her back to me, blocking the face of the other Braughn with her exactly-as-large head. "Sniper's dream," Howard often said, about his own enormous head. Once, he gave me a not-boring speech about head size in Hollywood and how big heads look better on camera: "It's why Vanna White is so successful." I thought about that phrase. I guessed Vanna White was successful, but still . . . she turned letters on a wall. Did she need a big head to look good doing that? It might have been those long lovely dresses that made her look fabulous. Every night she appeared as if she were on her way to the Academy Awards.

I picked up the phone and called my mom at Hardware Depot. It took two transfers to get her, and then, like Raquel had done, she answered by stating her name. Mom, however, wasn't breathy and Marilyn-like.

"Mom, some man called my apartment *and* my work and said he was my dad and that I should call him back."

I heard the clacking of registers, the sound of people talking in the checkout line.

"Mom? Did you hear what I said?"

"Uh-huh."

Someone asked my mother where the toilet plungers were. She said aisle nine.

"Mom? That wasn't actually my dad who called, was it?" I'd always assumed my father knew as little about my mother as she about him. That would make his ability to find her, or me, virtually impossible.

"You know, honey, he wanted nothing to do with us. So I don't understand why after nineteen years he's suddenly calling."

The feeling of brackish water in my brain dropped to my stomach. It sloshed back and forth like a small hurricane. "Wait. Did you talk to him?!"

"Well, yeah. He called me here and asked for your number. Honestly, Zippy, I didn't know what to say. But you've always asked about him, so I gave him your numbers. And, you know, we talked enough about what happened that I definitely know it's *the real him*. No question."

"Wow. I mean . . . was he nice?"

"Sure, he was nice. It was weird, he sounded so familiar. I mean, I know I only knew him that one night, but his voice and the way he spoke, well . . . I felt like I've known him all these years."

"That's . . . yeah, weird. And, like, what does he do? I mean, is he—" I stopped myself before I said what I was thinking, which was: Was he someone like Howard or someone like Raquel's dad, or something in between the two?

"I didn't get much information—I don't even know if he's married or has other kids. I shoulda asked questions, but honestly, I was so shocked that he was claiming to be who he is that the whole conversation was me figuring out if this guy was the real deal or not."

"Mom! I . . . I don't even know what to think." And I didn't. It was like my brain was faced with a situation that was so utterly alien that there was no place to understand it; nothing in my *past* helped me process this *present*.

"Call him. You might enjoy talking to him."

"What do I say?"

"Say hello! But, honey, don't expect much more than an interesting conversation. You know, someone who makes a baby and then disappears for nineteen years certainly isn't Mr. Perfect Pants."

"But you do think he's Mr. Nice Pants, right?" My heart felt like a self-banging timpani.

"Yeah, yeah. And like I said, I felt like I knew him already."

Neither of us spoke for a few seconds. I focused on what I heard from my mother's end: register *tick-tick*s, customers talking to employees, a mother scolding her kid. So many lives were being lived in Hardware Depot. Everyone was looking for what they needed: paint, brushes, a new sink, a plant, a mop head. While there in I. Magnin, my world was spinning and spinning and spinning into some new place that I had never thought existed. I had said a prayer with Miss Lena and now my one-night-stand dad wanted to talk to me.

"What's his name?" I finally asked.

"Blake. Well, that's his last name. Jack Blake."

"Jack Blake." I said the name as if the words would magically make him materialize in front of me. "Mom. Did you honestly never, ever see him again after that night?" According to my mother, my parents slipped off the nightclub floor to an empty stairwell where there was a flickering fluorescent light. They ended up having sex, *sort of but not really, standing up*. I didn't get the details of how exactly that worked. Knowing I was conceived in the stairwell was enough. I thought of my mother and the one-night-stand stranger doing *it* every time I was in one. When I confessed this to Raquel once, she said, "Why don't you look at it as the greatest moment in your life, since it created you?" She had a point.

"Nope, truly never caught sight of him again," my mother said. "I got a phone call and then a check from his parents. I didn't write his name on your birth certificate and I must have blocked it from my memory early on. The first five years of your life, I lived in terror that he or his family would ask for the money back and want to take you away from me."

"The Blake family."

"Yeah, if I'd ended up with him, you'd be Zippy Blake!"

"Someone named Jack Blake probably would never have agreed to name me Zippy."

"I bet you're right about that," my mother said. "Thank God I got you to myself! You were the best gift in the world."

My mother and I were so close, her friends used to call me Shadow. When Howard came on the scene, we had to separate. Still, I always felt like she was the one person who knew and loved me.

"Thanks, Mom." I watched as Miss Lena's yodeling customer walked out. Miss Lena was probably cleaning up the fitting room.

"I gotta go, honey. I'm at the return desk and there's a line now like they're waiting for Elvis or something. Will you call me back after you talk to him?"

"I can't call him from here; it's long-distance."

"Try your manager's office. Everyone here makes long-distance calls from the manager's phone. Either he doesn't notice or he doesn't care."

"Mom, I have no seniority. There's no way I can ask to make a long-distance call from my manager's office."

"Oh, Zippy, just ask! Who's your manager again? Miss Lena?"

"No, she's with me in Petite Dresses."

"Oh, Miss Liaskis."

"Formal Dresses."

"Miss Yolanda?"

"She's the mean one with the candy ball in her mouth."

"Damn. I can't remember anyone else."

"Miss Dani is the manager."

"Right! The fireplug. Ask her! She's not going to can you for asking. And if she does, you can get a job here like that—" I heard my mother's echoey snap. Two things she could do at an expert level: whistle and snap her fingers.

"Okay, I'll try," I said, with no enthusiasm. I wondered if Jack Blake, Raquel's parents, or even Sorority Girl's parents had ever snuck into an office to make long-distance phone calls for free. No. No way.

Before I left Petite Dresses, I searched for Miss Lena. She was in the first fitting room with the triptych mirror closed, on her knees, praying.

"Miss Lena?" I whispered.

She looked up at me but kept her hands at her heart. "What is it, dear?"

"I've gotta run into Miss Dani's office to talk to her. You okay covering the floor?"

"Of course, dear. Leave the door open and if I hear someone, I'll come out."

I was hesitant to leave Miss Lena exposed like that. I worried she'd be fired if she were discovered. Or, possibly worse, Miss Yolanda would find her and torment her about it every day from here on out. "Listen closely if you can, I mean, while you're still talking to God and all."

"Don't worry, dear. I'll hear if someone is walking around out there." She lowered her head and shut her eyes again, so I let her be.

Miss Dani was on the phone, gliding on her rolling stool from one corner of her office to the other, continuously laughing. It was a short distance; the phone cord stretched and recoiled as she moved. As I watched, she said, "No, you hang up first . . . No, you . . . You . . ." She laughed again, rolled back to her desk, and hung up the phone. "That was my best friend, Randi. Randi with an *i* on the end."

"Like you!"

"Huh?"

"Dani with an *i* on the end."

"Oh yeah!" She smiled. "Maybe that's why we became best

friends!" She threw her stumpy hands in the air and color flew from the multiple rings, all of them crammed with stones. "So, I hear you've never been on a date!" Miss Dani winked.

"Uh," I said. "Did the cosmetics girls say that?"

Miss Dani absently flipped through a thick stack of computer printouts. "I can't remember who said it. Pretty girl like you shouldn't be spending Friday nights alone."

There were two things that struck me about that sentence. One: I was being called *pretty* for the second time in one day. Two: Was she implying that not-pretty girls should spend Friday nights alone?! Also, I was starting to believe that everyone who was interesting or smiled or had kindness in their eyes (and who didn't smell bad, because let's face it, a bad smell coming off a person essentially cancels out all other qualities) was pretty. I suppose there were some Elephant Man people who couldn't seem pretty even with impeccable posture and a Certs "two mints in one" smile. And there were mean and bitter people who couldn't be pretty no matter what they actually looked like. But prettiness felt different in this world than it had in high school, where the definition of beauty was so slim, only the few born with particular A-plus qualities (silently decreed by some unknown teenaged force) were allowed into that rare, unapproachable club of prettiness.

"I have Raquel," I said. "So, I don't spend Fridays alone."

"Ah, right. Anyway . . . how's it going out there?"

"It's super slow. Bowling alley."

"Right. Have you moved any of those peplum-skirt dresses?"

"Not today. But Saturday, I sold one. Wait. Two."

"Great. Markdowns are coming soon, so try to sell through as much as you can."

"Okay. What's getting marked down?"

"All that knit stuff in the back. Wanna hide anything?"

"Huh?"

"The girls haven't shown you?" Miss Dani rolled to another corner and pointed to a rolling rack that was full of random items. "If you like something that's going on sale, you pull it, hide it in here, and then when we mark it down, you get the discount on top of the sale price."

"Oh, cool. I'm still rotating my three work outfits." That day I was in the Salvation Army sheath dress.

"I know. Use your discount! Hide some stuff!"

"Okay!"

"Okay. Good. So?"

"Oh, um, so a man, well, my birth father, called and I don't really know him—my parents were never even together, so I don't know him at all. But he called for the first time ever and he asked me to call him back."

"Cool. The reappearance of a disappeared dad!"

"Yeah. Exactly."

"So, are you gonna call him?"

"I'd like to, but it's long-distance."

"Oh—use my phone! Dial nine to get an outside number." Miss Dani stood and started to leave. Before closing the door, she stuck her head back in and said, "Think of it as a perk for being the best salesperson on the floor. And don't tell the other girls. Next thing you know, the Braughns will be in here calling all their Dudley Do-Right Mountie boyfriends in Canada."

"Do they have boyfriends who are Canadian Mounties?" I asked.

"Who knows!" Miss Dani shrugged and then left, closing the door behind her.

I put the hold tag next to the phone, dialed nine, and then dialed the other numbers. My fingers were shaking a little and I was glad that this first "meeting" was not in person.

A man answered the phone on the second ring. His voice was familiar, soothing. Was I feeling a genetic connection? "Is this Jimmy Blake?" I asked.

"This is Jack Blake," he said.

I laughed nervously. "Oh yeah, that's what I meant."

"Is this Zippy?"

"Yeah. Um. You called?"

"Zippy." I could hear the smile in his voice.

"That's me."

"Zippy, I'm your dad. I mean, I fathered you. I'm your biological dad."

"Yeah, that's what your message said. It's a little, uh, trippy for me."

"Yeah, me too. Listen, I'm sorry I . . . I'm sorry I never got to know you. Your mom told me you've been a dream child. The perfect kid."

"Well, she's a little biased."

There was silence for a second. I didn't know what to say.

"Zippy, I'd love to get to know you. Are you okay with that?"

I had prayed for him to show up, but now that he was here, I wondered if I was caroming toward disappointment. As my mother pointed out, could a guy who left before my birth turn out to be Mr. Perfect Pants? "Um," I finally said. "I guess we could try. A little?"

"How 'bout we start with some phone calls—easy stuff, okay? I'd love for you to catch me up on the last nineteen years."

"Um, yeah, I mean, a lot has happened in nineteen years." I wasn't sure why I said that. Mostly, I felt that *very little* had happened over the last nineteen years. As far as I was concerned, my life could be summarized in a single phone call.

"I'm game if you're game!"

He was so enthusiastic. And he did *sound* kind. Would I be

harmed somehow if I talked to him? "Yeah, I guess I'm game. But I can't really afford long-distance calls—"

"Oh, of course! What person your age can? How about if I call you, let's say once or twice a week? You tell me when's a good time—and I'll pay for all the calls."

"Okay. Yeah." My hands were still shaking, but I was smiling. He was making this easy.

We talked a couple minutes longer. He asked what my interests were, but I was too nervous to think of even one! Then he listed some of his interests, which included the moon, my favorite celestial body. Before the call ended, I asked, "Hey, what do you do? I mean, your career?"

"Oh, uh, I'm in advertising. Boring stuff."

"Boring stuff," I repeated.

"I'll tell you more another day," he said, and I let it go.

After we hung up, I remained in that hard wooden chair, staring at the phone. I'd fantasized and wondered about my father for so many years. Now, voilà: he'd appeared! I put my hands on my stomach. It was swirling with an unusual happy nausea. I was still smiling when I was overcome with an urge to cry, though I couldn't have said exactly why. Fear? An abundance of happiness? Sadness for what I'd missed out on? Maybe it was all of that, and *all of that* was simply too much to name.

# Chapter 5

**That night, I** visited my mother and Howard at home. Howard was splayed on the couch like a boneless breast of chicken. He saluted me, the white-thumbed Q-tip ball of his left arm rising and then lowering. "Ah, milady. Me thinks me got an infection," he mumbled in his drugged Elizabethan.

"There's now an infection in your hand?"

"Yeah, milady. Painkillahs and . . ." Howard closed his eyes and appeared to fall asleep.

"Antibiotics?"

He nodded and I left him to visit my mother in the open kitchen at the other end of the room. She was making Hamburger Helper in a frying pan and whistling the theme song from *Bonanza.*

"He okay?" I asked.

"Big infection, lotta drugs."

"How can I help out, Mom?"

"You can help out right now by chopping up that onion."

I got a knife from the drawer and then pulled a slice from the Wonder Bread bag on the counter. I stuck the slice in my mouth and chopped the onion. This was a trick my mother had taught me: the bread absorbs the tear-inducing fumes so you don't cry while cutting.

Howard sat up and looked over the back of the couch toward us. "AH AH AH AH!" He pointed toward his mouth with the Q-tip.

My mother put her hand to her heart as if that were the cutest thing she'd ever seen. "He's like a dog. He wants some Wonder Bread." She pulled out a couple of pieces, smashed them up into two doughy balls, and then went to the couch and fed Howard the balls while I continued chopping onions.

"Mom!" I mumble-shouted while keeping the bread slice in my mouth. My mother tilted her head my way. "Don't you want to hear about the phone call with my dad?"

"Tell me another time, honey." My mother looked at Howard and stroked his head. "I gotta focus on this guy now and not the guy I can barely remember."

My mother had always been interested in me, in my life. How could it be that she didn't want to know about the person who made up half my genetic material? Along with getting hired by I. Magnin, this was the biggest thing that had ever happened to me. I had thought that I knew my mother as well as . . . as well as *she knew me*. Then again, I never could understand how she fell in love with and married Howard (he wasn't a bad guy; it was the *love* part I didn't get). So, maybe she couldn't understand how I might feel about having talked to my dad. Also, since I'd moved in with Raquel, I was feeling like someone different from the girl who had slept in the hallway. I was feeling more separate, more complete—confused but complete. Like my mother was no longer the invisible governing force in my life.

"Okay, Mom." I looked toward my mother. Her gaze was focused on Howard, who was breathing with his mouth hanging open in a way that made me think the hinges of his jaw were broken.

It was a no-eating day, so I decided to leave once dinner was ready.

"Mom," I said when I kissed her goodbye, "I'll try to give you some money every two weeks when I get paid."

"Don't worry about it. I'll figure out something. But listen, honey, if you do want to make more money, Howard's slot at the Depot is open for you."

"Oh, Mom." I didn't know what to say without hurting her feelings. "You know how much I love my job. I . . . I like wearing dresses; I like how quiet and clean it is."

My mother said, "Yeah, you gotta love lumber and power tools if you take Howard's job."

"Sawdust is not my thing," I said, and my mother smiled at me in a way that let me know she understood.

**I felt like** a different person when I woke up the next day. It was as if I were no longer a single child whose mother was her only caregiver (Howard had never been a caregiver; rather, he was an anchor who entrenched our lives in muddy, still waters). Having a father who worked in advertising and lived in Los Angeles gave me a broader, more expansive sense of myself. I even felt more relaxed and less fraudulent posing as an I. Magnin salesgirl.

Still, the bowling alley at I. Magnin made me anxious about money. I didn't want to leave the floor in case a customer showed up, so I opened the supply drawer and took out the hold tags, tape, staplers, and all the other supplies so I could clean and organize.

Miss Lena joined me at the register. She wiped down the counter with a spray bottle and one of the thick napkin-like hand towels from the customer bathroom.

"Tell me more about your conversation with your father!" Miss Lena said. We had discussed the phone call previously and there wasn't much more to say. Still, her interest made me feel loved, so I told the story again, adding small details that were growing in time: the Harley-Davidson rumble of his voice, that I could hear talk radio on low in the background, that when I asked where specifically he lived, he'd said the Hollywood Hills, across the street from Richard Simmons.

"Why did he call *now*?" Miss Lena asked.

"Yeah, I don't know. That's a good question."

"Oh no!" Miss Lena put her hand over her mouth as if she wanted to stop herself from saying something. "What if he has cancer?"

"Cancer? No, we're not cancer people. At least, that's what I've gathered from the bits my mother's told me. Her father and everyone before him died of alcoholism . . . though I guess that has nothing to do with my dad." I spoke before I'd fully processed what she was saying. Then it hit me. "Yeah. Wow! What if he *does* have cancer? Would you contact the daughter you'd never met if you had cancer?"

"I would never *not* know a child I had, but you don't know his full story yet. You don't know why he disappeared."

"I should make a list of questions for him . . ." I pulled out a hold tag and a pen.

"Or," Miss Lena said, "what if he recently married and his new wife thinks it's wrong that he's never met you before, so she encouraged him to contact you?"

I tapped the pen on the hold tag. "Yeah, I guess it could be any number of things."

Maybe I looked worried, because Miss Lena took the pen from my hands and gave me a hug. She said, "The reason doesn't matter so much as the fact that he did contact you. And I am so happy that you know him now!"

"Ah, thanks." I pulled away from the hug and then Miss Lena clapped her hands once.

"Zippy!" Miss Lena said. "I'm going to go into the fitting room and pray for you and your dad to have a wonderful new relationship. And I'll also pray for customers for us. Well, for all the women on the fifth floor!"

I wanted to ask Miss Lena to pray that I could make enough money to help out my mother and Howard, but that felt greedy. She was already praying for customers. If they showed up, all I had to do was make the sales.

As soon as Miss Lena left, Miss Yolanda wandered over. She moved the candy ball from one cheek to the other, stood across from me, and said, "Well? Any sales at all today?"

"Only a couple of returns," I said.

"You finally changed your clothes," she said. I was wearing one of Raquel's skirts, which was too big for her now that she'd lost weight and which she, rightly, thought would fit me now that I'd lost some too. The blouse was also hers.

"Raquel gave me this." I ran my hands down the sides of the skirt. If I could borrow more of Raquel's tops, I could probably wear the skirt most shifts. It was a perfect sixties secretarial shape. Gray. Matched everything.

Miss Yolanda put a hand on each hip and turned in a complete circle, looking around. "What a waste of a day. At this point I'd be happy selling a ninety-nine-dollar French Connection frock to one of the rats."

"Are the rats the people who come in on sale days?" I asked.

Miss Yolanda shrugged. "They're all rats, I suppose. This place is one giant sewer system, something Baron Haussmann would have designed had he lived here instead of Paris."

"But it's a gorgeous store. And the clothes are beautiful. You make a nice living."

"For chrissakes, Zippy, it's all a fraud. Everyone dies and rots in the end. Who gives a monkey's arse what you wear until then?" She turned and walked away.

I watched her until she'd reached her station. How did Miss Yolanda spend her life, day after day (decades!), doing something she thought was fraudulent? Maybe everything about being alive—other than birth, love, and dying—was fraudulent. But you did it anyway. Buying clothes, putting on makeup, going to a bar—it was part of pretending you weren't en route to death. Simply breathing was a way of saying, *I'm here now, I'm here now, I'm here now.*

I returned to organizing the supply drawer, hoping my mind would drift out of the darkness brought on by Miss Yolanda. As I was putting the supplies back into the drawer, I paused at the box of short colored pencils. They looked like the pencils you got with the children's menu at Denny's. I left the pencils on the counter and picked up a hold tag. I was trying to remember if Mimi had given me any advice this morning. Only this: *Put a little white liner on the inside corner of each eye and it will make your eyes look wider.* Until then, I hadn't known that having wider eyes was something to want. But Mimi put white liner on the inside corner of each of my eyes, and I did look a little more awake and alert.

The weight and thickness of the hold tag reminded me of the paper dolls my mom used to buy me. I'd spent hours cutting out their clothes, folding the flaps at the shoulders and waist, and dressing my paper dolls. I'd designed clothes too. When the dolls got too flimsy (the clothes lost or torn or the flaps folded so many times that they fell off), my mom bought me new paper dolls. It was the one thing I never felt bad asking for. Unlike a pair of roller skates or clogs with leather butterflies snapped into the holes in the top, the price of a paper doll book never made my mother groan.

I placed a hold tag on the counter vertically. With the brown pencil, I drew Miss Yolanda with a bulging cheek. There was a slit down the middle of the tag where you slipped it over the hanger. I used that line as the center of her suit, putting black buttons down the front. When I pressed the red pencil down hard, it gave her lips a red that almost matched the lipstick she wore each day. I put reverse side-by-side parentheses between Miss Yolanda's brows and some lines radiating out from her eyes. She looked like she was scowling. On the back of the hold tag, I wrote, *All you rats can go bugger off.*

I propped up Miss Yolanda against the side of the register and made a paper doll hold tag of Miss Lena. Because she was so good and faithful, I drew a yellow halo around her head. On the back I wrote, *Jesus has blessed us today!*

A group of four women came up the escalator and walked around Petite Dresses. Their enthusiastic oohing and aaaahing gave them away as tourists. I smiled a hello their way, but stayed where I was, watching to see if they were shopping or only looking. They touched everything as if they were seeing with their hands, and they named people who would look good in each dress. One wandered over to the four-way rack near me, tugged on a Vittadini, and said, "Celeste. Celeste. Celeste. Celeste—" Another woman looked at her and said, "No, that's not Celeste." She plucked a much shorter Calvin Klein off a different rack, held it against her mighty chest, and said, "Well, Celeste or Stacy." Then she looked at me.

"Do you need my help?" I smiled hopefully but then tried to stop the smile so I didn't look too desperate.

"Nah-uh," she said, and then she yelled, "CELESTE!"

Celeste, who was standing with the fourth woman at the Donna Karan rack, finally looked over.

"Huh?"

"Wouldn't this be cute on you or Stacy?" She flapped the dress like a flag she was about to fold.

"Stacy, maybe. What about this for Anne Marie?" Celeste held up one of the Andrea Jovine blue-swirl dresses.

"Uh-huh. What about this for Mary Beth?" The woman now

held up a Vittadini that was so colorful, it was like the Pollock painting hanging at the museum where my mom used to take me before Howard entered the scene.

The two of them went back and forth like this while the other two met at the rack behind my back and talked about chocolate, who had the best chocolate, and where you could buy it.

I approached the woman who wanted to buy something for Stacy or Mary Beth and said, "I'm Zippy. If you need anything, call my name."

"Stacy needs a man. Can you help her find one?" the barrel-chested woman said, and they all laughed.

"I can try," I said, "but there aren't many who hang around the Petite Dresses department." They laughed harder than one would expect. Vacation giddiness, I supposed.

They moved closer toward me, as if I were suddenly more interesting. "We're from Michigan," Celeste said. "We have to bring presents home for our daughters and nieces. I have three daughters, she has . . ."

They each gave me the names and ages of their offspring while I held my mouth turned up so it wouldn't look like I was bored or scowling. I was fairly certain the nieces and nephews were going to get Coit Tower–shaped bars of Ghirardelli chocolate and I wasn't losing a sale here. And I wanted to get back to my paper dolls.

When the offspring listing ended, I said, "So, anything you need, ask. I'll be right there." I pointed to my station. The barrel-chested one started talking again, and I nodded while slowly backing away, one foot behind the other like Scooby-Doo sneaking out of a shuttered warehouse.

Soon enough, the four women moved on to the Braughn sisters' section and I was able to do my doll work without keeping an ear open to them. I put tears on the Miss Liaskis doll and wrote on the back, *But WHY did they have to change the registers?!* On Miss Dani, I put loads of jewelry. For her quote, I wrote, *I got nice legs!* The Braughn sisters were fun to draw, almost like a Charlie Brown cartoon. Blond hair. Pinpoint blue eyes. A pursed mouth. I didn't give them noses (only dots for nostrils), and that made them look snootier. I used a thick Sharpie to make their moles even darker and bigger than they were in real life. Their quote started on one doll and ended on the other. *Pizza is so much less expensive in CANADA and we get free healthcare in CANADA and everyone is polite and proper and kind in CANADA!*

As I was finishing Miss Lee, one of the regulars, a stylish woman whose age was blurred by excellent skincare—and, maybe, surgery—came up the escalator. I gathered the paper dolls and put them in the drawer with the pencils.

"We're going to Sonoma for the weekend," she said. "Anything cute?"

Even though I'd never been to Sonoma, I knew the perfect dress: a chambray button-front with a dirndl skirt and a sash tie. It was playful, cowboyish, but still chic. That dress was in the Braughn sisters' section, so I led the woman over there, pulled out the dress (which she loved), and then walked the floor with her to pull dresses from Miss Liaskis's and Miss Lee's and Miss Karen's sections, too.

Miss Lena stayed in the fitting room as the regular tried on all the dresses and then bought two. When I was ringing her up, Miss Lena emerged and was treated to the same stories I'd already heard about the mud baths in Sonoma. Miss Lena nodded and asked nice questions as she took off the security sensors and bagged the dresses.

Once the regular left, there were no other shoppers in our area, so I pulled out the paper dolls and colored pencils. Miss Lena looked down. She picked them up one by one and laughed as she said their names. She shifted Miss Yolanda back and forth as she had her "walk" across the counter. "What are you hyenas doing?" she said in Miss Yolanda's phlegmy French voice. "Get back to work!"

I picked up Miss Dani and said, "Don't tell anyone I'm the manager! I don't want customers to talk to me!"

"Go back to that tiny office! Where's my candy?! Who ate my candy?! Did someone give my candy to the rats?!"

Miss Lena put down Miss Yolanda and picked up Miss Braughn L. "Dahling," she said, as if Miss Braughn L spoke like Eva Gabor on *Green Acres*.

I picked up Miss Braughn R and said in that same Gabor voice, "Dahling, the clothes are so much nicer in Canada."

"Isn't your mother Canadian?" Miss Lena said in her own voice. She put her Braughn doll face down on the counter. "Would she be hurt by this?"

"My mother is French Canadian, but once she left Quebec, it was like the entire province disappeared. She likes to pretend she's American."

"WAIT!" Miss Lena said. "Where are you? You have to make the doll of you! And Cecil. Please, can you make Cecil?!"

I drew myself while Miss Lena leaned over my shoulder and said things like, "Your mouth is bigger, you have a huge smile!" Next, I made Cecil, the stock boy who was around Miss Lena's age (just as all saleswomen were called *girls*, the men who worked in the stockroom were all called *boys*). Miss Lena's face looked like a glowing night-light every time Cecil was on our floor. Once I caught them singing Cole Porter songs together. He'd had one giant muscled arm atop the rolling rack, and Miss Lena's pale wisp of an arm held on to the side bar. They'd stared at each other, singing while smiling so widely, you could have thrown a tennis ball into each of their mouths.

When I was done drawing Cecil, Miss Lena picked up the hold

tag and kissed Cecil on the lips. "I'll do Cecil and you do me," she said, and then she lowered her voice and said, "Hello, Miss Lena, don't you look charming today?"

I picked up Miss Lena and delicately pranced her across the counter until she was face-to-face with Cecil. "Oh, Cecil! I'm worried about Yugo, I'm worried about Miss Zippy's new relationship with her father, and I'm worried that we don't have enough customers."

"Don't you worry, Miss Lena! Here, come a little closer."

"Is this close enough?" I asked in Miss Lena's voice.

Miss Lena pushed the Cecil doll against the Miss Lena doll and we both rotated our hands so they were sliding in half circles against each other. And then we broke apart laughing. So hard, we drew the attention of the other salesgirls, all of whom stood like alert birds listening to another breed's song, until finally Miss Yolanda walked over to us.

Miss Lena quickly gathered the paper dolls and threw them into the supply drawer.

"Well?!" Miss Yolanda said sharply, as if she were angry.

"Jesus has blessed us today," Miss Lena said. "He has blessed us with joy."

"I think you're confusing a blessing with a bonk on the head," Miss Yolanda said, and then she snapped her face toward the escalators and watched as three women glided up onto our floor.

The women walked straight into Petite Dresses. Miss Yolanda approached the one who was shaped like a very long Popsicle stick.

"You don't belong here," Miss Yolanda said to her. "These dresses will barely cover your bottom. Follow me." She marched away and the woman obeyed.

I kept an eye on the other two, and then I nudged Miss Lena and nodded toward the one wearing Ferragamo mules. She would be a more likely buyer than the woman in hiking boots and a utility vest. The sale score for the day was me: one; Miss Lena: zero. I was working against my impulse to grab every sale I could. I had to try, at least, to be as good as Miss Lena.

**The rest of** the day was too busy to play paper dolls. Unfortunately, the busyness didn't generate sales. The woman in hiking boots had barely glanced at the dresses and didn't try on anything. She was a tourist from Seattle who claimed she only shopped at REI, where she worked. When she passed through again on her way out, she waved and shouted, "If you're ever in Seattle, stop in REI and I'll take you to lunch!"

I waved and said, "Of course," though I'd never thought about Seattle before, and thought I'd probably never go.

About an hour before closing, when there were no more customers on the floor, Miss Dani came out of her office and circled from station to station.

"Meeting!" she said to each of us. When she got to Petite Dresses, she took my arm and whispered in my ear, "See me in my office after the meeting."

Everyone gathered around Miss Dani in the center of the floor near the Braughn sisters' station.

Miss Yolanda popped a new candy ball into her mouth. "How long is this going to take? We're not closed yet."

"There are no customers on the floor; we'll be fine." Miss Dani seemed more serious than usual. She even looked uncomfortable; she kept tugging at the sleeve of her lime-green suit jacket. "So, as you all know, those stupid complaint cards have been placed beside each register—"

"Let's call them praise cards!" Miss Lena said, and everyone looked at her a second before turning back to Miss Dani.

"Well, unfortunately, they've been used mostly for complaints, and mostly to complain about a person, or maybe people, on this floor."

Miss Lena and I both jerked our heads toward Miss Yolanda and then back to Miss Dani.

"Why does anyone want to hear what the customers have to say anyway?" Miss Yolanda said. "The masses are asses."

"Eh, not always. Sometimes the masses are asses and sometimes the masses have something important to say. But what I want to say is this: Any more complaints and Miss Kitty will have me trim my sales staff. No department got more complaints than ours."

Miss Liaskis gasped and covered her mouth. Miss Lena hooked her arm through mine and whispered, "Oh no."

"What exactly are the complaints?" I asked.

"And about which one of us, exactly, are the rats complaining?" Miss Yolanda asked.

"I'll be talking to the people who got the most complaints. But what they said on the cards was that you steal each other's customers, you boss people around, you load on shoes and accessories without being asked, you grab customers off the floor without giving them the time or space to choose you, and you then cajole them into buying dresses they're too afraid to return . . . Basically it's pushiness and rudeness."

Miss Lena and I looked at each other quickly. Of course we both were thinking of Miss Yolanda. But no matter how awful she was to me, I didn't want her to lose her job.

"Remember, our customers are like fine jewels—"

"HA!" Miss Yolanda said, and she moved the candy ball from one cheek to another.

Miss Dani shook her head at Miss Yolanda and said, "Treat the customers with respect, kindness, graciousness. And for godssakes, treat each other like that too. No more stealing customers!"

"If they took away the damn complaint cards, we wouldn't have a problem," Miss Yolanda said.

"If we took away the customers, we wouldn't have a problem either," Miss Dani said. "And none of us would have a job. Everyone shape up! That's it."

Miss Dani walked away, her little legs moving quickly.

I didn't want to follow Miss Dani into her office, lest the other ladies think the complaint cards were about me. So I sauntered back to Petite Dresses, where Miss Lena and I reconvened. She looked around to see that no one was in hearing distance and then said, "Even though Miss Yolanda is very unkind, I do not want her to be fired."

"I know. Me neither! I've learned so much from her."

"She's been here much longer than Miss Kitty. It doesn't seem right that Miss Kitty could fire her." Miss Kitty, the store manager, carried herself in a way that made her unapproachable. It was the same action I'd seen in the few celebrities I'd spotted in San Francisco: no eye contact, a stiff and still body, shoulders at an angle, turned away from whoever was staring. She only wore clothes from the designer floors: suits and dresses that were so structured they looked like fabric glued to plywood. Even her hair was a stiff blond helmet that flipped at her shoulders and looked like it wouldn't blow apart on a fast motorcycle ride. Within the walls of I. Magnin, Miss Kitty was the queen, or the president—the most powerful person in most of our lives. I, of course, had never had the nerve to speak to her.

"Miss Dani asked me to come to her office after the meeting," I said. "Do you think I'm the person who got the bad reviews?" The only reason I could say it aloud was that I was certain she was describing Miss Yolanda.

Miss Lena shook her head. "She probably wants to ask if she's been stealing sales from you. You're the newest and the youngest. The rest of us are very used to her."

"Well, I'll tell Miss Dani how much I've learned from Miss Yolanda and—" I stopped. I wasn't sure what the *and* would be.

"Tell her there are many customers who value Miss Yolanda's opinion."

"Okay. Good one!" I turned and headed toward Miss Dani's office.

Miss Dani's door was ajar. I peeked in and she did a *Circle in* wave. She was on the phone, doodling on the edges of a computer printout that was two inches thick. It was the markdowns for the upcoming sale, I realized.

"I'll come see you after," she said, and then she hung up and pointed at the chair beside her desk.

I sat and then leaned over to see the list of markdowns. I still hadn't pulled anything to hide in her office. Maybe after my next couple paychecks.

Miss Dani asked, "How are you feeling on the sales floor?"

"Good. Fine. I mean, I hope I can make more sales."

She stared at me like she was mulling over something. "You feel comfortable with the customers?"

"Yeah. Or, I do now. I was intimidated by our customers when I first started because everyone's so rich. And I didn't know what a Rolex was or what Ferragamo was. You know, I was a little behind."

"You're a fast learner, Zip." Miss Dani did a little fist swipe in the air, like she was saying *A-OK!*

"Thanks." I was feeling nervous. Did I do something wrong? "Was there a complaint card about me?" I couldn't bear the suspense of this odd meeting that appeared to have no end point.

"No, no . . . It's . . . You know, with these complaint cards coming in, I want to make sure you don't do any of the things people are grousing about."

"Is it Miss Yolanda? Because I know she's mean and bossy, but I respect her in so many ways. She knows everything about every dress on the floor and—"

"Don't worry about anyone but yourself, okay?"

"Okay." I was embarrassed that I'd asked about Miss Yolanda. Of course it was none of my business, and, as odd and hidden-shellfishy as Miss Dani was, she was loyal to her salesgirls.

"I really want to make sure you don't start any of these bad habits: don't steal customers—"

"Oh, I never would!" I wanted to tell her that every single day, I tried to ring up sales for Miss Lena. But I said nothing, as telling Miss Dani about it would be bragging and that would take away the goodness of the act. "Really. I wouldn't steal a sale."

"Good, and don't push shoes on a customer unless she wants them, don't push a bra unless she's interested, and don't try to talk someone into something they don't appear to really want." She was speaking firmly, as if I were getting a scolding. Was she worried that I was going to *become* Miss Yolanda?

"Okay. I'll try to never do any of that." I looked at Miss Dani. She looked back and her eyes were a little funny, like she was sad or worried. Just then her phone rang.

"This is Dani," she barked into the phone. And then, "Uh-huh . . . yeah . . . yeah . . . one minute." She stood and fingered through a rolling rack in the corner.

"Do you need help?" I asked.

"Yolanda wants this Bill Blass dress I haven't even put out yet. She claims she'll sell one this second. I'll be right back, Zip." Miss Dani pulled two dresses from the rack and dashed out.

I sat up in my chair and examined the clutter and mess of the office. Soon I was reorganizing the space in my mind. I'd have the rolling racks lined up with gaps between them so I could see what was on each one. And the desk, wow: it looked like someone had upended a moving box of bits and ends on it. I stood and perused the scattered papers on the desk to see what Miss Dani's daily workday entailed. There was the markdown printout, a memo pad that listed damaged items to be returned to the vendor, and an inter-store nylon envelope that was open and had the complaint cards spilling out.

I leaned closer to try to read one. Miss Yolanda's name wasn't there. Instead it said *Zippy.* I took a fingernail and slid the card out a little farther and there it was: a handwritten screed about me being pushy and bossy.

My heart thumped in my chest; I felt my face burning. I was both horrified that someone had complained about me and scared that Miss Dani would return and find me poking around where I had no business poking around.

I looked toward Miss Dani's door, then back to the complaint cards. Very gingerly, I pushed the top card aside to see what was beneath it. Again my name. I went one deeper. My name again.

I felt light-headed and slightly nauseous. Was Miss Kitty going to fire me?

Miss Dani came into the office and I dropped into the chair.

"Sorry," she said. "Once I was on the floor, Miss Liaskis needed help closing out her register. This is why I should never go out there—I get sucked into helping!"

I tried to laugh, but all I could do was eke out a smile.

"Yeah, Miss Liaskis—" My mind was stuck on the complaint cards and my name spread across them like blood at a crime scene. I felt a watery rush of shame. Embarrassment. I thought I was having fun, getting to know the customers, putting them in my Blue Book, getting to know the merchandise, when in fact I was shoving people into clothes they didn't want to buy and stealing sales! Was I so blissfully happy at I. Magnin that I couldn't even tell that the customers actually loathed me? And were they afraid to make returns to *me*? ME? I was a girl in a starch-ironed Salvation Army dress. Who would be afraid of me?

"Anyway, Zip. Try to tune into the customers better, okay? You're doing an excellent job. You're my strongest seller on the floor. But see if you can keep up the sales while also dialing it back a little."

"Dialing it back." I swallowed hard, as if I were pushing down peanut butter. "Okay. Okay, thanks!" I stood up and sensed that my knees might buckle. I wanted to get out of there. Quickly! I wanted to go home, undress, and eat Ka Ka Lucky Seafood Barbecue Restaurant food while watching TV with Raquel. I wanted to forget what I had seen and not feel all the terrible things I was feeling about . . . about myself.

**I tried to** leave the store without talking to anyone, but Mimi spotted me across the first floor as I was headed to the employee exit.

"GIRLIE! Get over here!"

I blinked hard and tried to erase what I'd seen in Miss Dani's office. It was like I was changing the channel in my brain.

"Hey, sorry, I was rushing out because it's an eating day and Raquel and I are getting Ka Ka Lucky Seafood Barbecue Restaurant tonight."

"I love that place!" Mimi typed in her sales number, slid open her register, and started counting out the cash.

"Us too."

"Raquel still taking you to Blue Light?" Mimi glanced up from the piles of twenties she was making.

"Yeah, we went on Saturday." I deliberately focused on the crowd at Blue Light in my mind.

"You'll be losing your virginity within the month if you keep hanging out at that place." Mimi wrote down her total on the slip of paper that went with the cash into the nylon zip bag.

I cringed. "I dunno. Sex, like everything else in adulthood, seems a little scary and overwhelming to me. And I'm not looking forward to holes and smells if I don't go blind, as you say."

Mimi waved her hand. "Don't overthink it! Your friends in high school didn't have sex, did they?"

"Um, my only friends were the theater kids and I never saw them outside of school or rehearsal. But I don't think any of them had had sex. Oh wait, Kelly Tameretti. He was the hottest boy in theater and everyone said he was having sex with the homecoming queen though no one ever saw them together in public." This was good. This conversation was taking me away from thoughts of the complaint cards and Miss Kitty.

"I've found that the best indicator of whether or not someone has had sex is if their friends have had sex. So when you have kids, if you don't want them to have sex, make them hang out with the kids who aren't having sex. The same is true for affairs."

"What do you mean?"

"If someone's friends are having affairs, they're more likely to have affairs themselves. So if you're dating someone and you want to know if they'll be faithful, ask if their friends are having affairs. If the answer is yes, stay away. If the answer is no, then you're good to go. Unless, of course, you don't care about affairs."

I repeated her words in my head so I could memorize this for the hold tag advice file. "The dress ladies don't talk about sex or affairs."

"We cosmetic girls are all about sex." Mimi reached out an arm and lifted my face from below my chin. "You've got some shine. Can I powder you before we leave?"

"It's Chinese food and TV tonight, remember? I don't need to be pretty."

"You're pretty no matter what," Mimi said. "Makeup doesn't make you pretty; it just gives out signals that make people want to mate with you. Or, if they don't want to mate with you, they want to *be you* so that other people will want to mate with them."

"What do you mean?"

"It's biology. Most men will say they love a clean-faced woman without makeup, right? But they don't recognize makeup. What they're actually saying is they love a woman who isn't wearing so much makeup that she looks like a man in drag. She needs to look like a *woman*."

I leaned to the right and glanced in the mirror on a stand. "Do I look like I'm in drag?"

"No! You look healthy. Did you know that when you get sick, like seriously ill, your brows and eyelashes fall out? So if you have sparse eyebrows or lashes, you need to fill them in so that the dense male brain sees: *Yes, she is not sick, you dumbass; she has lashes!* The same for bronzer: *No anemia here, you lizard-brained fools.*"

"Do you think all men are lizard-brained fools?" I asked.

"Of course not. But my boyfriend broke up with me, so I'm a little down on men right now. He said he didn't have the time." She shrugged and rolled her eyes.

"I'm sorry." I felt her feelings even though I'd never had a grown-up boyfriend. We both, it occurred to me then, were in the middle of heartbreak and rejection.

Mimi waved her hands around as if she were clearing away smoke. "Easy come, easy go. But I gotta tell you, I'm tired of trying to adjust myself for people whose desires are merely the imprint of evolutionary biology."

"Are we talking about eyebrows and bronzer again?" Mimi talked so much about men, women, sex, and dating that I often wished I had a tape recorder running so I didn't have to concentrate so hard.

"Now I'm talking about bodies. You see, men like breasts because it shows that you can nurse a baby: *their* baby. They like hips because you need hips to carry a baby. A flat stomach means you're not carrying anyone else's baby. Blah blah blah."

"Breasts, hips, belly . . . the *Venus de Milo*." Of course I'd never seen the *Venus de Milo* in person, but I had loved art history class in school. Sitting in the dark room watching slideshows of art was like getting a meditation break.

"Here." Mimi leaned over the counter and brushed powder over my face. It felt nice and feathery—a soothing sensation that helped me let go of what had just happened in Miss Dani's office. I could sense Mimi relaxing too.

"Healthy face," I whispered.

"Open your blouse and I'll do your cleavage."

"Okay." I undid one button and held my blouse open at the sides. When she was done, I quickly buttoned it up again.

"Maybe I resent men a little," Mimi said. "My shape categorically makes them not see me as mating material. It's cruel, you know? I can't help but wonder what God expected to happen when I was born into this hulking man-sized body."

"You're not *hulking*!" She was man-sized, but I hated that she was feeling bad about it. "You're a bit taller than most women and . . . I mean, so is Brooke Shields, right?"

Mimi shrugged. "Can I put mascara on you?" She opened the wand and held it in front of my face.

"Yes. It will signal to Raquel that I'm mateable." I leaned forward.

"Ha." She put the wand against my lashes. "Blink. Blink. Blink. Blink. Blink. Blink. You'll have a nice relationship with a guy one day. I can see these things. Other eye."

She moved the wand to my other eye. I blinked without being told.

"What do you see?"

"It's more of a sense. A glow you give off." Mimi got out lipstick and cleaned the tip with a tissue. "You're lovable and feel intense love for people." She slathered my lips, back and forth. It was so relaxing, I could have sat there for the whole tube. "Do this—" Mimi stuck her first finger in her mouth, wrapped her lips around it, and then pulled the finger out like she was popping a cork on a wine bottle. I did the same.

"Good?" I looked at myself in the mirror on the counter. It was like a magic act—my eyes looked bigger, my lips looked sexier.

"Bronzer," Mimi said, and before I even turned my face to her, she was brushing something under my jawbone, on my cheeks, and above my brows.

I sighed as I relaxed again. "No anemia here."

At last she stepped back and examined me the way my art teacher in high school used to examine our paintings.

"Well?"

"Perfect." Mimi put the bronzer away. "Enjoy Ka Ka Lucky and I'll see you tomorrow."

"See you tomorrow." I waved, even though we were standing on either side of the counter, and then I turned and walked off.

In line at the employee exit, where the security team checked each person's bags for stolen goods, a salesgirl I recognized from

Designer Sportswear looked me up and down. She was shaped like a cartoon character of a curvy woman and she had long blond hair in a ponytail that went halfway down her back. Her face was so deeply lined that she looked like two versions of the same person twenty years apart depending on if you viewed her from the front or behind. From any direction, she was the universal idea of gorgeous.

"Who are you?" she asked in a voice as deep as the grooves on her face.

"Miss Zippy. Fifth-Floor Dresses." I smiled at her.

"You're so pretty and I love that outfit." She held her gaze on me as she opened her capacious Louis Vuitton bag, which the security man inspected.

"I love *your* outfit!" I said to her as she closed her bag and walked out the door.

I opened the fake-leather satchel I'd found on the floor in my mother's hall closet and watched as the security man shined his light inside.

"Good to go, Miss Zippy." He waved the flashlight like he was ringing a bell.

As I walked toward the bus stop, I wondered who I was to the security man. Did he see the difference between me and the old/young woman from Designer Sportswear? Or were we the same breed of human as we each opened our bags: one (waxed canvas) that cost a couple thousand dollars and one that probably couldn't be resold for two dollars (pure plastic, which, when I found it, was filled with dusty, sticky coins; loose tobacco from my mother's occasional cigarette; crumpled receipts that had never needed saving; and old balls of gum mummified in silver wrappers).

The bus pulled up as I arrived at the stop. I lined up, followed the others on, and then let my coins drop with a tinny clink into the change box. There were no visible seats, so I walked to the back, examining the faces and clothes, until I found a spot near the rear window.

Riding a bus was a great equalizer. All of us passengers were alike in that moment: me, the woman in the hotel maid outfit, the man in a three-piece suit, the man in the car mechanic's jumpsuit, the old woman whose body folded like layered doughnuts, the guy wearing shorts and no shoes even though it was about fifty-five degrees outside . . . Why did I think I should have a "fancier" life than anyone else? The complaint cards clearly attested to my incompetence. Maybe me in the I. Magnin world was no more real than the Miss Lena paper doll making out with the Cecil paper doll: dreams and aspirations with no solid ground against which any of it could gain purchase.

# Chapter 6

**The next day** was the start of the big sale. It was so busy, I couldn't have fetched shoes or bras for anyone if I'd wanted to. There was no time to take a lunch break until four, and even then I planned to only go for a half hour so as not to leave Miss Lena alone too long.

I grabbed my purse from under the counter, and Miss Lena, who was ringing up a customer, stopped me. She opened the drawer, pulled out a stack of hold tags and the colored pencils, and dropped them in my bag.

"Do Jesus," she whispered, and then she turned back to her customer and smiled as she continued to ring up.

I sat alone in a corner of the lunchroom and, with as much stealth as possible, made three more dolls: Spin-Art Eyes and Mimi from cosmetics, and—as Miss Lena had asked—Jesus. Before leaving, I stopped in at a table where Mimi sat with a boisterous gang of women, including three elegant ladies from Designer Dresses. I tried to examine them without staring. They were so polished and poised, even their jewelry was nicer than that worn by everyone else at the table. Still, the words that came out of their mouths weren't any different from any other woman's. If I'd been listening to a tape, I wouldn't have been able to tell who was wearing a Chanel suit with a Rolex and who was in a Hunt Club sweater and skirt. It was interesting to think of clothes as mere wrappings of a person and not the person herself.

When I returned, I showed Miss Lena the new paper dolls and

she did a little jump in her tiny ballet flats and then clapped her hands. "Tomorrow we can play before opening," she said. The sale was going on until Sunday; bowling alley freedom wouldn't return until Monday.

"Okay. Maybe I'll take some hold tags home and make more."

We couldn't finish that conversation, as everything amped up the last hour of the sale. There were people swirling around us, needing fitting rooms, needing to be rung up, needing bigger or smaller sizes, needing one of the Italian women from alterations to be brought in to shorten a hem or take up a sleeve. There was a strange panic in the air, as if people were buying for their lives or a bomb would explode at closing hour and everyone had to get what they could before then.

By the time the store was closed, I understood Miss Yolanda's distaste for sale days. Even though I was selling loads of dresses, I wasn't enjoying myself. Part of the joy of I. Magnin was the stillness and quiet, the way it felt removed from the chaos, crowds, and black-gum-on-the-sidewalk right outside the door. It was a different realm, a soothing spaceship hovering in Union Square. Of course, most people (including me) couldn't afford to buy anything there. But *everyone* was free to wander the lovely sunlit open floors.

**After work I** rushed home to change. It was my mom and Howard's best friend, Toby's, birthday. Toby's wife, Jo, was throwing a party that started at my mom and Howard's place for drinks and appetizers and would end at Toby and Jo's place for dinner and dessert. Raquel had insisted on coming with me—she wanted to meet my mom, Howard, Toby, and Jo. After what she'd learned of my conception in a stairwell, having her meet my mom and Howard seemed a lot more manageable. Also, it was a no-eating day, and it seemed like it would be easier for me not to eat if I had Raquel by my side, also not eating.

"What are you wearing?" Raquel shouted from her bedroom.

"Jeans and I don't know what else," I shouted back.

The phone rang. I ran in my underwear to get it.

"Hey, Zippy, my daughter!" my dad said in his Harley-Davidson rumble.

I looked down at my bare belly and legs. Was it okay to talk to your dad in your underwear even though he couldn't see you? I'd never had a dad—how could I know?

"Hey!" I was happy to hear his voice, even when uncomfortably in my underwear.

"I was in the yard this morning," my dad said, "and there were a bunch of dandelions—you know, the fuzzy bloomed ones—"

"Oh, did you blow on one and make a wish?" I loved dandelions. Had my mother told him this in their one brief chat?

"I was going to and then I was staring at it, at the pattern—"

"Was it in the Fibonacci sequence?!"

"Yes! I love the Fibonacci sequence!"

"Or the golden ratio!"

"Or the divine proportion!" my father said.

"I even love all the names for it," I said. "That was my favorite unit in math class."

"I think of it often," my dad said. "Every time I see a snail or a shell—"

"I think of it with hurricanes." I had never discussed the Fibonacci sequence with anyone other than my high school math teacher. That my father was as thrilled by it as I was made me feel like I had anchored my space capsule with his—I'd found my fellow human.

"You know what I like best about it?"

"What?" I asked.

"That it's a mathematical sequence that creates a design that is both bigger than anything on Earth—like galaxies—and smaller than anything we can see with the human eye, like cell division. I love the range."

Raquel walked out of her room. She was wearing bright red leather pants and a red top that was so thin and fitted, it looked like it could outline a mole on her chest. She tilted her head and watched me, trying to figure out who was on the other end of this call.

"Uh," I had a hard time saying *Dad* and I didn't want to say *Jack,* so I avoided calling my father anything. "I love talking to you, but Raquel and I are going to a party and I have to get dressed."

"Ah, fun. Okay, remember all the details of the party so you can tell me the next time I call. And look for the golden ratio when you're out. I want to make a list of things I see that have perfect radial symmetry."

"Perfect radial symmetry," I repeated. "Okay. I love this assignment."

I could feel my dad smiling, though there was no way to know if he really was.

"I'll search too," my father said, "and we'll compare lists next time I call."

"You got it," I said.

When we hung up, I felt a contentment in my skin. It was like I'd been a coloring book drawing and now that I was getting to know my dad, the drawing of me was starting to be filled in.

"Your father?" Raquel asked.

"Yeah. I like him. Hey, could you wear that to work? Because if you did and you saw Jason, he would follow you home like a hungry dog."

Raquel smiled and threw her glossy, thick hair over one shoulder. "It's too sexy for work," she said with the confidence of someone who knew exactly how great she looked. No one on the street would have ever guessed that this was a woman who, twenty-four hours earlier, had topped off her kung pao chicken and lo mein with a Sara Lee cheesecake eaten straight from the tin while wearing stained, baggy sweatpants and an oversized men's T-shirt.

As Raquel and I sifted through her drawers looking for a top for me, I thought about clothes again, wrappings, and wondered if what you wore *could* change who you were. I felt like a different person when I was dressed up for work. Maybe molecules moved, synapses fired, muscle and fat shifted to fit whatever wrappings one decided defined their ideal self. Was I a different person now that I was working at I. Magnin? When I was carrying dresses into fitting rooms, zipping someone up, finding shoes to match the dress—was there any difference between me and the rich wife from Marin who worked as a floater simply for fun? How was *being* someone not like *pretending to be* someone? Did acting the part (as I did every day I worked) help you become the part?

The other day a customer thought that I was a girl she'd seen in the hot tub at Canyon Ranch guzzling cucumber water with her mother. There it was: Raquel's old skirt and my freshly pressed blouse, a makeup job via Mimi, and I looked like someone who traveled with her mother to Canyon Ranch and drank cucumber water. In fact, I had no idea what or where Canyon Ranch was, and the only water my mother drank had four heaping teaspoons of Tang mixed in. (In order to get Tang, which was no longer carried at the large grocery stores, she had to make a trip to a corner grocer in Chinatown. Sometimes, Mom brought the jar of Tang to the living room and ate the dry powder off a spoon while she watched TV. Howard liked it too. She often nudged him with her elbow, told him to open his mouth, and then spoon-fed him Tang powder, his eyes still pinned on the television.)

Who would I pretend to be if I were dressed in the Hardware Depot apron? My mother had worn that apron my whole life and she never seemed to feel like she was pretending. If you knew exactly who you were inside, did it matter if you had on the apron or the skirt?

Meanwhile, I had to dress like someone who might hang out with the gorgeous Raquel.

"Can I wear this one?" I held up a black silk tank with a scalloped hem on the bottom.

"You better," she said. "It would look great on you."

**There were about** forty people at Toby's birthday party and they filled my mom's apartment from window to window. Most were variations on Toby and Jo: happy weirdos, people who either exploded with personality or were the audience for exploding personalities. One woman wore a red plastic medallion the size of a saucer that lay at an angle across her shelf of breasts. I couldn't help but think about someone trying to balance a cracker and some cheese on it. Her earrings were almost as big as the medallion. They pulled so heavily that her earlobes looked like pale little worms hanging on either side of her face. I could see the elongated slits of the earring hole, too, and decided then to only wear posts so as to preserve the tidiness of my earlobes.

In middle school I'd had a gym teacher who talked about loving your body no matter what shape and size it was. But other than Ms. Walker, I'd never heard a person say that a girl or woman should accept her body. Everything I read about female bodies in magazines, and everything that was said to me about them, was with the intention of improvement, shaping, manipulating, and reworking. So, like all the girls and women I knew (save my mother, who didn't ever look at or think about her body), I had at different times wished or imagined each isolated exterior part of me changed. Except my ears. I thought my ears were perfect. They were two compact flesh-shells nuzzled against the sides of my face.

Raquel looped her arm in mine and said, "This is fabulous. I can't believe you have a mother who hangs out with these kinds of people!"

"Would your parents ever throw or go to a party like this?" I asked. We inched our way forward into the room. The deeper we got, the louder it was.

"WHAT?"

"WOULD YOUR PARENTS EVER GO TO A PARTY LIKE THIS?"

"MY PARENTS WOULDN'T WALK DOWN THIS STREET!" Raquel shouted, and I laughed. She wasn't being insulting. She was being straight.

"DO YOU FEEL BAD FOR ME THAT THIS IS WHERE I GREW UP?"

Raquel turned her head and stared at me. She mouthed, *ARE YOU CRAZY?* And then she shouted, "YOU'RE LUCKY! WHAT A FUN LIFE! YOU'VE MET SO MANY INTERESTING PEOPLE! NOW LET'S GET A DRINK AND LOOK AT THE APPETIZERS!"

We threaded through the crowd to the dining room table. Ritz Crackers and Triscuits circled a plate that held a Velveeta wine ball in the center. The cracker boxes were on the table next to the plate and many people put a hand in there and avoided the plate. Another plate held a bowl of ranch dressing dip surrounded by cut carrots and celery sticks. A bowl overflowing with green grapes appeared to be untouched. Potato chips filled four cereal bowls. And there was a salad bowl filled with fun size candy bars, like the kind given out for

Halloween. Surely that was Howard's addition to the table: he loved candy and hoarded bags of it that he bought on sale the day after Halloween.

From there Raquel and I squeezed into the kitchen. Someone turned down the music and my body relaxed a little.

Toby was playing bartender, standing on one side of the counter mixing margaritas in the blender. A green plastic trash can beside him was filled with ice, beer, and some pink cans of Tab. Toby turned around and caught sight of me. "Zippy!" he shouted, and reached over and hugged me. He then looked Raquel up and down as if she were something he was going to buy. "Zippy said you were beautiful, but no one ever expects a person to be *this* beautiful."

Raquel opened her arms and the two of them hugged. From the hug, she turned her head toward me and said, "Oh my God, I love this party!"

My mother and Jo came into the kitchen together, each carrying an empty margarita glass.

"My turn?" Jo said, and she and Toby switched places so she could tend bar.

"Jo, this is Raquel!" I was so excited for the people who had known me forever to meet the person with whom I spent all my time outside of work.

Jo smiled as if she hadn't heard me and then said, "The only job better than bartender is photographer. You get to hide out and watch rather than participate."

My mother was staring at the oven. "Mom!" I said, eager to introduce her to Raquel.

She opened the oven door and then reached her hand in and started to remove a cookie sheet before screaming, jumping back, and abandoning it.

"You have to use oven mitts!" I took her to the sink and ran cold water over her hand. When I turned back, Raquel had found a dish towel and removed the cookie sheet. Blackened pigs in a blanket.

"Do you have more?" Raquel asked. "We could start over again."

"Howard likes them black like that," Mom said. "Put 'em on the table."

Raquel shrugged, found a plate, and then tilted the cookie sheet over it so the pigs in a blanket tumbled off. I released my mother, who stuck her hand in the trash can full of ice.

"It's like fishing in a frozen lake!" She pulled out a can of Budweiser, removed the metal tab, and left the kitchen.

"MOM!" I called after her. "This is Raquel!" But she didn't hear.

"They started celebrating at noon," Jo said. "Well, we all did, but I was drunk so early that I'm entirely sober now." She was pouring out margaritas that the rotating kitchen crowd picked up before she could pull the blender away. Pink slush trailed along the counter. Even with the music lowered, the crowd noise was like a wall. I had to strain to hear Jo speak at a normal volume.

Raquel stepped closer to Jo and the two of them talked—Jo still working the blender—while I watched the party from the safety of the kitchen. As a kid, I loved my mom's parties. Her friends spoke to me like I was interesting or fun. And they told me fascinating stories about their lives or people they were dating or a dinner they'd had. I was never dismissed or left out because I was a kid. But it was like a dirty secret that my life was like this. I never brought kids from school home because I couldn't imagine what anyone from the outside would think, looking at the way we lived. When I saw it all through Raquel's eyes, however, it didn't feel so shameful. It hadn't been the ideal way to raise a kid, but it was a life full of joy. Energy. Entertainment. And love!

Jo handed Raquel and me a margarita each and then someone changed the music to the Commodores and turned it up even louder. When "Brick House" came on, Howard lifted his bound ball and shouted, "'TIS TIME FOR THINE SOUL TRAIN!"

"THAT'S HOWARD!" I shouted into Raquel's ear. "OBVIOUSLY." I lifted my fist.

The soul train snaked from the living room couch, past the dining room table, and then to the kitchen counter. One guy walked on his hands with his bare feet pointed like a ballerina. This inspired the next guy, who was wearing a dashiki that fell toward his head as he flipped into a handstand. His neon-pink underwear looked like they were shrink-wrapped around his crotch. The hooting and clapping drowned out the music for an instant.

"THIS IS THE GREATEST PARTY EVER!" Raquel shouted, and for the first time in my life, I actually felt an unfamiliar sense of pride about my ad hoc family. It was short-lived, as my mother had started down the soul train line.

"THAT'S HARD TO WATCH," I shouted.

"ARE YOU KIDDING?! SHE'S SO TERRIBLE, IT'S GREAT!!" Raquel shouted back.

What my mother didn't have in rhythm or skill she made up for with enthusiasm. She was like a bundle of triangles trying to escape—elbows flying hither and yon, knees lifting in a herky-jerky un-tempoed march. And then she stopped in the middle of the train line, dropped to all fours, and swung her tiny butt like a cat switching its tail. This made no sense, dance-wise, but it drew a lot of cheering. Raquel lifted her fist and hooted so loudly, I expected everyone to turn and look at her. No one did, of course; they were equally raucous.

Next, Howard bopped in, his giant thumb-nosed Q-tip waving in the air like his personal flag. The way he moved made me wonder if he needed medical help.

"JESUS!" Raquel shouted. "AND I THOUGHT YOUR MOM WAS BAD!"

"IT'S LIKE HE'S SUFFERING FROM SOMETHING. MAYBE AN ITCHINESS IN ALL HIS DARK SPOTS BUT HE CAN'T USE HIS HAND TO GET TO THEM." I waved my hitchhiking fist as I spoke.

"OR HE HAS TO POOP VERY BADLY AND IS MOVING TO HOLD IT IN!" Raquel shouted, and then she leaned into my ear so close, I could feel her lips against me when she said, "Our turn."

I pretended not to hear. Even though I loved dancing, the idea of being the *only* one dancing made me nervous.

"WE HAVE TO DO IT!" Raquel took my hand. "NO CHOICE!" She led me through the crowd to the end of the train line. When our turn came, I emptied my thoughts and let it happen—I entered the flow. Raquel did the small, tight moves she always did at home, at a club, standing beside a bar with the thumping music. She was good, but there was an air of containment in her dancing, as if she were watching her body in a mirror and needed to keep it all intact. Raquel dancing versus excellent dancing was like the difference between someone who can draw an exact likeness of a face (Raquel dancing) and someone who creates *art* (many of the people I'd seen dancing at the clubs where Raquel had taken me). At theater parties, I was often told I was a good dancer, but I was certain that sometimes I was good and sometimes I was terrible. The more I thought about how I moved or what I was doing, the worse I was. Dancing only worked for me when I was so absorbed, it was like I wasn't there.

When we made it to the end, my mother rushed up to us and shouted, "ARE YOU RAQUEL?"

Raquel nodded and my mother hugged her and then said, "THANKS FOR LOOKING OUT FOR MY ZIPPY!"

My mother held on to Raquel, one hand on each of her upper arms, as the two of them talked, their faces a pantomime wall away from each other so they wouldn't have to shout. I alternately watched them, only slightly curious as to what they were saying, and the people at the party. Few people wore anything that would be considered stylish at I. Magnin, yet many displayed a distinct fashion sense. There were a lot of bright colors and big shoulders, sequins, and bulky, weighty jewelry. I liked most of it on the people themselves, but none of it was something I wanted, the way I wanted so many of the clothes I hung, straightened, handed over, and rung up.

Raquel broke my spiraling thoughts when she grabbed my hand and said, "THE PARTY'S MOVING NOW!"

My mother pushed ahead of the people pouring out of her place and down the stairs to Toby and Jo's for the dinner buffet. Raquel and I inched our way down the crowded slanted staircase.

When we entered Toby and Jo's place, classical music was playing at a volume that allowed conversation without shouting. Raquel's head swiveled from side to side as we went down the hall and into the living room.

"This is decorated like my grandmother's place," she said.

"Yeah, I bet. If the furniture your mother gave you for our place is your mother's generation, then one above her would be like this." Everything was ornate, floral, tapestry-detailed: lion-clawed lamps, turned-out legs holding up every table.

"Exactly! It's funny that Toby and Jo are so close with your mother. She's such a tack-the-canvas-on-the-wall person and they're—"

"Send-it-out-for-mat-board-and-a-gilt-edged-frame people."

"But I guess they have the same energy and humor."

"And they all love to eat, drink, laugh, and dance," I said.

"Let's look at the food." Raquel took my hand and we made our way to the dining room, where we circled the table.

"Did you ever see that movie *Arsenic and Old Lace*?" she asked.

"With Cary Grant? Yes, my mom and I watched that one together."

"This food looks like something those two murderous old ladies would serve."

She was right: it was dowager food. Everything was bitty, fishy, eggy, and smelly. Even the meat was thinly sliced, slimy, and shiny. All of it was displayed on patterned china with a gold-rippled edge. The only thing that caused me no-eating-day regrets was the pan of mac 'n' cheese. I stood near it, admiring it the way Raquel and I looked at babies in strollers. But when I overheard Jo explain to a man in a seersucker suit that it was made with bacon fat, bacon, and sardines, I was relieved of desire. This was, perhaps, the best dinner party to attend on a no-eating day.

The only alcohol Toby and Jo were serving was wine. Raquel and I slipped back upstairs to Mom and Howard's apartment, which looked like it had been ransacked by teenage boys, and made more margaritas. It wasn't until we were downstairs again that I could feel that I was drunk. Spinny, fat-tongued drunk.

Raquel was in conversation with a man in a fishnet top when my mother sidled up beside me. She held a near-empty glass of wine in one hand and a deviled egg in the other. She finished the wine and then lopped off half the egg in one bite. "How you doin', honey?"

"You mean, like, how am I doing because I've been talking to my dad?"

"Yeah. Still Mr. Nice Pants?"

"Yeah. He's super nice. He mostly asks questions about me."

"Hmm. Is he married?"

"Would you want to date him again?"

"Of course not! I'm married to Howard! Besides, your dad and I didn't date. That was a one-night stand. The only one I ever had and look what it got me!" My mother nudged the side of my cheek with her hand holding the remaining deviled egg, which she then dropped into her mouth. "I was lucky," she said, with her mouth full. "He got laid, but I got you."

"I think you'd like him. He's interested in a lot of the same things that interest me—the Fibonacci sequence—"

My mother cut me off. "I'm glad you're getting to know him, honey, and I'm glad he's nice, but he better not try to take you for Christmas or Thanksgiving."

Now I understood that her lack of curiosity had been a simple fear that I'd prefer him to her. "Oh, Mom," I said. "I'll never abandon you."

My mother didn't respond. Or maybe she was hiding her response, as she immediately bent down so I couldn't see her face. She opened a lower cupboard in the kitchen, as if this were her own home, and pulled out a bottle of vodka on which the word *ABSOLUT* was written in a big bold font. "I bought this for them. It's sooooo good."

She opened a top cupboard and pulled out four shot glasses, then poured vodka into each glass.

She took a shot and then tried to hand one to me. I waved it away.

Mom picked up one of the other shot glasses and tapped Raquel's shoulder with it. Raquel turned around, took the glass from my mother, and slugged back the vodka. The guy in fishnet walked away.

Raquel picked up another shot from the counter and tossed it back.

My mother took another shot. When I looked directly into her face, her eyes appeared wobbly, as if her inability to focus physically blurred her eyes. Then I remembered that I was drunk too.

Toby whooped and we all looked out toward the living room. He was roping people with his boa and doing a slow ballet with them.

Raquel grabbed my hand and led me to the center of the living room, where people were now slow dancing—dramatically, comically. I put my arms around her neck, she put hers around my waist, and we danced too.

"Remember middle school mixers?" she asked.

"I never went to one," I said.

"I went with West Jones and he did this the whole time—" Raquel pulled me in and breathed like a panting asthmatic dog into my ear.

We danced with Raquel switching up characters every few steps until I understood what it was like to be her in eighth grade and to have had every boy in the school want to dance with you. (Flattering, claustrophobic, overwhelming.)

It wasn't long before the music was turned off and a spoon was clinked against a wineglass to call everyone into the living room. Toby stood on the ottoman in the center of the room and gave a speech that was so funny, I couldn't believe he hadn't practiced it for hours in front of the mirror. When he was done, Jo put on an Earth, Wind & Fire album, and it was a new kind of dance party with Raquel and I in the center, singing along the whole time.

Eventually Howard went upstairs and crashed out in his own bed and my mother fell asleep (or passed out) on the velvet fainting couch, where several people decorated her with costume jewelry and Toby's boa.

Raquel and I stood together and I looked at my festooned mother the way you look at a pair of dropped underwear on the pavement of a parking lot. It's a curious sight, but no one wants to do a close examination. "I'm too drunk to drive home," Raquel said.

"Me too."

"Cab?"

"Let's try." I never took cabs; I used buses, cable cars, and the BART train. This was part of the greatness of being with Raquel: I was exposed to a larger life than the one I'd had with my mother (who also never took cabs and who owned a twenty-year-old car that she spent months *not* driving every time she found a good parking space).

By the time we left, the temperature had dropped by twenty degrees. My teeth chattered as Raquel and I walked arm in arm to the Darien, the closest hotel to my mom's place, where we thought we could find a cab. Before we got there, a cable car stopped near us. Neither of us spoke; we simply ran to the rear middle of the car and jumped on. Only tourists bought tickets for cable cars. Locals boarded away from the brakemen and hung on until they were close enough to where they were going.

This car was packed with what may have been a bachelorette party. The women were around Raquel's age and dressed like they were about to receive awards. Everything was skimpy, short, with big shoulders and puffy sleeves. Only half of them wore coats—the others must have been freezing. I recognized a Betsey Johnson dress from Miss Liaskis's section that had chunky life-sized silk roses sewn all over the skirt. An older couple, sitting and clinging hands, stared out at the girls as if they were a stage show. Raquel and I stared too, and then I realized we were about to zoom down a steep street and the cable car would pick up speed.

"Come on!" I worked my way to the back and Raquel followed. We both stepped onto the runner and double-hand-gripped the bar at each corner of the rear. The cable car crested the hill and started dropping straight down. The party girls screamed like they were on a roller coaster. I hung on and leaned back so my hair was flying and the wind was stinging my face. Even as cold as I was, I was flushed with exhilaration. I looked up at the full moon and was thrilled by the simple fact that there was no fog dimming that perfect disc of light.

"Raquel!" I shouted. "The moon! Look at the moon!"

Raquel threw her head back and stared up. Her hair undulated in the wind like a silk flag. She was smiling so big, I knew she'd forgotten about Jason and that it was a no-eating day and the case she was working on then, which involved forty-seven people, all of whom were bossy and difficult.

When the cable car made it to the bottom of the hill, Raquel and I jumped off. I was still shivering, my teeth clattering, but I was no longer cold. Raquel held my hand as we stumbled along toward our apartment.

"Day-Timers!" Raquel said once we'd taken off our shoes and changed into sweats and T-shirts.

I returned to my room and got my Day-Timer and also the collection of hold tags that held all the advice I'd been given since the last time I wrote in the book.

We sat on the couch with stacks of colored pens and a stick of pink glitter glue. "We need to write two things tonight," Raquel said. "One: personal goals. Two: career goals."

"I don't have a career," I said.

"Yes, you do. How do you think Miss Lee would feel if you said what she'd been doing for fifty years wasn't a career?"

"Yeah. You're right."

"Hell yeah, I'm right. Third—"

"I thought you said *two things*."

"These are subcategories." Raquel rocked her shoulder into

mine. "So, sub-cat-three is love goals. And for sub-cat-four write down one way in which you can be a better person."

"Jesus. Do you think I'm awful because I didn't realize right away that selling dresses is a career?"

"NOOOO!" Raquel said. "But we both could improve, right?"

"Okay, sure. But I have to write down the hold tag advice first."

Raquel already had her head down and was writing. She alternated between a pink pen and a baby-blue one so that her writing looked like a sherbet swirl. I entered the latest: (1.) *Never get in a hot tub. It's like a bacteria soup.*—Sulinda, Lancôme. (2.) *If you're with a man, make sure you can tolerate his testicles, because those only get smellier and saggier—like super uneven, too—with time.*—Natalia, Fendi. (3.) *Your body has a set weight that you'll be no matter what. Forget that Day On/Day Off diet and eat. Wherever you land weight-wise is where you should be.*—Mimi, Estée Lauder. (4.) *Every time you apply a cream to your face, stroke up. UP! UP! If you don't, you'll pull down your skin and you'll have one of those long, hangy hound dog faces by the time you're thirty-five.*—Vivi, La Mer (face as taut as an overblown balloon). (5.) *If you eat sushi, you have nice poop. Like, there's nothing better than a sushi poop. It slips out so cleanly, you don't even have to wipe.*—Mirabelle, the model-looking woman who sold Chanel cosmetics and said she only ate raw fish and raw vegetables.

The last entries I had were from Mimi again: sex and affairs.

"How are you doing there?" Raquel asked.

"I'll start my goals now."

"Do it!" Raquel said. "Committing on paper helps it materialize in real life."

I picked up a dark blue pen and wrote, *Personal goal: Get to know my dad better. He mentioned the moon briefly that first call; ask him if he likes staring at the moon as much as I do. Stop talking about myself and my life and find out about him! Career Goals:*

I tapped the pen on the book. A career at I. Magnin would be a dream come true. But a dream was exactly what it was right then. Now that I'd seen the complaint cards, my worries about being fired had quadrupled. To even imagine a career in "San Francisco's Finest Department Store" felt childish. Like dreaming of being a princess.

"I can't figure out my career goals," I mumbled.

Raquel looked up from her book. "Who are you jealous of?"

"What? Why are you asking that?"

"If you're jealous of someone, it's probably because you want what they have or you want to be them but aren't . . . yet, like, you want to be them but right then . . . I can't talk clear. Those drinks! But jealousy tells you a lot about yourself. Who makes you jealous?" Raquel looked back to her Day-Timer and continued writing as if she hadn't even stopped.

"I'm jealous of Christie Brinkley."

"Huh?" Raquel looked up at me.

"I could say that I want to be a model, but I'm five six and chubby, so that's impossible."

"Do you want to be a model?" Raquel asked.

"I don't think so. It seems like a waste to *want* something that's impossible."

"Very little is *impossible*."

"I couldn't be a world-class gymnast. I couldn't be a horse jockey. I couldn't be a professional football player."

"Are you jealous of any of those people?"

"No."

"Zippy! Who do you see who makes you jealous?!"

I looked down at my Day-Timer and tapped it with my pen. Raquel went back to writing in hers. I had been jealous of Sorority Girl—of the fact that she got to go to college and of her relationship with her dad—but I'd pretty much cured myself of that by trying to appreciate her as a customer. Raquel was someone I should have been jealous of. After all, she had a perfect family, a perfect childhood, and a perfect career. But I wasn't jealous of her at all. I was proud of her, proud to be her friend.

"I was jealous of the buyer who showed up at work one day. That seems like the single best and most amazing job in the world. But how could *I* ever be a buyer? They wouldn't let me be a buyer any sooner than they'd let the homeless guy who sleeps in the shrubs on Union Square be a buyer."

Raquel stared at me. She said, "Uh, Zippy. You're kinda killing me with the pathetic sob story. You already work there. You're learning about fashion every day. *Why not you?* You think that buyer knew anything more than you at your age? Everyone starts at zero. Get over it and get on it."

"Get over it and get on it." My voice was listless and sad. How could I get on with it when no one—not the customers and not the other salesgirls (minus Miss Lena and Miss Liaskis)—wanted me there.

"YES." Raquel tapped her pen on her book. "In order to achieve, you start at the bottom—no one is too good for the bottom!"

"No, oh . . . I mean, I don't think I'm too good for anything. It's . . . well . . . I'm kinda on probation there."

Raquel threw her pen across the room. "PROBATION?! NO WAY!"

"Way. Or . . . well, something happened and Miss Dani didn't quite tell me about it. But she told me to simmer down when it came to dealing with customers. And Miss Kitty, who's never said a word to me, knows about it."

"ABOUT WHAT? What exactly happened?" Raquel picked up another pen and then put it on the open page of the Day-Timer as a bookmark.

"I got a pile of customer complaints. Like, a whole batch of them." Tears pooled in my eyes.

"I honestly can't believe anyone would complain about *you*."

"They said I was pushy and forcing bras and shoes on customers and that they were afraid to return stuff when I was there." More tears gathered. I'd only have to move my head and they'd skate down my cheeks.

"That sounds like Miss Yolanda. It doesn't sound like you. You're not pushy. You need to be pushier."

"Not according to the Magnin shoppers. Meanwhile, I'm not sure how I can make enough money to help out my mom while Howard's walking around with his giant Q-tip and . . . I dunno. I could take Howard's job at the Hardware Depot. I'd make a lot more money and I bet nobody would complain about me there."

"You're *actually* considering going to the Hardware Depot and taking Howard's job?" Raquel was suddenly serious. "Look. If you do get fired because of those complaints, and if you do take Howard's job at Hardware Depot, this isn't the end of your dreams."

"No?" I looked over at her.

"No," Raquel said. "It's like a commercial break from the main attraction. Then, once Howard's back at work, you apply for a job at another department store, like Neiman Marcus. There will always be obstacles to any career you choose. Just accept that there are problems and then push your way through until you get where you want to be."

I stared at Raquel. She stared back. It was like we were playing that staring contest where you tried to hold your gaze and not be the first one to look away. This one ended in a tie—we both burst out laughing.

"As I said." Raquel lifted her pen, ready to write again. "Why not you?"

I put my pen to the book and wrote, *Why not me?* If I wrote down the big dream of being a buyer at I. Magnin, it might be jinxed. I knew what I meant by *Why not me?* The Day-Timer knew what I meant. And God, if He ever bothered to listen to me, would know too.

Raquel was reading over my shoulder. "Good," she said. "Did you already do love goals? Or how to be a better person?"

"Oh, yeah. I'll do those now."

For *Love Goals,* I wrote: *Date someone. Like, a grown-up date. Like, dinner or something. And, maybe, have sex? Wait, that's too much. Maybe kiss. But without slobber pooling in the divots of my clavicles. And then, after kissing, other stuff. Like sex eventually? Holy moly!*

For the *Better Person* topic, I wrote: *Ring up more sales for Miss Lena. Seriously.* I paused for a minute and then I added, *Day-Timer, I know I will likely end up at the Hardware Depot, so maybe it doesn't matter how many sales I make at I. Magnin. But if you and God can help me figure out a way to not be pushy while making more sales, ringing up sales for Miss Lena, and keeping my job at I. Magnin, well, that would be swell. I don't know why I wrote SWELL; no one my age says SWELL. Even my mother doesn't say SWELL! I'm not sure who says SWELL, but someone does because damn if that word's not stuck in my brain right now.*

"Done." I looked over at Raquel. Her head had dropped back. Her pen was still in her hand. She was passed out.

# Chapter 7

**About a week** later, my father called me at work before the store opened, while Miss Lena was picking up our cash bag.

"Oh, I wanted to talk to you about an ear!" I said, into the phone. "And the moon."

"An ear and the moon?" my father asked.

"I was looking at Miss Lena's ear," I said. "It spirals like a shell. The Fibonacci sequence!"

"That's beautiful," my dad said. "And what about the moon?"

"I wanted to know if you like it as much as I do," I said. "Because I love looking at it and reading about it and even thinking about it."

"The Sea of Tranquility is a place I've always wanted to go," my father said, and I had the chills. Could I have somehow inherited my interest in the lunar mare where Neil Armstrong and Buzz Aldrin left their footprints?

We talked for a few more minutes while Miss Lena opened the register, and then my father said he'd call again soon and I hung up.

Miss Lena opened the supply drawer and pulled out the hold tags and pencils.

"You must make your dad," Miss Lena said.

"Hmm, okay. But I don't know what he looks like. I mailed him my senior picture from school and he said he looks exactly like me, only he's six feet three inches tall, has super-wide shoulders, and is never mistaken for a woman."

"You can draw that!" Miss Lena said, and she watched as I did.

"Good?" I stood the Dad doll up and wiggle-walked him across the counter.

"Excellent," Miss Lena said. "Now make my parents."

"What do they look like?"

"They are both in Heaven now. My mother looked exactly like me and my father looked like that Robert actor."

"Robert De Niro?"

"No, the handsome Rob man."

"Rob Lowe?"

"No, older. He was in that baseball movie."

"Robert Duvall?"

"No, he's more leading-man handsome—"

"Robert Redford?"

Miss Lena clapped her hands and jumped. "Exactly. But my father was taller. He was very tall and narrow and my mother was very small and round."

"Like the number ten," I said.

"Yes!" Miss Lena said. "They were the number ten!"

I felt blissfully absent, my mind nowhere but on the hold tags, as I worked on Miss Lena's parents.

Miss Lena took out the other paper dolls and walked them across the counter. She hopped Jesus to the keys of the register, where he hovered (silently) over the other dolls. Then she started a conversation about Yugo between Cecil and Miss Lena. Cecil was very curious about Yugo, and Miss Lena had many stories to tell about the Kingdom of Serbs, Croats, and Slovenes. I continued to work on her parents. When I was done, I asked, "From which kingdom does your family come?"

"We are Serbian," Miss Lena said. "But together we are all Yugo!"

I wrote on the back of her father, *We are all Yugo!* On the back of her mother, I wrote, *We come from a proud history of Serbians.*

"Maybe I should do some customers," I said.

"Oh yes! Do the twins."

"The twins! Perfect. And I'll do Sorority Girl."

When I finished the first twin, Miss Lena picked her up, pranced her across the counter, and then picked up the Miss Yolanda doll. In a near-perfect imitation of Miss Yolanda's muted bark she said, "You look like a cow in that dress! Come here—I'll tell you exactly what to buy . . . dumb cow."

I was laughing as I finished the second twin, and then I bopped her across the table and said in a fancy old-lady voice, "Excuse me? Can you help me find—"

Miss Lena, in Miss Yolanda's voice, grumbled, "I'm already helping you! What is wrong with you, you stupid rat cow!"

I screamed with laughter and then startled as Miss Lena gathered up the dolls and threw them in the drawer before slamming it shut.

Miss Dani was approaching with a rolling rack of dresses, Miss Yolanda beside her. Miss Lee and Miss Karen were crossing the floor toward us. They were having a low, fast chat that sounded like the *ch-ch-ch* of slippers shuffling across a wood floor. Next, Miss Braughn R sauntered over. I looked across the floor toward Miss Liaskis. She was waving her arms at me and was, maybe, crying.

"Quick meeting," Miss Dani said.

"Lemme go open Miss Liaskis's register real fast." I ran off and sent Miss Liaskis to the meeting. I didn't count out her bills, as I'd yet to see a cash bag that didn't have the correct opening numbers. Once her register was ready, I ran back to the meeting.

"What'd I miss?"

"Blathering bullcrap," Miss Yolanda said.

Miss Dani shook her head. "Nope. I told everyone I'm in love. There is no BS in love. Love is love."

"Wait. You have a boyfriend?" I asked.

"She and the Blondie's Pizza guy are in love!" Miss Lena said.

"The cute guy everyone has a crush on?!" Was that possible? He looked at least a decade younger than Miss Dani, and salesgirls who looked like models were in love with him. I tried to imagine him making out with Miss Dani. It would be like wrapping a suede coat around a fireplug. But why not wrap a suede coat around a fireplug? What a beautiful and interesting combination that would be.

"Well, he's no Berber Coffee guy, but hell yeah, the gorgeous one!" Miss Dani kicked out her little calf and punched the air.

Miss Lee and Miss Karen whispered to each other. I could tell they thought this was inappropriate talk for work. Miss Braughn R stared into space as if we were kids and she was a grown-up whose ears weren't even taking in this conversation. Miss Yolanda was rolling her eyes and clucking on her candy ball. Miss Liaskis had teared up with joy and Miss Lena was smiling.

Right then Miss Meredith, the most popular salesgirl from Designer Dresses, walked by. She looked over at us, waved, and did a quick closemouthed smile. She was so chic, it was like she'd walked off the runway in a fashion show. No one spoke until she was out of hearing distance and then Miss Yolanda said, "Who the hell is she getting dressed up like that for?!"

"Her job," I said. "I mean, who are you dressing up for?"

"I'm dressed to sell. I'm not dressed *to kill,*" Miss Yolanda said. "That woman looks like she wants men to bow down before her."

"Even the handsome Berber Coffee guy would bow down before *her,*" Miss Dani said.

"I dress up for me!" Miss Liaskis said. "Mr. Liaskis doesn't even notice what I'm wearing. Unless I'm in red. He's like a bull when he sees red! If you look through my underwear drawer—"

Miss Karen wagged her first finger at Miss Liaskis. Miss Liaskis quieted.

"I think when I'm not dressing for work—" I started.

"In one of your two outfits," Miss Yolanda said.

"I now have four," I said. "But I think when I'm going out at night, I'm dressing for my roommate, Raquel. For her approval."

"Okay, enough of this ridiculousness," Miss Yolanda said. "What are we meeting about? These dresses?" Miss Yolanda tugged one out, the hanger still attached to the bar, and then let it drop.

"Oh, there's nothing ridiculous about love!" Miss Dani said. "But yes, these are the latest Vittadini. Maybe one of you can try one on before we open." Miss Dani picked up her wrist, which was covered in bangles and jewels, and glanced at her watch, which was buried in the bric-a-brac.

"Hell if I'm taking off my clothes." Miss Yolanda fingered the dresses on the rack. The dresses came in gray or red. The red dresses had gold buttons on the epaulets and down the front. The gray dresses had silver buttons. Some dresses were sleeveless and they were all knee-length.

"Miss Zippy should try one on," Miss Lena said. "She's the youngest."

"Hm," Miss Karen said, and I wondered if she was younger than I thought. But she'd been there ten years, so she couldn't have started at age nine!

"Sure, hand me a ten."

Miss Yolanda looked me up and down. "You're an eight now."

"No way," I said. My skirt was fitting loosely (I assumed this was because of the Day On/Day Off diet) and I did fit into Raquel's old skirt. Still, I didn't believe that I'd actually gone down a full size.

"Suit yourself." Miss Yolanda shrugged.

Miss Dani handed me a size eight. It was red with short sleeves and gold buttons. I went into the fitting room, unzipped, and then dropped my skirt on the floor. I took off my blouse and draped it over the chair. I stepped into the dress, reached my arm back, and zipped it almost to the top.

It fit perfectly. I felt taller and stronger when I walked out of the dressing room.

"You look like Sgt. Pepper," Miss Yolanda said.

"She looks beautiful!" Miss Liaskis said.

"Yes, gorgeous," Miss Lena said.

Miss Braughn R, Miss Lee, and Miss Karen were murmuring to each other about the dress as if they had ways to sell it that they didn't want the rest of us to know.

"I think you all can sell the heck out of this line," Miss Dani said. "It's got that military—"

"Sgt. Pepper," Miss Yolanda said.

"Yeah!" Miss Dani laughed. "It's got that Sgt. Pepper thing happening. That's *very* in now. It was all over *Women's Wear Daily* yesterday. Tell you what, Zippy, since Miss Yolanda is sick and tired of your three outfits—"

"Four now. Raquel gave me a skirt."

"Right," Miss Dani said. "Still, why don't you wear the dress today? It looks dynamite on you and might help the sales."

"Can I?" I knew the store had a policy that you could not wear stock unless you bought it. Was this a parting gift because Miss Dani suspected I might soon be fired? I didn't want to think about that, and I did *love* the dress. How cool would it be to actually *wear* an I. Magnin dress while working at I. Magnin?

"If you think you can sell at least two of them, then keep it on," Miss Dani said.

"Okay!" I said.

"And please buy the thing," Miss Yolanda said. "We need to see you in more than those damn skirts—even if you're dressed like an officer in the military."

Miss Braughn R turned and walked off. Her departure started a ripple of other departures, and soon it was only Miss Lena and me standing there as Miss Dani arranged the dresses on a four-way rack near the front of Petite Dresses.

I hung my blouse and skirt up on the hook near the register. Miss Dani glanced over at them and said, "Put those in my office so we can keep the area clean." I blushed, grabbed them, and rushed toward her office. Did she really think they made the area look messy, or did she want them off the floor because they were obviously used and refurbished clothes?

The office felt odd, spooky, almost, without Miss Dani in it. I hung the clothes on a rack in the corner that held damaged dresses. Each dress had a plastic tag attached to it that said *RTV. Return to Vendor.*

I was about to leave when I glanced at the complaint cards still spilling out of the envelope on Miss Dani's desk. I hovered over the desk and saw that a couple new ones had come in: *Miss Zippy didn't know that Bill Blass was the one who said, "When in doubt, wear red."*

The moment I read that card was the moment I learned the quote. Was someone mistaking me for another salesgirl? I didn't resemble anyone on the fifth floor. In fact, other than the perfectly self-replicated Braughns, no one on the floor looked like anyone else. It was like the United Nations of faces.

As if I didn't want to leave a fingerprint, I used the knuckle on my pointer finger to push the Bill Blass complaint card aside in order to read the one beneath it: *What a dumb name Zippy is. Why would you hire anyone that young and inexperienced?* Could I disagree with this person? Even I had been astounded that a store this established and prestigious would hire someone who had never, ever, and still never (!) shopped there. And, regarding my name, I'd been alternately embarrassed and confused by it since I started kindergarten, when the kids called me Zipper. I had even asked my mother, who was zipping my dress one morning, if I had been named Zippy because my mom liked pulling up zippers. (No, she liked the idea of speediness and pep.)

Tears were going into my mouth now, salty and slick. I gingerly picked up a stack of sweaters (from a different department, of course, who knows what they were doing on Miss Dani's desk) so I could get to the tissue box, when Miss Dani entered.

"Oh boy," she said, watching me blow my nose.

"Maybe if I were named Stephanie or Katie, the customers wouldn't hate me so much."

"Oh, for goodness' sake!" Miss Dani waved a stumpy jewel-clanging arm. "It's a great name. These customers are snobs. You'll figure it out."

"But I have to figure it out before you fire me . . . I hate my stupid name!" I blew my nose again to hide the fact that the tears were flowing now.

Miss Dani rubbed the top of my back. "Listen: try to back down a little with the customers, keep smiling, and stay the course. I'd never fire you. You're doing an excellent job and I'm not sure these cards are all . . . I'm not sure what's going on with the cards."

"But what about Miss Kitty? Won't she fire me?" My voice was stuttering with tears. I felt like quivering Jell-O that needed to be set on a table. In a quiet room.

"I can't control that woman. But listen, Zip, do the best you can and I'll do the best I can on your behalf. Okay?"

"Okay," I said, only to please her. "I'll do the best I can. I'll stay the course." As far as I could see, the course was leading me out of the store and over to the Hardware Depot, where I'd make more money and no one (probably) would complain about me.

"Now go in the bathroom and splash some water on your puss so you look fresh again."

"My puss?"

"Face. Your puss!"

"Ah okay, another thing I didn't know. Bill Blass thinks, *When in doubt, wear red,* and *puss* is another word for *face*."

Miss Dani gave me a thumbs-up as I left.

**I splashed water** on my *puss,* which splattered mascara down my cheeks. The more I splashed, the more I had jailhouse stripes. I dried my face on a hand towel, and then left the bathroom and jumped in an open elevator car to visit Mimi.

Mimi wiped my face clean with makeup remover. It felt like licks from a kitten. "Were you crying?" she asked.

"Yeah. I need to make more money to help my mom with the bills while her husband is out of commission. So maybe I should go take a job at the Hardware Depot, but . . . I don't want to."

"Why is your mom's husband out of commission?"

"Uh . . . he hurt his hand in a power saw accident."

"Of course he was playing with a power saw! You know, as far as I can tell, men are more simian than human." Mimi opened a mascara and held it near my eye. "Blink. Blink. Blink. Blink."

"Howard isn't very simian. He's more . . . like a turkey. What's the word for that?" I closed my eyes quickly, as Mimi was coming at the other eye with the mascara wand.

The wand hovered as Mimi said, "Well . . . *anserine* means 'goose-like' and a goose is sort of turkey-like, right?"

"I guess."

Mimi put the mascara away. "In the meantime, you've moved out of the house and you support yourself. Why do you need to help support your mom and her anserine husband?"

"Oh, you know. I mean, my mom supported me without any help from anyone my whole life, and now they have these Mount Vesuvius–sized medical bills, so don't you think I should—"

"The only thing you *should* do is dictate your own life. You be the chooser for where you go or what you do or who gets the money you earn."

My life so far had been spent lining up in order to be chosen: for a position in the costume department in high school shows, for friends to invite me to their parties, for any boy to like me, and for my job at this gorgeous store. My mom chose how I spent my time when I lived with her, and Raquel now chose how I spent my weekends and when I ate. It had never before occurred to me that I was not the chooser in my life but, obviously, that was so.

"Are you the chooser in your life?" I asked.

"Yeah, as much as possible," Mimi said. "I mean, none of us can control everything, but I can control what I aim for and how I respond to the things I don't choose."

"Huh. Okay, I'll try to think of myself as a chooser."

A customer approached and stood directly behind me. I turned my head and looked at her. She had two full I. Magnin bags in her hands and an impatient smirk on her face. Mimi gave her a big smile, a hello, and then a few words about the new eye cream. I whispered *thank you* before I quietly slipped away and returned to the fifth floor.

When I came up the escalator, Miss Lena was rushing in my direction. Stripes of blond hair, loosened from her bun, lined her face. She pushed the loose strands aside and said, "Every room is full! You take the first two and I'll take the last two."

"Are you sure?"

"Yes, dear, you always share your sales with me! Now please go! The woman in room one needs something, but I'm—" She ran off toward Miss Lee and Miss Karen's section, mumbling words I couldn't catch.

I knocked on the door. It opened immediately to a woman in her bra, panties, and high heels. Her hair was thick and swooping; Howard would have loved the size of her head.

"Well?"

"Hey!" I smiled. "I'm Miss Zippy and I'm taking care of you now."

"Where's that little woman?"

"That was Miss Lena and she has so many customers, she asked me to help."

The woman huffed and turned her head away as if there were something to see behind her. She turned back. "Fine. Can you get me this in a four?"

I stumbled back a step as she pushed a detached dress and hanger into my hands. "No problem, I'll be back in a sec."

She shut the door and I went to the next room and knocked. There was movement on the other side, but it was slow, quiet, as if someone were hiding from me. "Hello?" I knocked again.

"What?" The voice was low but young-sounding.

"I'm Miss Zippy. Can I get you something?"

"No."

I listened to the whispery shuffling on the other side of the door. "Okay," I said at last. "Call my name if you need anything."

"You want me to call out your name?"

"Yeah. I'll hear you."

The door opened and a tiny woman craned her head out, hiding her body. Her face was as white as tapioca pudding and almost as mushy-looking. Acne scars marred her cheeks and mascara flecked under her eyes. "How will you hear me?"

"Uh, well, I'll be back and forth, so—"

"Are there cameras here? Am I being recorded?"

"Not that I know of." I hoped there were none, or Miss Lena and I would probably be fired for praying!

"That you *know* of?!"

"There aren't any. Period." I tried to peer over her shoulder to see what she was trying on. Or was she stealing something? "What kind of dress are you looking for? Can I bring you something?"

"I need blue. Blue! Why is it so hard to find a blue dress!"

"I know, it's not the color this season." I shrugged. "But there's a blue jumpsuit downstairs. Size?"

"Ten."

"Okay, I'll be right back."

I stepped away and she shut the door and then shouted, "Twelve! Or maybe a fourteen!"

"No problem!" I hurried out of there, holding the crumpled dress and hanger the woman in the first room had handed me. It was a Donna Karan and there were no more fours on the floor. I went to the phone, called the I. Magnin in South Coast Plaza, and connected to Petite Dresses.

The woman on the other end sounded like me. "Welcome to I. Magnin, this is Libby, how can I help you?"

"Hi, Libby, it's Zippy in San Francisco. Do you have that new Donna Karan with the sash tie in a size four?" I rattled off the words so quickly, I reminded myself of a newsie from a 1940s movie.

"It's in my hand! I was about to put it out."

"Great. Don't sell it—lemme call you back in a sec. I think my customer will want it sent."

"Fabulous," Libby said. "I'm standing by!"

I rushed to the first fitting room and knocked. The door opened. She was still in her bra and panties.

"We don't have the four here, but I can have it sent from South Coast Plaza."

"Okay." She turned around, dug through her purse, and pulled out an I. Magnin credit card and her driver's license. "Address is there, charge it to the card."

"Great!" I started to leave when she did a quick whistle. I turned back to her and, as if I were reading her mind, said, "Let me get you shoes and a bra that will work with the low front."

"Excellent!" she said.

"Strappy heels?"

"Duh."

"Black or silver?"

"Double duh," she said, and she pushed the door shut.

"What size?" I said to the slatted door.

"Seven and a half."

"Bra?"

"YOU ALREADY SAID YOU'D GET ME A BRA!"

I looked down the row of fitting rooms, waiting for someone to open a door, pop her head out, and see what all the ruckus was about. No one did. I said, quietly and calmly, "Yes, I need to know your bra size."

"Oh. Thirty-two C."

"I'll grab matching panties, too," I said.

"I should hope so," she mumbled from behind the closed door.

"Back in a sec!" I had a chipper upbeat in my voice. These women, like all the hard ones, were almost fun. It was like a game winning them over, ringing them up, and getting them the heck outta there!

"ACTUALLY, I'M A THIRTY-EIGHT C!" she shouted as I

was happily hurrying away. There wasn't time to worry about being too pushy or simmering down. I was in the groove.

**When the floor** was quiet again, Miss Yolanda stopped by.

"We've had a pretty good day so far," Miss Lena said.

"How much?" Miss Yolanda asked. Her mouth was smirk-puckered around a rotating candy ball in a way that made me think she was outselling me by far.

"We haven't added it up. There're still a couple hours left, so—" I shrugged as if I weren't worried. In truth, my only sales were the two women Miss Lena had given me and they had only bought one dress each (plus a bra and a pair of shoes).

"Hm," Miss Yolanda huffed, and then left us so she could snatch a customer who was stepping off the escalator.

Miss Lena waited until Miss Yolanda and her customer were out of hearing distance, and then she opened the supply drawer. She pulled out the paper dolls and waved them in the air.

"Let's do it," I said.

Miss Lena propped Jesus onto the register keys where he could silently watch. We'd already agreed that neither of us would dare speak in His voice. Next, like dealing out cards, Miss Lena separated the dolls into two piles.

On the top of her pile was my dad. On the top of my pile was me. Miss Lena picked up my dad and then said a low voice that strangely resembled my father's telephone grumble, "Zippy! I am so happy we're talking now. I know we haven't met in person yet, but that doesn't mean I don't love you."

"Oh, Dad . . ." I wasn't quite sure what to say. I put down the Zippy doll and picked up the Miss Braughn R doll. With a teetering walk, I moved the Miss Braughn R doll to the dad doll. As we had done before, I had her speak in the voice of Eva Gabor.

"Mr. Zippy's father, dahling," I said to the doll, "I can't wait to get back to Canada, where everything, even the water, even the coffee, even the air, is better than it is here!"

Miss Lena snickered. "Well, if you had Berber Coffee, you would see that it's the best in the world. And it is not Canadian!"

"Are you offering me a second cup? I think I will have a second cup!"

Miss Lena put down the dad doll and then picked up the Miss Yolanda doll. She said in Miss Yolanda's shrill roll, "Why don't you ever want a second cup of *my* coffee! You only want that gosh darn Berber Coffee?!"

Miss Lena and I both laughed and then she said, "Wait! Make the Berber Coffee guy and then we can do the Berber Coffee commercials exactly as they are on television."

"Why don't we make Miss Yolanda play the wife? I'll make the neighbor who serves the Berber Coffee."

"Yes!" Miss Lena jumped a little and clapped her hands.

I pulled out more hold tags and worked on the Berber Coffee guy. Maybe, after he'd had his coffee, we could have the Miss Dani doll make out with him since the real Miss Dani was in love with the real Berber Coffee guy.

"And here." Miss Lena laid some more hold tags beside the one I was working on. "Draw some coffee cups and the coffeepot. I'll color them and cut them out."

Miss Lena was focused, in a serious way, as she removed things from the drawer to stage the living room where the coffee would be served. A white plastic sensor was the coffee table and the stapler was the couch.

"Should we glue the coffee cups to their hands?" I asked.

The air cracked open with the sound of Miss Yolanda's shrill voice. "What are you idiots doing now?!"

Miss Lena opened the drawer and brushed in all the paper dolls, the stapler, and the sensors. Jesus was still leaning against the cash drawer, facing us. I deliberately didn't look at Him, as I didn't want Miss Yolanda to look there.

"What are *you* doing?" I asked.

"We're not doing anything!" Miss Lena opened her palms and straightened up. I could feel her suppressing a giggle as I aligned myself beside her.

"The way you two are standing side by side, you're like the goddamned Braughn sisters!"

"Only another Canadian could stand as still and straight as the Braughn sisters," I said, "because everyone knows people stand up better in Canada."

Miss Yolanda actually laughed. This made Miss Lena laugh and then I laughed as well.

"You ever been to Canada?" Miss Yolanda asked. She reached a hand into her suit jacket pocket, grabbed one of her candy balls, and popped it in her mouth.

"I have only been to Yugo, Italy, and America," Miss Lena said.

"I've never been anywhere," I said. "Well, Disneyland. And a lake once, with my mom and Howard."

"You should hear how they speak French in Montreal," Miss Yolanda said. And then she affected a French Canadian accent and said, "*Tu veut du painnnn?!* Painnnn, not PEH. They pronounce the final consonant. Idiots, like all our customers." She had no idea that my mother was from Montreal and I had no interest in sharing that fact.

"What happened with that woman you were helping?" I asked.

"She belongs at Kmart, where she can shop the Jaclyn Smith collection."

I felt blood paint the inside of my face. The former Charlie's Angel had started a clothing line that year. My mother and I went to Kmart the week it was out and splurged on two gorgeous cozy sweaters (size large so they could be shared). My mother wore them both so regularly, I'd never had a chance.

"I like those clothes," Miss Lena said. "I bought lounge pants."

Right then three things happened simultaneously: the phone rang, a heavy stream of customers stepped out of the elevators, and Miss Meredith from Designer Dresses floated off the *down* escalator. Miss Meredith smiled and delicately waved toward Miss Lena and me. She moved across the marble so lightly and elegantly, it was as if her feet weren't touching the ground. How did anyone ever end up with so much grace? Even Miss Lee and Miss Karen stopped rearranging clothes and watched. It felt like there was silence until Miss Meredith had disappeared on the next escalator. And then, sound resumed. Miss Lena answered the phone while surreptitiously putting Jesus in the drawer with the other paper dolls. The rest of us moved quickly to catch the customers who were now so numerous, it was like casting a fishing line into a stocked pond. I took a deep breath and, like an athlete with muscle memory, dove in and found my next customer.

# Chapter 8

**Raquel was back** on the floor in the shape of the letter X. It was a no-eating day. Her ribs arched out in a way that made me think of beached dolphins.

I stood with my feet at her head and looked down. "Is this a happy pose?" Her face was upside down to me, pointed chin on the top, hair flowing out on the bottom. Her eyes looked wider from this angle. Her thick black eyelashes along with her blacker eyebrows (below her eyes, from this perspective) created two sets of uneven equal signs on her face.

"Ooooh my God. Zippeeeeeeeee." Raquel rolled from side to side and then resumed the X.

"Jason?"

"Jason has been erased by Paul."

"Paul? Does he work at the firm? Or—"

"No, he's a reporter for the *Chronicle*. I've seen him on the BART train about five times. Thick brown hair, this accent—"

"You talked to him before? What kind of accent?"

"No, I'd never talked to him until now! This morning. But we'd seen each other many, many times. And then we started talking today—it's an Irish accent—and . . . OH MY GOD, he's so sexy. We went to lunch—"

"Raquel! It's a no-eating day!"

"I KNOW, but, Zippy! There are times when you have to say *screw it*. There are times when love or passion needs to supersede whatever rules have been put into place. In fact, that can be chapter ten—"

"Are we already on chapter ten?"

"Yeah. Right? Nine was 'Drinking Your Meals on a No-Eating Day.'"

"Okay, so ten is 'When Lust Supersedes—'"

"Exactly! We went to Fog City and I had a grilled cheese. He had the fried chicken, which is good because fried chicken breath is sort of sweet and crunchy, like it made me want to bite his lips."

"So you made out already?"

"YES! Zippy! He walked me back to the office, and before we got to the glass doors, he stopped on the sidewalk, pulled me into him, and kissed me so deeply, I almost melted right there. I even saw it in my brain—"

"Saw what?"

"Me, melting! Like in *The Wizard of Oz* when that witch melts and only her shoes are left."

"No, the house lands on the witch and the shoes are left. Her sister is hit by a bucket of water and then *she* melts. Wait. Maybe *she's* wearing the shoes by then—"

"Well, whatever. I was seeing myself melting. We're going out Friday night and I can feel it, Zippy. I mean, I feel it deeply: he's as into me as I am into him."

"Wow." I sat on the floor next to Raquel. She scooted so that her head was on my crossed legs. Theater people were like that: always flopping over each other like puppies and constantly playing with each other's hair. Raquel wasn't usually this touchy.

"Zippy, I have something very important to tell you."

"Are you drunk? You seem slightly drunk."

"No, well— No. I mean, yes. But no. I had a little Tanqueray and tonic, because, um, because we love T and T with lime, don't we?"

"We do love T and T."

"But, Zippy, grasshopper, what I have to say I'm not saying because I'm buzzed. It's super important."

"Okay. Say it."

"There is no way I can have sex with Paul before you at least make out with a grown human boy-man who doesn't drill into your mouth with his sea slug tongue and drool down your neck."

"He also has to not have fuzzy buttons." I had once overheard Toby tell Howard about a venereal disease he got years ago that gave him caterpillar-textured dots on his testicles.

"I'm not sure I believe Toby's fuzzy buttons story, because I sure as hell have never seen fuzzy pink dots on any man's *anything*."

"I think he said they were purply gray—"

"DO NOT FEAR FUZZY BUTTONS!" Raquel threw all her limbs in the air and then let them flop back to the floor.

"Fine. There's still AIDS, pregnancy—"

"Stop. Condoms. Okay? But listen, if you were in college, this would be freshman year. And most people who haven't lost it already lose their virginity freshman year. Your mother had you when she was your age. She wasn't a virgin."

"I love my mother, but I don't want her life in any way. I mean, I really, really, really don't want to work at the Hardware Depot and end up with my generation's version of Howard."

"You work at I. Magnin."

"For now. I'm not sure how long they'll keep me at I. Magnin."

Raquel sat up, turned around, looked at me very seriously, and said, "First of all, *how long they'll keep you*? You're outselling Miss Yolanda—of course they'll keep you! You'll earn more and more the longer you're there and the more regulars you get . . . I'm telling you all the things *you* have told me! Secondly, we need to go to Blue Light. You need to be out in the world like the I. Magnin girl you are and make out with someone who is nothing like Howard so you can see you're *not your mom.* You get to choose how you live your life."

"Sometimes it seems like *you* choose how I live my life!" I was only half-joking.

"Fine. I'm simply making suggestions!"

"Fine," I said. "But two things: One, Mimi also said I should be *the chooser.* And you two are my very best advisers. Two, what if no one wants to make out with me?"

"Stop. Anyone will make out with you. Like Mimi said, you have to be the chooser. All you do is choose the guy, but let him think that he's choosing you. Then, if you decide you want to make out with him, you give the signal."

"But I don't know the signal! This is the problem, Raquel! I don't know how any of these things work! I don't know the signal! I don't know how to kiss! I don't know how to choose a guy and be the chooser, or how to decide that you want to be the choosee and let them think they're being the chooser when, in fact, you're choosing them to choose you—"

"Enough!" Raquel stood. "Undo the top two buttons of your blouse and meet me in your room for the Jordache jeans." Raquel's Jordache jeans had become too big for her since she'd lost weight. They now fit me, but I could only wear them when Raquel was home to help me get them on.

"I guess you're being the chooser of what I wear too." I slipped off my skirt as we walked to the bedroom. The jeans were sitting on top of my dresser. Raquel handed them to me and I stepped in and pulled them up; the fly remained open in a wide letter V.

"Ready?" Raquel asked.

"Go for it." I lay back on the bed, sucked in my stomach, and held the button as close to the buttonhole as possible. Raquel straddled my legs, grabbed the pull tab, and worked the zipper up. It was like trying to close an overstuffed suitcase.

"Help me stand," I said, once the button was secure. I couldn't bend to sit up and would have to work on loosening the jeans in the car.

**We had a** roomy, clean parking spot four blocks from our apartment, but Raquel seemed to feel there was urgency enough to give it up. It didn't take long to get to Blue Light and then, as He often did, Air Freshener Jesus pulled through for us.

"Thank you, Jesus." Raquel killed the engine and yanked up the parking brake. She kissed her first two fingers and tapped Jesus, setting the air freshener swinging back and forth.

"Amen," I said, and I kissed my fingers and tapped Him too.

Blue Light was surprisingly crowded for midweek. The band in the back sounded twangy and cool, like the Allman Brothers if they'd had a sister singing along. The music was so loud, Raquel had to shout-order two Tanqueray and tonics for us. As the bartender was making our drinks, Raquel stood on a rung of the barstool and turned her head, scanning the crowd. I stood on the rung of my barstool so our heads were even, and scanned with her.

"HOW WILL THIS WORK?" I shouted. We had planned to discuss methodology in the car, but a series of great songs came on the radio (starting with Chaka Khan, "I Feel for You," then Wham!, Whitney Houston, and Dire Straits in the middle, and ending with Huey Lewis and the News, "The Power of Love"), so we sang as if we were on a stage holding mics the whole ride over.

"WHEN WE FIND THE RIGHT GUY," Raquel shouted back, "YOU GET CLOSE, DANCE A LITTLE. BUT DO NOT DANCE TOO ENTHUSIASTICALLY OR YOU'LL LOOK

LIKE A CRAZY LADY! ONLY A LITTLE *I'M INTO MUSIC* KIND OF MOVEMENT. THEN YOU LOOK AT HIM, MAKE EYE CONTACT, AND THEN LOOK AWAY."

"LOOK AWAY?! WHY LOOK AWAY IF I WANT TO MAKE OUT WITH HIM?"

"IT'S A GAME. AN ANIMAL GAME. LOOK, LOOK AWAY. COUNT TO THREE, LOOK BACK, CATCH HIS EYE, SMILE, LOOK AWAY, COUNT TO FIVE, LOOK BACK, SMILE, HOLD HIS LOOK FOR THREE FULL SECONDS! THEN LOOK AWAY—"

The bartender set our drinks before us. Raquel sat and I sort of bent onto my stool. I chugged my drink and then clunked my empty glass on the bar.

"HOW CAN I POSSIBLY REMEMBER ALL THIS? IT'S LIKE A DANCE ROUTINE I'D NEED A THREE-HOUR-LONG CLASS TO MEMORIZE!"

Raquel sipped her drink and thought about it. Then she smiled and leaned into my ear. "WHEN WE FIND THE GUY, I'LL DO IT IN THE AIR. YOU THEN FOLLOW ME. LIKE IN ELEMENTARY SCHOOL WHEN THE TEACHER STOOD IN FRONT OF THE CLASS AND DID THE STEPS AND MOTIONS YOU WERE SUPPOSED TO DO IN THE CHRISTMAS PAGEANT."

I remembered that. I could do that. "YOU DON'T THINK I COULD GET FUZZY BUTTONS FROM A KISS, DO YOU?"

Raquel shook her head and then stood on the rung again and searched for my first real kiss. Her gaze was far off into the crowd when a guy with Frankenstein shoulders scooted in beside me to order a drink. I looked at him until he locked his eyes with mine. I looked away and counted to three. When I looked back, he was staring at me. I looked away and counted to five. I looked back.

"DO WE KNOW EACH OTHER?" he shouted.

I tried to imagine kissing him. His face was a beautiful display of rectangles: his eyes were two sideways rectangles, his nose was a vertical rectangle, his mouth was another sideways one. His lips, however, were ragged and chapped. Was kissing chapped lips as dangerous as having sex without a condom? Could there be blood in the cracks of his lips that would enter my bloodstream and infect me with something like fuzzy buttons, if not AIDS?

"NO, WE'VE NEVER MET!" I said, and then for the first time I looked at Raquel, who was frozen in place watching the two of us like a retriever staring at a duck.

"MAYBE WE SHOULD KNOW EACH OTHER," he said into my ear.

I turned to him again and felt our joined focus lock into place like two Lego pieces snapping together. "YOUR LIPS ARE SO CHAPPED," I said.

"SKIING," he said. "YOUR LIPS ARE GORGEOUS."

I reached up to my lips as if to feel what he was talking about. He put his hand on mine and then placed my hand against his chest before leaning in and kissing me. A slow lip to lip. And then another but with tongue. It tasted like silver and I liked that.

No drilling.

No drool.

No pneumatic pump against my mouth.

It was a weirdly novel and explosive sensation. Like trying a new food and instantly wondering why you'd never eaten it before.

I felt Raquel's eyes on us, but I didn't look at her. My eyes were shutting and opening and shutting and opening. Each time they were open, they met his.

The bartender put a drink down right in front of him. He pulled out of the kiss, reached into his pocket, and laid a bill on the counter.

"KEEP THE CHANGE," he shouted. Then he picked up the drink and offered me a sip. I took a too-large gulp and felt my sinuses bloom open like a flower. He took a sip and then leaned in again and the kissing resumed. This time I glanced at Raquel, whose mouth was actually open. Like a cartoon's.

When we finally pulled out of the kiss, I said, "THIS IS RAQUEL."

He looked at Raquel, nodded, and then turned to me and said, "BUT WHO ARE YOU?!"

"SHE'S ZIPPY!" Raquel said.

"ZIPPY!" I said.

"I LOVE YOUR NAME," he said.

"WHO ARE YOU?" Raquel asked him.

"JUST JOHN. BORING NAME."

"NICE TO MEET YOU, JUST JOHN," I said, and he leaned in and kissed me once more.

I once saw a meteor shower and it made my brain feel like an electrocuted animal was trapped in my skull. I could barely contain the thrill. Making out with Just John was like that. It was as strange and stunning as watching an exploding star that took two million years to be seen from Earth.

Here are the things I liked that I previously didn't know *were* things to like: (1.) The way his body felt dense and warm against me; (2.) The gentleness of his silver-tasting tongue; (3.) The waves of sensation that ran through my body when he squeezed my lower back, touched my neck, wove his fingers in my hair; (4.) The way his skin smelled like freshly mown dewy-green grass.

Here's what I didn't like: (1.) When Raquel interrupted us and said we had to go because she had to be at work early tomorrow; (2.) When Just John told me he was visiting from Michigan and would be returning there, to Ann Arbor, tomorrow.

"Wait," I said, "you mean you don't live here?" Raquel was gently tugging my arm, trying to pull me out the door. It was late and she had patiently waited through a lot of kissing.

"Well, I don't live here now." Just John looked between me and Raquel, as if he were begging her to stay another minute. "But I'll be back in a couple months. So, will you see me then? Like, we could go to dinner or something."

"Dinner or something sounds good."

"NUMBERS!" Raquel shouted. We had one more kiss while Raquel procured two pens and two cocktail napkins from a bartender. She waved them in front of us and we broke apart so quickly that it felt like arctic air was rushing past my lips.

We each wrote down our information and then exchanged napkins. When I looked down at Just John's spiky handwriting, I knew I'd remember his address the rest of my life. *1432 White Street.*

Raquel took my hand and pulled me toward the door. I walked backward, she walked forward, and Just John stood in the middle of the noise watching, smiling, and waving the napkin with my address on it like a small white flag.

"Not yet!" I said to Raquel when we were out on the sidewalk. I knew it was impossible for Just John, who was inside Blue Light, to hear us, but I wanted to be in the car, with the doors locked, before we spoke of him.

Once we'd pulled away from the curb, I turned to Raquel and let out a moaning scream. "RAQUEL! THAT WAS AMAZING!"

Raquel slammed her fist into the middle of the steering wheel where the horn was, though it didn't beep. She hooted and hollered, "YOU'RE NO LONGER A KISS-VIRGIN!"

We both screamed and cheered. And then Raquel laid her palm into the horn and let it wail.

"Wow. I had no idea."

"Right? And sex, if it's with the right person, is even better than that."

"I dunno, that was clean. No one was naked, nothing spilled out of another body. It all smelled good."

"Trust me about sex."

"Why does kissing change everything? Why does physical contact make the brain want the person more? So much more!"

"The wanting and waiting is half the fun," Raquel said. "If you automatically had everything you wanted, there would be no joy in the having."

When we got home, Raquel threw her purse on the counter and shouted, "Day-Timers!" She gathered them while I sat on the couch and rearranged the colored pens we had left out.

Once she was tucked into the couch beside me, Raquel said, "I'm going to write the dream scenario with Paul. Not what happens, because if I write it the way I did with Jason, it can't happen, right?"

"You mean, like, if you write it, you take away the chance of it happening because when does anything in life ever turn out as you imagine it?"

"Exactly. To imagine it is to take away that iteration of the event. It's better to describe only how I will feel. My feelings could be applied to an infinite number of scenarios."

"Okay, I get it."

"And you do the same with Just John, even though it might be two or three months before you see him. Write down the feelings you will have before, during, and after you lose your virginity."

"So we're assuming I'm going to lose it to Just John?"

"For now. It doesn't matter so much that it's him. It's more that you're taking the step toward having sex by imagining the feelings around it."

"What I'm feeling at the time of penetration?! I mean, I have no idea what that feels like? Is it like a tampon? Or like what it feels like when you stick a Q-tip in your ear?"

Raquel thought about it a second and then said, "More the filled-up surprise of the Q-tip, but I'm not talking about physical sensations as much as I'm talking about what you feel in your heart and soul."

"My heart and soul," I said.

"And you're not allowed to write that you feel terrified of *fuzzy buttons.*" Raquel looked down at her Day-Timer and began writing.

I tapped my pen against the open page. "Wait."

"Yeah?" Raquel looked up, her pen still poised on the page.

"I know I'm supposed to write only my feelings, but I can't imagine my feelings unless I'm imagining an act. So, if I move ahead according to the bases, I have to give him a hand job and then we have oral sex. A hand job seems fairly simple, but how do you even do oral sex? I mean, is it like a hand job but with your mouth? And what about when he's doing it to you? Do you just lie there?"

Raquel tapped her pen on the Day-Timer and then shut her eyes for a long second as if she really needed to work this through. She opened her eyes again and said, "To receive oral sex, you close your eyes and stop thinking. If you think, you'll be doomed. If you *have* to think, think about something sexy: a scene you saw in a movie or something you've fantasized about forever. Anything."

"You're telling me to fantasize about something outside of reality *in the midst of my reality being sex with some guy*? I mean, why even have oral sex if that's what you have to do?"

"Yeah, I know it's weird. I'm not saying you always have to do that. And eventually you won't. All I'm saying is that if self-consciousness enters and blocks everything, the only way to get rid of it is to enter some scene in your head and then be *there,* in that imagined place. Your body will respond to the real place on its own."

"You are not doing a good job selling me on receiving oral sex."

"Yeah, you know, you can ignore that one for now. Guys don't always do it right away anyway."

"Fine. What about when I do him? Let's say it's Just John."

"Hold Just John's dick in your right hand, down low. Then put your mouth over it. Hide your teeth. This is essential. *Cover your teeth with your lips.*" Raquel covered her teeth with her lips; she looked ninety years old. I laughed and then she broke apart laughing. I made the face and she laughed harder. "Wait, go on the ground between my legs and look up at me. I want to see what that face looks like from the angle a guy sees it."

I climbed off the couch, got on my knees in front of Raquel, and made the toothless-old-lady-sucking face. Raquel laughed so hard, she snorted.

"Is it bad?" I asked.

"I think we need to only do it in the dark," she said.

"But wait, if your mouth is actually over his penis, it won't look the same." I got up, went to the kitchen, and then returned with a banana. I got down on the floor in front of Raquel again. I made the hideous face and put my mouth over the banana. Raquel stared down at me intently.

"Move your head up and down a little."

I did. She watched, still concentrating. And then I pushed the banana too far back in my throat and started coughing. Raquel fell back on the couch laughing.

"Okay, okay," she said, when my coughing and her laughing had subsided. "It doesn't look as freaky with something in your mouth, so make sure he doesn't see you prep your mouth. Like, hide behind your hair or something."

"Do guys look down and watch?"

"Most do. They're so happy it's happening, they have to watch it as well as feel it in order to double up the sensation."

"Men are strange," I said.

"Yeah," Raquel said. "They're essentially bundles of muscle and bone and brains that are flooded with hormones that make them want to mate with some people and dominate others either by being a lawyer or simply being the smartest guy in the room."

"Do they honestly think about that?"

"About what?"

"About being the smartest guy in the room."

"Totally. Every single one of them does."

"I've never had that thought," I said. "Also, I can't imagine being the smartest person in any room. My favorite part of the newspaper is the Pink Section on Sunday."

"That doesn't mean you're not smart," Raquel said. "It means you're not competing over smarts. Now, we have to stop all this chatter and get back to work." She picked up a new pen and hunched over her Day-Timer. I watched her for a couple minutes and then leaned over mine. At the top of the page I wrote, *How I Hope I'll Feel During and After I Have Sex for the First Time*. Underneath that I wrote, *Connected, loved, safe, cozy, adored, adoring* . . . I lifted my pen and thought about it some more and then I added: *sexy, passionate, excited. Not scared. Not grossed out. Not embarrassed. Not ashamed.* I paused again and then I wrote, *And no matter what my body looks like, or how much I happen to weigh, I will NOT feel fat or ugly.*

**I wasn't scheduled** to work the next day. I woke at seven and was showered and dressed by eight. It was an eating day, so I planned to grocery shop at the corner market and actually cook a meal for

Raquel and me (pasta with cream sauce). But first I wanted to clean the apartment. Prince was on the record player and I was vacuuming when the phone rang. I answered before it went to the machine.

It was my mother.

"What's that music?" she asked.

"Prince," I said.

"Prince who? Prince of what?"

"Just Prince. A musician."

"Huh. Funny name. Anyway, they haven't filled Howard's position and they're doing training for new hires today. So, if you wanna come down and try it out . . ."

Of course I didn't *want* to try it out. What I wanted was to have a bigger, better life than that which my mother had. "Oh, I dunno, Mom. I love my job so much."

"I thought you needed more money."

"I do. To help you and Howard—"

"You don't have to help us, sweetheart. We'll figure something out."

My stomach plummeted to my feet. I leaned over the kitchen counter and laid my head down, the phone against my outside ear. At this rate, as the top seller on the floor, I was making about $24,000 a year. There wasn't an extra dime to help anybody. And what would I do if Raquel wanted to move in with a boyfriend? I could only afford my rent now because I paid less than Raquel, on account of my room being smaller. Most people wouldn't offer that discount—you split the rent no matter which room you had! I couldn't see far enough beyond the paychecks I was getting then to understand how this dream job could be sustainable.

"Maybe I should go down there and see what it's like—" Was there a chance that I'd actually enjoy working there?

"The training starts at ten. If you grab the number eleven bus, you could be here in time."

I stood up straight and looked at the wall clock in the shape of a cat with a switching tail and ticktocking eyes. Raquel's old roommate had left it behind. I could feel myself breathing. "Fine. See you in a few."

"You're going to love everyone!" my mom said. "And there's nothing more exciting than pushing a power saw through something as strong and solid as wood."

"Nothing more dangerous," I said.

"It's not dangerous!"

"Mom, your husband has no fingers because of a power saw."

"My husband has no fingers because he was a dumbass *with* a power saw. Saws don't chop up people; people with saws chop up people."

"That's beautiful, Mom." I wanted to weep. "See you at ten."

**Because of my** mother's and Howard's senior positions, I skipped the whole interview process and was welcomed in as a new hire. Five of us showed up for the training: me, a very pale and skinny woman named Sparkalee, a young guy named LeDaryl, a thirty-year-old(ish) man named Troy, and a grandmother-looking woman named Flor. The manager, Roberto, was so enthusiastic, it was contagious. There was clapping, there was jumping up and down (Sparkalee when we were told we'd each get a turn at the paint shaker), and there was laughter (toilet plunger jokes). After a three-hour overview and tour of the entire store, we broke for a thirty-minute lunch (my mother split her leftover pizza with me) and then we were sent off to the area where we'd each work.

I was put in the lumber department with Jeff, who had been there for sixteen years. Jeff looked me up and down like I was livestock to be purchased and then he said, "You don't look like Howard at all."

"We're not related," I said.

"I thought he was your dad."

"Nope."

"But Marie is your mother, right?"

"Yeah. She and Howard are married, but he's not my dad."

"So, Howard raised you."

"No. He didn't do any of the parenting stuff. It was like he was my roommate. He moved in when I was a teenager. I'm not even sure when exactly they got married—neither one told me about it."

"Huh." Jeff stared at me some more. I looked back without looking away. If the look-away-look-back was a flirt (as Raquel had taught me), the look-without-looking-away must be the opposite of that.

"So," Jeff finally said. "You want to be a woodcutter."

"Um, no. But I will consider being a woodcutter."

"You don't want to?"

"Well, I have other aspirations. I mean, I'll do it. For the paycheck. But it's not what I truly want."

He seemed angry. His face went a shade darker and he said, "Do you know how many people in San Francisco would kill for this job? I mean actually kill! Between the health insurance, the double-pay holidays, and the multiple breaks during the day, this is a primo job."

I nodded. "I'm not sure how great the health insurance is since it's barely covering all the stuff with Howard's hand."

"Assuming you don't cut off your own hand, and that you only go in for checkups and such, it's pretty darn great. In fact, Phil over in paint even suggested that Howard deliberately cut off his fingers so he'd get out of working and his daughter would get a good job from the deal." His stare became more intense as if he could read on my face whether or not that were true.

"I'm not his daughter. And it was my mother who suggested that I replace Howard. I don't think it even occurred to him." I was starting to feel confused. Did he truly think someone might cut off their own fingers to give a nineteen-year-old girl a job at the Hardware Depot?

Jeff nodded and bit his lip. "And you think you'll be as good at this as your dad?"

"Again, Howard's not my dad, and no, I . . . I honestly don't think I'll be as good." Speaking with Jeff was a conversational Tilt-A-Whirl and I wanted off.

"But you want to try. You're aiming for that?"

"If I'm going to do it, I want to be the best I can be."

"Last thing." Jeff held up his pointer finger. "You're not afraid of a power saw that could cut through bone as if it were butter?"

"I am terrified of holding a saw that could cut through bone as if it were butter," I said.

Eventually Jeff took me to the supply room, where I was fitted for goggles and an apron. The next three hours were spent learning about the different types of hardwood, how to measure it ("measure twice, cut once!"), and how to cut two-by-fours (using a less scary saw than what I saw the seasoned employees using). The lessons on plywood, particleboard, the miter saw, the band saw, and the scroll saw would come the next training day.

"Okay," Jeff said when we were done for the day. "Same time tomorrow."

"I can't come tomorrow. I haven't given notice at my current job yet." Also, I hadn't actually decided that I'd leave the greatest job I could imagine for more money cutting lumber.

Jeff and I sat in silence for a long time. Finally, Jeff said, "Because you're Marie and Howard's kid—"

"Not Howard's," I whispered.

"We'll give you a break."

"I can train again Tuesday next week."

Silence and lip-chewing. Then: "You're on. See you Tuesday."

I didn't cry until I was riding the number 11 bus home.

# Chapter 9

**First thing Wednesday** morning, Miss Dani called a meeting on the floor in Miss Liaskis's area. I was opening her register.

"So everyone's gossiping about who got arrested," Miss Dani said.

"We already know exactly who it was," Miss Yolanda said, and she moved her candy ball to the other cheek.

"Who?" I asked. Miss Karen raised her eyebrows at me as if I shouldn't be prying.

"Miss Tammy. That blond dingbat from San Diego. She never should have been hired. No one from Southern California is worth a damn." Miss Yolanda popped another candy ball into her mouth and I wondered about the one I'd seen only seconds ago. Did she swallow it? Had that been her tongue and she'd only been prepping for the candy ball?

"*Was* it Miss Tammy?" I asked.

"Yes, it was. I'm not supposed to tell anyone, so don't say I told you!" Miss Dani did a little punch in the air.

"She looks like a beauty pageant winner," I said. Miss Tammy, like Sorority Girl, was someone I tried not to envy. She was skinny in the way that every girl I knew wanted to be. Her yellow-white hair was so thick, she probably had to wear special rubber bands to put it in the fist-width ponytail she wore most days. Her clothes were magnificent. Always exactly what was in season. And everything looked brand-new.

"Oh, she was!" Miss Lena said. "Cecil told me she'd been Miss San Diego."

I closed the till on Miss Liaskis's register, put the empty money bag in the drawer, and came around to the other side of the counter, where everyone circled Miss Dani.

"She was a liar and a thief," Miss Yolanda said. "I have no patience for degenerates. I work too damn hard to buy the clothes I'm wearing."

"How did she do it and how did they catch her?" I asked. Everyone moved in a step, even Miss Braughn L, who never seemed interested in anything.

"They put a goddamned camera in the fitting room where she always went to try on clothes," Miss Yolanda said.

"Are you serious?! Are there actually cameras in the fitting rooms?!" I thought about the woman who had asked me if there were cameras. (I had thought the question was paranoid, loony!) And, of course, I thought about all that praying with Miss Lena! Also, a couple days ago when I was trying on a dress for fun, I pulled the three-way mirrors in and looked at the full view of my butt from behind. In my underwear. It didn't look like anything special. A big beach ball of a butt jutting out with two soft, fleshy legs descending beneath it. I started to pull down my underwear to see what my bare bottom looked like but was saved by the voice of a customer in the hall.

"Of course there are cameras!" Miss Yolanda said.

"No, no, no!" Miss Dani waved her arms. "There are no cameras! And no men or cops can spy on women in fitting rooms. But there are women who can legally look. And it's not through cameras."

"How do they look?" Miss Lena asked.

"No one is supposed to know, but"—Miss Dani was clearly someone who should never have the responsibility of holding a secret—"there's a crawl space above the fitting rooms, and the security women, if they have a reason to believe someone is stealing, can go in and look down into a fitting room."

"Oh my!" Miss Lena put her hand to her mouth. Maybe she was worried about the praying too. Though no one would ever be suspicious enough of her to climb into a crawl space and look down.

"She was removing sensors before she tried things on," Miss Dani said. "And then she was going into the fitting rooms and putting on clothes under her clothes. Every day!"

"EVERY DAY!" Miss Liaskis had a hand on each cheek. I had a feeling she'd never known anyone, anywhere, who had broken a law.

"They got a search warrant, went to her apartment, and found tens of thousands of dollars of missing stock. It's a felony. She could do jail time." Miss Dani nodded over and over again.

This put all my jealousies in perspective. If I had met Miss Tammy the day before she went to jail, and was unaware that she was going to go to jail, I'd have been jealous of her. I guess you never know the life of most people outside the bounds of the moment when you intersect with them.

"I've never met anyone who went to jail!" Miss Liaskis said.

"You've probably sold dresses to white-collar criminals who are minutes out of jail," Miss Yolanda said.

"My mom's husband, Howard, had a childhood friend who went to prison and when he got out, he needed a place to stay, so he stayed with us for a couple weeks," I volunteered. Two weeks ago I'd have been too embarrassed to tell this story. But now that I might be at the Depot soon, what difference did it make if I told a story about Howard's jailbird pal?

"I hope he wasn't a perv!" Miss Dani said, and this time she did a little kick.

"No, he slept on the couch. He was a pretty nice guy; he cooked dinner for us every night. And he liked to name the meals he made after his sisters and aunts. So pasta was Pasta Marsha. And hot dogs were Wieners Jill."

"What was salad?" Miss Liaskis asked.

"We never had salad. The sides were always Ore-Ida frozen french fries and Wonder Bread with Parkay. The mains were usually Wieners Jill and Pasta Marsha. Maybe a Hamburger Helen once a week."

"Did you ever have mac 'n' cheese?" Miss Lena asked. Miss Lena loved mac 'n' cheese.

Miss Karen rolled her eyes and elbowed Miss Lee. I ignored them and answered, "Macky-Missy!"

"Americans eat like pigs," Miss Yolanda said, and she moved the candy ball to the other cheek. "We done here?"

"Yup! Now go sell the heck outta everything!" Miss Dani did a final fist swoop and then turned and scuttled away.

Around four, Miss Lena opened the supply drawer and nodded down to the paper dolls. I looked across the sales floor, saw that no one was coming our way, and nodded back.

Miss Lena set up the Jesus doll on the keys of the register, looking over us, and then she dealt out dolls. To herself: Cecil, Miss Liaskis, and me. To me: Miss Braughn R, Miss Lena, and Miss Dani. The other dolls were lined up across the counter so that either one of us could pick one up and play it if we felt it helped the story.

I tried to make the game all about Miss Tammy getting arrested, but Miss Lena kept turning the game toward Cecil, who wanted to talk about Cole Porter, Louis Armstrong, Ella Fitzgerald, and Louis Prima. I let the game go Miss Lena's way. Louis Prima was completely unfamiliar to me until Miss Lena picked up the Cecil doll and had him dance and sing the "I Wan'na Be Like You" song from *The Jungle Book*. I knew and loved every song from that movie (my mother took me to see it three times when it was playing at the Coronet), so I sang along, bouncing the Miss Lena doll to the beat. Right when Miss Lena held the Cecil doll so he was dancing cheek to cheek with the Miss Lena doll, I looked up and saw a good-looking guy with a lion's mop of hair on his head walking straight toward me. I opened the drawer and pushed in all the dolls. Miss Lena threw Cecil in but continued to hold the note she was singing.

The man stood at the counter and said, "You must be Zippy?" He had an Irish accent.

"Yeah," I said. Miss Lena took a step closer to me so our shoulders touched.

"And who are you, dear?" Miss Lena asked.

"Ah, I'm Paul. Raquel's man." He placed a cassette tape on the counter. "I'm leaving the country for a couple weeks and I have an appointment a block away from here, so . . ." He slid the cassette closer to me, like it was a Mafia payment.

"Is this for me?" I picked it up.

"Nay! It's for Raquel, but I don't have time to stop by her office and she said you'd be here. It's time we met anyway! I hear that if I'm with Raquel, you're part of the package."

What I felt then could only be described as love. For Raquel. "I *am* part of the package! This is Miss Lena."

"Pleasure," Paul said, and he smiled in the nicest way that made me believe he was a boyfriend who was nice to mothers and aunts and best friends and sisters and brothers and waiters and hotel staff and stewardesses and . . . everyone. He was a good guy.

"Oh, the pleasure's ours, dear!" Miss Lena seemed excited to have a great-looking guy standing in Petite Dresses.

"Well, if I weren't in such a rush to leave the country, I'd do some shopping. But if you see anything that you think Raquel would love, call me and leave a message. I need to give her more than a silly mixtape."

"I'll keep my eyes out," I said, and I picked up the tape.

"Thanks a million." Paul winked and it felt directed at both Miss Lena and me, and then he walked away.

Neither of us spoke until he was in the elevator. Then I looked down at the tape and saw he'd listed the songs in tiny, perfectly legible, boxy handwriting. I read the tape:

"I'm on Fire,""Time After Time,""Here Comes the Rain Again," "Crazy for You," "I Want to Know What Love Is," "The Power of Love," "Heaven," "Little Red Corvette," "You Give Good Love," "I Feel for You," "What About Love," "Slave to Love," "Every Breath You Take," "Lawyers in Love."

Miss Lena looked at me, her eyes as bright as flashlights. "I don't know those songs, but—"

"They're all love songs," I said, and Miss Lena gasped and laid one hand over the other on her heart.

**Once the store** closed, when Miss Lena was closing out our register and I was closing out Miss Liaskis's, Miss Dani emerged.

"Zippy." She waved her hand as if to motion me to her. "Can we talk in my office?"

I nodded and swallowed down what felt like a walnut in my throat.

As we walked to her office, Miss Dani chattered away about Miss Tammy and the clothes she'd stolen. Once inside, she shut the door behind me. I sat on the schoolroom chair beside her desk.

"Did I get more complaints?"

"A couple more."

"Did Miss Kitty say to fire me?"

"Well, not exactly. But yeah, maybe exactly." She sat at her chair and moved piles of clothes and papers around, searching for something. "She'll listen to me, though. You're the best salesgirl on the floor. And I never see you doing any of these horrible things. There's gotta be some kind of mistake here."

"Well . . ." I wanted to point out that she was rarely on the floor when the store was open. There was no way for her to know what was going on while she hid in this musty, dark closet.

"I'm refusing to fire you. But I need you to somehow make this stop." Miss Dani picked up one of the cards and waved it like a fan.

I felt like my body was melting into the chair. "I don't know how to make sales without doing the things they're complaining about. And I mean, there's nothing I can do about my name or the fact that I haven't memorized every Bill Blass quote—"

"Listen, Zip, you're smart as a whip with that mind like a steel trap. You can figure this out. Try to chill a little. Okay?"

"Okay. I'll try to chill." My eyes stung from tears; I sniffed.

"Ah, come on, it's going to be okay." Miss Dani leaned forward and rubbed my shoulder.

"Miss Dani"—I almost had to choke the words out—"I think I should go work at the Hardware Depot."

Miss Dani scowled. "Why would you work at the Hardware Depot?"

"Because they offered me a job, I guess." I could barely look her in the eye. Each additional complaint card seemed to confirm, in my mind, that I was not a real I. Magnin girl.

"Ah, Zip." Miss Dani continued to rub my shoulder. "You're doing a great job here. Something wacky is going on and I'll figure it out. I'm only telling you so you can dodge some bullets."

"I feel like Reagan, if he had to show up and work *with* John Hinckley Jr. in the White House."

"Ha," Miss Dani said. "Good one. I didn't realize you were interested in politics."

I shrugged. "I'm actually more of a Pink Section person when it comes to reading the paper."

"Me too." Miss Dani patted my hand twice and then glanced at the papers on her desk and I knew the meeting was over.

**I spent the** next few days trying to be as low-key with the customers as possible, playing paper dolls whenever Miss Lena felt like it, and (to keep hope alive) daydreaming about the magic kiss with Just John, which I had described to Miss Lena in the most chaste way possible (it *was* chaste! I simply left out the deliberation, the search, the look-look-away bits of the story).

Howard called on Monday. He said he'd heard about the great lunchroom at I. Magnin and wanted to know if the food was cheap and if I could bring home some dinner for him and my mother.

"As you know, your mother's a terrible cook," he said. "It's peanut butter every damn meal. How can I heal without some real food in my body?!"

**On Tuesday, I** went to the Hardware Depot for my second day of training.

"What's the most important rule?" Jeff asked me. I was in my apron and goggles. We were standing at the miter saw.

"Always wear your goggles?"

"No." Jeff stared at me. I stared back through the scratched plastic and rummaged around the Depot file in my brain.

"The customer is always right?" I didn't remember him saying that, but I'd heard it at I. Magnin, so why not?

"No. We never say that here. When it comes to cutting wood, the customer is *never* right." Stare. Stare. Stare.

"Do I have to keep guessing until I get it?"

"Yes."

I looked around the lumber area. It smelled woodsy and fresh—like a clean barn. I looked at the wood. I looked at the sawdust on the floor. I looked at the saws. I looked at the men in aprons, and other men in tool belts, coveralls, and jeans. I looked at the one woman I could see, a customer, who had a baby in a stroller and a piece of plywood, which she handed to the salesman. He laid it on the table and started measuring.

"Oh! Measure twice, cut once!"

"Exactly," Jeff said. "Your job depends on correct measuring. You can't start sawing through Depot wood and then toss it out because you cut it wrong. Every cut needs to be perfect."

"Right."

"Measure, measure, measure."

"Measure, measure, measure," I repeated.

"In fact, since you're new to all this, let's say measure three times, cut once."

"You got it. I'll measure three times." I looked at the baby in the stroller; she looked back and held my gaze. Her cheeks were so fat, they looked like someone had blown air in them. Her face went red and she frowned. I frowned too. *I don't want to be here either,* I said to her, in my mind.

I took my lunch break with my mom, who had brought food for us both in a brown Safeway bag. We sat in the employee lounge on a long stained couch with a low coffee table in front of us. Mom's friends Lucinda, Brian, and Brie were at the little table nearby.

"She looks exactly like you!" Brie said.

"Like a larger version of me," my always-skinny mother said.

"Why larger?" Brie asked.

"'Cause she's heavier."

"She don't look no heavier," Brian said. "I think you have that dysphoria."

"Dysmorphobia," I said.

"What are you talking about?" my mom asked.

"I read about it in a fashion magazine," I said. "It was about Japanese women who think they're fat when they're not."

"That's exactly what I read!" Brian said. "That's what your mom has! She thinks she's smaller than you!"

"Uh-huh," Lucinda said. She reminded me of Miss Karen, who could convey so much distaste in only a couple syllables and a nod.

"Since when do you read fashion magazines?" my mother asked Brian.

"My wife gets a bunch of mags. I read them when the ads are on TV."

"That article was in *Vogue,*" I said. "But I don't think my mother has that illness—she doesn't think she's bigger than she is. She thinks she's smaller than me. Which she is."

"Not by much," Brian said.

"Barely," Brie said.

My mother leaned forward and examined me. I was corn-on-the-cob-style nibbling across one side of the uncut sandwich I'd been told Howard had made. It was ridiculous but delicious: peanut butter with Marshmallow Fluff and semisweet chocolate chips. A lunch-dessert.

"I guess you have lost weight," my mother said, still assessing me.

"How did Howard make this with one hand?" I asked, hoping to change the subject.

"He's getting pretty good at being single-handed. And he can do wonders with that thumb."

"Poor Howard," Brie said.

"Nah, no one has to *poor Howard* Howard," my mother said. "The man's never been happier! He watches TV all day and then walks over to the Buena Vista around three or four to meet his friend Sean, who bartends there."

"I love those Irish coffees," Brie said.

"I like it on his breath," my mom said. "It's sexy!"

I needed another subject change. "Don't you think Howard could do phone sales or something?" I asked. Seeing as he could make these sandwiches, it did seem like he could take a job somewhere.

"What do you mean?" my mother asked.

"He could work in phone sales," I said.

Lucinda did another Miss Karen and made a sound deep in her chest that conveyed both agreement with what I was saying and disgust for Howard's slothfulness.

"You know Howard doesn't like the phone!" my mother said, and I thought, *And you know I don't like cutting lumber!*

Brie and Brian started discussing all the jobs Howard could do with one hand while my mother defended him and Lucinda grunted. I listened and watched. There were no windows in this lunchroom and no food to purchase—it was a sealed box where people ate what they'd brought. At I. Magnin, the lunchroom was blanched with light from the windows that looked out onto Union Square. The food the Depot employees had brought in that day ranged from elegant-looking sushi (the middle-aged woman alone at a table) to a box of McNuggets (the skinny boy with acne that ran from his temples to his clavicles). At I. Magnin, the lunch ladies (with their thin, baggie hair caps) served a variety of things, all of which were a few steps better than a school cafeteria and only a couple steps down from a real restaurant. The chatter at I. Magnin was about sex, relationships, known people, and customers. The chatter here, well, when I tuned in to the people beyond my mother and her friends, it wasn't far off from what the Magnin girls discussed: customers, bosses, and there were even a couple of women (who I believe worked in returns) talking about dating. When the returns ladies got up to leave, I got a good look at their faces. Mimi would have approved of their no-shine makeup and perfectly brushed-on mascara.

People were more or less the same, I decided. They were just hanging out in different surroundings. Some of them had more money (Sorority Girl); some were dressed better (Miss Meredith); some were a little crazy (Jeff); some were a little mean (Miss Yolanda); some had pure hearts (Miss Lena); and some loved me purely (my mother). Still, they were all simple humans.

Eventually I tuned out the chatter and thought about the kiss with Just John. That, and Howard's gorgeous sandwich, made the afternoon not so painful after all.

**I didn't cry** on the bus home. Instead I thought about how lucky I was that I had been employed at I. Magnin for as long, or short, as I had. I was the child of a woman who was married to a man who had sawed off his own fingers. I had a father I'd only met on the phone. I hadn't gone to college. I had never shopped at I. Magnin. And though I hoped to have many more days or years at I. Magnin, it wouldn't be tragic if I had to leave and work at the Hardware Depot instead. If my mother could do it, why couldn't I?

When I got home, Raquel called from the Oakland office of her firm, where she'd been at meetings all day. "Everyone says Zachary's Pizza is the best in the world. Should I pick one up?"

"Yeah, sounds great." I was already eating cheddar cheese off the brick.

When we hung up, the phone rang again instantly.

"Zippy!" my mom said. "You know, I think you did lose a ton on that diet!"

"It's strange," I said, "but I'm starting not to care how much I weigh."

"Are you depressed? Or morsdysphia?"

"*Dysmorphobic,*" I said. "But I don't think I have that, or depression. It's . . . well . . . Nothing's changed since I lost the weight. I'm still me. You're still you. Howard and my dad are still themselves. I dunno. It feels inconsequential."

"It will bring boys to you! That's consequential!"

"I think going out of the house and making eye contact for the correct number of seconds is what brings boys to me."

My mom made a clucking sound, and I could hear her pouring a glass of wine. Howard said something in the background, but I couldn't understand.

"Howard said boys like all girls no matter what the size," my mother said.

"Tell Howard that girls . . ." I started to say that girls liked boys with all their fingers, but I knew it was mean. I realized I was mad at Howard. And mad at my mother, too. I wanted to be the chooser, as Mimi (and Raquel!) had said. I wanted to choose what job I had and how I spent my money. But every day Howard wasn't working, every day those complaint cards came in, I felt like I had fewer options from which to choose.

"Have you heard from your dad again?"

I swallowed down the cheese ball. "We've talked on the phone a few times. He finds every ridiculous second of my nineteen years of life interesting."

"Huh." The greater my contact with my father, the less happy my mother seemed about his having found me. "I never talked to my father. And then he was gone."

"Yeah, neither of us has much experience with dads." Hers had died after falling down the basement stairs when my mother was nine. The more I dug into that story, the more it sounded like he died of alcoholism. The stairs were merely his final act.

"Mom, do you know when Howard might be back at work? I mean, when is he getting his claw?"

"It's a hook, not a claw. And he's on a waiting list to get it, which is sort of fine because the out-of-pocket for that thing is outrageous. I'm on the phone every day negotiating and setting up payment plans."

"Do you have any savings?"

"Oh, Zippy, I've never been able to save! Listen, do yourself a favor: Never lose a digit or a limb! I'm telling you, the only thing worse than losing that thing is trying to pay for whatever you need *after* you lose it!"

"Lesson learned, Mom," I said.

By the time Raquel got home with the pizza, I was no longer hungry. Still, I picked at a slice and we watched *Who's the Boss?* After the show was over, Raquel talked about what kind of nanny she would have and if she'd ever even consider having a boy nanny.

"I bet if he looked like Tony Danza you would," I said.

"Day-Timers!" she shouted, and she ran to fetch them.

I wasn't in the mood. As far as my career went . . . Well, it was feeling as solid as a mirage. And my love life amounted to one great kiss from a guy who lived in Ann Arbor, whom I'd probably never see again. Still, I took my Day-Timer from Raquel and flipped to the first blank page.

Raquel flopped down next to me on the couch and then leaned over the coffee table and sorted the markers into two piles the way Miss Lena sorted out the paper dolls.

"I don't want to imagine anything about my career because that's a bit hopeless right now. And I don't want to imagine sex with Just John," I said. "He'll never call; it's too depressing."

"No, we're advancing past sex. We're on to children: how many, gender, and names. And then describe the nanny you'll have." Raquel leaned her head over her book and started writing.

I put the pink pen to the page. I would have loved to have felt as certain about my future as Raquel did about hers. Certain that there'd be a marriage, children, enough money for a nanny. Was I going to be one of those single women with a dog that sleeps in her bed, who talks to the dog while in line at the bank, and who limits her travel to places where the dog is welcome? What if I had to spend the rest of my life helping to pay off Howard's medical bills?

"Do you think I could ever afford a nanny on the Hardware Depot salary?"

Raquel looked over at me. "No. Just because you went to training there today doesn't mean you're taking that job. As far as I know, you're still employed at I. Magnin. Stay the course!"

"I know." I sighed. "I've got to be *the chooser*."

"Duh. I mean, I like your mother! And I even like Howard with his giant white baseball-shaped fingerless hand. But hell if they get to decide how you live your life. And hell if Just John gets to decide if the two of you ever see each other again. And the I. Magnin complainers, well, they can all go to hell!"

I finally smiled. "Lotta *hell* in there."

"This is it, Zippy. This is *your* life."

"I might not have the kind of choices you imagine I do."

"Boo-hoo. Imagine a greater life. Imagine your kids!" She went back to writing.

I drew eyes all over my page. Lots of eyelashes and some good eyebrow shapes. A couple of them had tears running down.

Eventually Raquel looked up. "Ready?"

"You read me yours. I'm not done."

"Fine. Six kids—"

"Six?!"

"I'll have a nanny to help! Four girls and two boys. The girls are Jessica, Ashley, Sarah, and Elizabeth."

"Nice," I said, though I wouldn't have chosen any of those names.

"And the boys are Michael and Joshua."

"I might name a boy Josh too."

"I'll have two nannies and one will be a boy who's from Sweden who will speak Swedish to the kids all day. The other will be a girl from Spain or Mexico who speaks Spanish to them all day."

"Couldn't you speak Spanish to them?" None of Raquel's grandparents spoke English.

"I could, but my husband won't be able to speak Spanish, so it would be unfair to him."

"Your imaginary husband."

"My imaginary husband who will likely be Paul who speaks no Spanish."

"Excellent. Okay, I'll have two kids: Josh and Jemima. The nanny will speak French." I hadn't written it down and had only decided all that as I spoke. But it did feel nice to imagine this future. "And my husband will be Just John."

"And NO DEPOT!" Raquel shouted.

"Nope! Let's say *NO-PO*!" I shut my eyes and did a fast-motion silent prayer that everything I'd said was how it would be. It felt funny to pray without Miss Lena, but I figured I had to start sometime; I had to grow up.

# Chapter 10

**A week later,** Raquel and I were watching Roz Abrams on the news when my mother called because she wanted to give Raquel a fifteen-year-old first aid kit she had in the trunk of the car.

"Mom, throw it away. I mean, the Band-Aids have probably dissolved by now."

"Just ask her if she wants it!"

I looked over at Raquel, who was talking to Roz on the screen—she liked the blouse Roz was wearing. "Raquel has a first aid kit already. Leave it in the trunk."

"I sold the car tonight and I didn't say the kit was included—"

"You sold your car?" As far as I knew, she hadn't driven it for months, as she had a primo parking spot right in front of the building.

"Can you believe I got enough to pay for almost half of Howard's hook!"

"You sold the car to pay for his hook?" My heart hurt. I knew it was only a car, and she rarely used it, but when she did use it, she used it well, driving to Stinson Beach or over to Berkeley to walk around Telegraph Avenue. My mother was happy when she went on outings—her enthusiasm and joy when she crossed the Bay Bridge or the Golden Gate Bridge rivaled that of any out-of-towner.

"I already let the auto insurance lapse anyway," my mother said, "so it's better I don't have it."

"Yeah, that sounds right," I said.

**The next day.** I went to talk to Miss Dani before the store opened.

"Any more complaint cards?" I asked.

"Zippy, those cards are useless! I'm not buying it." Miss Dani moved aside several piles of papers until she found the inter-store envelope with the cards. She opened the envelope and emptied it into the trash can, which was already full. Most of the cards fell to the floor.

I stared at the cards and then looked up and took a long, deep breath. "So, I need to help out my mom because her husband—" I lifted my left hand and chopped at my fingers with my right hand as I was suddenly overwhelmed with the urge to sob.

Miss Dani did the same move back at me with her head tilted. "What is this?"

"He—" I kept chopping. She chopped right back at me. And then I burst out laughing and crying at the same time. "He chopped off his fingers!"

"Jesus! Why?"

"Power saw accident." My words stuttered out in a choking way.

"Holy moly! Poor guy! Do you need some time off?"

"No." I shored up, the crying stopped. "He did it a while ago. But the medical insurance they have barely covers anything, the bills are piling up, and . . . I don't know. It's my mother. How could I not help?"

"Oh, Zip, of course. But I can't give you more hours. You're already here five days a week—"

"No, I'm saying I have to go work at the Hardware Depot, where I'll make a lot more money." My head dropped; I felt like Eeyore the donkey.

"Yeah, you will make more money. My boyfriend—"

"The Blondie's Pizza guy?" I looked up at her. "That going okay?"

"It's . . . dreamy." Miss Dani smiled. "Anyway, he used to work at the Depot and he made a killing there. He quit because he needed more flexible hours. He's an actor, you know. He needs to go to auditions and such."

"Yeah, the people who work at the Depot are pretty committed."

"Can't you just pick up a day there and use that money to help out your mom and dad?" Miss Dani scooted her rolling stool closer to me.

"He's not my dad," I said.

"Oh yeah, the LA guy is your dad. How's that going?"

"Okay, I guess."

"Would *he* give your mother money to help with the bills?"

"Nah. They had a one-night stand and"—I put my hands up like I was curtsying—"voilà."

"Only thing I ever got from a one-night stand," Miss Dani said, "was a nasty little sore on my mouth that visits regularly, uninvited. I call it Aunt Trudy because that's what Aunt Trudy does."

*Poor Aunt Trudy,* I thought, *being categorized as oral herpes.* "So . . . anyway. I guess this is my two weeks' notice."

"Oh, no, Zip. I don't accept it." Miss Dani rolled back and crossed her tiny fit legs, as if that was that.

"I'm worried she'll spiral down to . . . Well, I could imagine her mortgaging the house, not being able to pay the mortgage, yadda yadda homeless."

"Yadda yadda homeless?"

"She's not a plan-ahead person," I said. "No savings, no cushion, no family, and now her husband has no salary and she's paying all the medical bills. It's . . . I don't know, it's sad."

Miss Dani took a deep, audible breath. "This really is a shame."

"Can you imagine what the Braughns would say about the superiority of socialized medicine in Canada if they knew what I was dealing with here?"

Miss Dani nodded. "Yeah, they'd have a field day with that."

"So . . ." I shrugged.

"I get it," Miss Dani said. "But listen, when things straighten out with your mother's finances, I'll hire you back, assuming there's a spot. I promise."

I wanted to cry again, but instead I forced a smile and held my breath for a few seconds until the urge to cry left me. "Thanks," I finally said. "But will there ever be another spot? People stay in this store for decades."

"They stay a long time. But things happen. Pablo in shoes left."

"He did?! Why?" I barely knew him, but I felt hurt that he hadn't warned me.

"His best friend." Miss Dani. "He's got some kind of rare cancer. They're traveling to Mexico, where there's supposed to be some guy who can save people with wild herbs that are grown down there."

I felt a murky nausea. Cancer was, according to Toby and Jo who had lots of gay friends, what people with AIDS said they had. Pablo's *best friend* was likely his boyfriend. Suddenly, my needing to go to the Hardware Depot didn't feel so tragic. What Pablo was going through, *that* was tragic. "That makes me so sad," I said. "I really, really hope the treatment works."

"Here—" Miss Dani picked up what looked like a balled-up sweater and pulled out a *Cathy* coffee mug. "Don't think about Pablo's best friend or the medical bills your mother's paying. For now, have a drink with me and we'll toast to better things for *everyone* who's sick and for your one-handed stepdad."

"We're going to *drink* now?"

Miss Dani shook her head and then unburied a thermos under another sweater and opened it. "It's Berber Coffee. God, I love that Berber Coffee guy." She poured some coffee into the mug and then into the little plastic cup that had sat atop the thermos.

"Who doesn't?" I picked up the mug and took a sip.

"You should hear my boyfriend do the voice of the Berber Coffee guy. Makes me love him even more than the Berber Coffee guy. Which is damn near impossible." Miss Dani took another slurping sip. When she pulled the cup from her mouth she sloshed a wet trail over the papers on her desk. The smell of that coffee, the sight of it splattered on the coming markdowns, made me feel nostalgia for I. Magnin even though it wasn't yet in the past.

**All day long** I tried to find the right time to tell Miss Lena I had given notice. Miss Dani had promised me she wouldn't announce my departure to the Fifth-Floor Dresses girls until the day I left. I couldn't predict how any of them, other than Miss Lena and Miss Liaskis, would react. It would be too painful to spend two weeks witnessing relief or joy or whatever it was that any of them might feel. Miss Yolanda, at the very least, would be thrilled to resume her position of top salesgirl on the floor.

We had a moment of quiet and I meant to tell Miss Lena then, but instead I told her about Pablo's *best friend*. Tears filled Miss Lena's eyes and she said, "I'll pray for him tonight, and you should pray too."

I nodded and then threw on a smile as a customer approached holding a red Donna Karan wrap dress. "Miss Lena can help you," I said, placing the dress in Miss Lena's hands as I turned to another woman who was running her fingers along a Bill Blass as if she were testing the temperature of water.

Later that day, when the bowling alley effect set in, and Miss Yolanda was on her break, Miss Lena pulled out the paper dolls. I held my breath as she dealt them out. She had Miss Zippy and I had Miss Lena. I picked them up and swapped, so we each had ourself. My lip was shaking a little; I could sense Miss Lena examining me.

"What's going on, dear?" Miss Lena asked through her doll, which she wiggle-walked across the counter so she was only a millimeter from the Miss Zippy doll. "Are you distressed about Pablo's friend?"

I wiggled the paper doll of me as I made her (me) speak. "Yes. But also, my mom and Howard can't pay their medical bills. They had to sell my mom's car. So I took a job at the Hardware Depot and—" My voice abruptly stopped, like it had hit a cement wall. Miss Lena took the paper doll from my hand and put both of them face down on the counter. She wrapped her arms around me and we hugged. Miss Lena rocked me a little, as if I were a baby. Even though I was so much larger than she, it felt good to be held like that.

"You are a very, very good daughter" was all Miss Lena said, but those words alone made me feel like I'd done the right thing. Like all would be okay.

**On my last** morning at I. Magnin, I was at Mimi's counter, my eyes shut, as she applied foundation. It was so soothing to have my face stroked that I had to repress a sigh.

"Well."

"Well what?" I squinted my eyes open. I could barely speak in my current state.

"Eye shadow," Mimi said. "Shut your eyes."

I did as asked. "Feels good."

"Are you ever going to tell me?"

"Tell you what?"

"Everyone in the store knows."

"Knows what?"

"That you gave notice because you have to take another job somewhere so you can help your mom with medical bills accrued by your power-saw-injured dad—"

"Not my dad."

"Right, the Howard."

"*The* Howard!" I said. I liked how that sounded. "Does *everyone* in the store even know who I am? The Designer Dresses ladies don't appear to see me when I run into them."

"Yes, everyone does know you. You're the cute girl with the cute name!"

"Ha. Weird. Are you making that up?"

"No, I'm serious. Mascara?"

"Yes." I opened my eyes as she drew the wand toward me.

"Blink. Blink. Blink. Blink. Blink. Other eye." Mimi moved the wand to the other eye. "Blink. Blink. Blink. Blink. Blink."

I stopped blinking and stared at her. "Did Miss Dani tell anyone about the complaint cards that named me?"

Mimi held the mascara aloft. "Miss Dani told some people who told some people—"

"God, I'm so ashamed."

"According to Miss Justine, who is friends with Miss Pippa, who is friends with Miss Dani—Miss Dani doesn't think they were legit." Mimi cleaned the mascara wand with alcohol and then put it back in the tube.

"She's just being nice," I said.

"Miss Karen also said she didn't believe it." Mimi opened a drawer beneath her counter and pulled out a compact of blush and a big bushy brush.

"Miss Karen from my department? I thought I was invisible to her. She doesn't speak. Or, she doesn't speak to me."

"She spoke in the lunchroom. She said the cards said that you're bossy and that she's watched you in action and you're not bossy at all. You're smart."

"She said that about *me*? Are you sure she was talking about me?"

"Yup." Mimi put blush on my cheeks and jawline. She took a step back, examined me, and then brushed on some more. "She said Miss Lee and Miss Yolanda are both way bossier than you."

"Wow. Well, I don't know about Miss Lee—she and Miss Karen are running a stealth operation. But I often hear Miss Yolanda yelling at customers."

"Anyway." Mimi put the blush brush away and pulled out some perfume samples.

"Anyway," I said. "Those complaints were . . . devastating. But none of it matters now. I have a job at the Hardware Depot."

"Seriously?" Mimi stepped back and examined me.

"I'll be in lumber."

Mimi laughed. "Sorry, I'm not laughing at you. It's just funny to think of you going from Fifth-Floor Dresses to lumber." Mimi spritzed perfume on my neck.

"Sad, not funny." I stopped talking as a lump grew in my throat. With some effort, I swallowed away my sadness. "Okay, gotta go open Miss Liaskis's register. Thanks for putting on my face."

"You got it." Mimi squeezed my hand. "Wait, don't go yet." She bent down beneath the counter and rummaged through the drawers. When she shot up, she had a shopping bag, which she handed to me. "Here are a bunch of samples to get you through the next couple months."

I looked into the bag. It was like Halloween loot, only for the face. "Wow. Thanks!"

"When's your last day? I'll gather bags of samples from other departments, too."

"Today's my last day."

"Today?" Mimi's eyes went glassy. "Oh no. I'll miss you."

"I'll miss you, too. But I'll come in and visit."

"You better."

"Maybe I'll even buy something one day," I said.

Mimi came around to the other side of the counter and gave me a hug. My head was buried somewhere atop her breasts.

I got another hug from Miss Lena when I showed up at our station. "Make a doll of a mean customer who wrote one of those complaint cards," she said when she pulled out of the hug. "We will scold her!"

"Wait! You know about those cards too?!" Was there anything anyone didn't know?

"Lunchroom chatter," Miss Lena said, and then she opened the drawer, looked at the dolls, and then looked at me with her lips pursed as if she were holding in a secret. "Want to play?"

"Sure, why not." I took out Jesus and placed Him on the register while Miss Lena put all the dolls face down on the counter and shuffled them around before randomly dealing out three to each of us and lining up the rest to be picked when needed.

**Miss Dani called** a meeting at the end of the day. I felt shaky and ill. I knew she was going to announce my departure.

"Well, some of you might already know this, but today's Miss Zippy's last day," Miss Dani said.

Miss Liaskis gasped, teared up, and then hugged me. "I learned the terrible news only an hour ago!"

"I'm okay," I said, squirmy and uncomfortable.

"We will all miss you, Zip!" Miss Dani said, and she handed me an I. Magnin bag.

"Open it!" Miss Lena clapped her hands and did one of her little jumps.

"It's a gift from everyone. We all chipped in." Miss Dani executed her fist swipe.

"That's when I learned you were leaving!" Miss Liaskis said, and she wiped away tears. "When I chipped in."

I looked at the other faces encircling me. Both Braughns, L and R, were there that day and neither was looking at me. Miss Lee had a sweet smile, as if maybe she'd liked me all along. Though, maybe not. Miss Karen tilted her head and gave me a closemouthed smile. Miss Yolanda fingered her pocket for a new candy ball, and Miss Lena leaned into my side.

"Well, open the damn bag," Miss Yolanda said after she popped in the new candy. "Even with the discount, we each had to give more than I would have for any of my stupid nieces for Christmas."

I turned to her. "But you did it, right? You, personally, gave?"

"Hell yeah, I did! Open it!"

I reached into the bag and pulled out the Sgt. Pepper dress I'd worn that one day. "Ahhhhh, I love this dress! Thank you." I held the dress against my heart and smiled at each of them. Except the Braughns, L and R, who looked like mannequins waiting to be put in storage.

When the meeting ended, Miss Dani hugged me and then everyone dispersed, leaving Miss Lena and me alone in Petite Dresses.

"I wish you were staying," Miss Lena said, and to that I could only nod vigorously. I opened the supply drawer and looked down at the paper dolls.

"Do you want to take them, dear?" Miss Lena asked.

"No. They belong here." I shut the drawer and Miss Lena and I both got our purses from under the counter. As we walked toward the customer elevators, Miss Lena took my hand, the way my mother did every now and then. She let go before we stepped into the elevator, joining the women from the floors above us. The designer ladies were discussing the Ungaro dresses that had come in that afternoon. The sleeves were far too big, like a chef's hat starting at each shoulder, according to the elegant Miss Meredith. The others disagreed with her.

When we got off the elevator, Miss Lena and I silently followed the Designer Dresses ladies to the employee entrance and exit where everyone had their bags checked. Neither of us spoke until we were out on the sidewalk.

"You'll come see me soon, won't you, dear?"

"Of course," I said, though I wondered.

"I'll pray for you," Miss Lena said, and she leaned in, hugged me fast and hard, and then scurried off. Her tiny body was soon swallowed up by the crowds on the sidewalk. I tilted my head and searched for her, and then I squatted down. Yes, I could see her tiny ballet flats, briefly, before the feet on the sidewalk closed in around her again.

**I wore my** Vittadini military-style dress the first day of work at the Hardware Depot. A few people whipped their heads toward me as I put my purse and sweater into a locker in the employee lounge.

"Are you in customer service?" a guy asked. His right pant leg looked empty and he limped. His upper body was like a weightlifter's. If he could work with one leg, couldn't Howard work with one hand?

"Lumber," I said.

"No kidding!" He revealed a powerful, broad smile. "Dressed like that?"

"Well, as long as I have on the goggles, I should be okay, right?"

"I guess so. You're the fanciest lady here." He tied his apron behind his back and then loped out in his half-stiff way.

It seemed funny, fun actually, to be the most elegant lady at the Hardware Depot. At I. Magnin, I had been the least elegant. Everything in life, I realized, was measured in context: rich, poor, family or no family, dad or no dad, fancy or not fancy. Whether or not any of it mattered depended on the backdrop against which you measured it.

Jeff looked me up and down when I showed up in lumber. "Why are you wearing that?" he asked.

"I like this dress."

"But you're cutting wood in it. You're going to have sawdust clinging to the fabric, or whatever you call it."

"Yeah. Fabric." I had thought of that, but the dress wasn't made of angora. It was tightly knit and anything—sawdust included—could be brushed away.

"Suit yourself," Jeff said.

**The morning went** by quickly. There was sawdust in my hair, on my dress, in my mouth and ears. I washed my hands in the employee bathrooms and tried to clean my dress before meeting my mother in the lounge for a lunch that I had packed for both of us: croissants cut open and stuffed with Swiss cheese and apples.

"You doubling up?" my mother asked when I walked into the windowless linoleum-floored room.

"Huh?" I sat on the stained couch beside her and placed the grocery bag on the coffee table in front of us.

"You still at I. Magnin?"

"No. That was a full-time job. I couldn't do both even if I wanted." My employment at the Depot was somewhat like the situation with my dad: my mother and I both knew what was what, but to talk about it too deeply would make one or the other of us feel things we didn't have the fortitude to face.

My mother reached into the bag, pulled out both sandwiches, and handed me one. "If you're not working at Magnin's, why are you wearing that dress? You look way too fancy."

I shrugged, unwrapped the Saran from around my croissant, and took a bite. "I like this dress."

"You still eating every other day?"

"Pretty much." Raquel was a little more lax about it now that she was dating Paul. When she ate on non-eating days, so did I.

My mother looked up at the plump woman across from us. She was staring down into a Tupperware container as she forked something smelly and fishy into her mouth. "My daughter only eats every other day!"

"Oh yeah?" The woman looked up for a second, then looked back down and took another bite. "Why?"

"A fancy diet. She's writing a book about it."

"Doesn't sound fancy to me," the woman said. "Sounds dumb."

I laughed and so did my mother. The woman didn't laugh; she kept eating.

By late afternoon I was only measuring twice. My mistakes hadn't been about measuring; they were about control. The bandsaw with the circle-cutting jig wobbled in my hands so much that Jeff had to rescue the plywood I was mutilating. Another time, I cut along a knot, creating divots that did not please the tall, skinny man who wanted solid, narrow planks. Overall, the day wasn't as bad as I had anticipated. I was too busy to dwell on what I wanted and didn't have. Too busy to think about how I would carry on differently if I were the chooser in my life.

# Chapter 11

**My father called** and I told him all about my first day at the Depot. "And guess what?" I added after a particularly long run-on.

"What?"

"I was walking through the area where they sell plants and I was examining the succulents—"

"Fibonacci!" my dad said.

"Yes! The most perfect spiral pattern. I'd never noticed it before."

"I have succulents lining the window in the kitchen. They were picked out for exactly that reason."

"That's so cool!" I would have loved to have a kitchen with a window that was lined with beautiful plants, the leaves of which were patterned in a perfect mathematical equation.

"Zippy," my dad said. "I think it's time we met in person. I want you to be a part of my life and . . . Well, there are plenty of hardware stores here—maybe you'll consider moving to LA."

"My mom's worst nightmare!" I said.

"Okay, I'm jumping ahead. What if I buy you a ticket for Saturday? People Express has a flight every couple hours. You can spend the day with me, fly home at night, and wake up in your own place in time to have brunch with Raquel."

"Wow. Yeah. Okay." There was so much to be afraid of here: flying, figuring out how to get through the airport in LA and then get to my father in his house across the street from Richard Simmons, *being* with my father in person *for a whole day* (what if we ran out of things to talk about?!), and even reporting it all to my mother without hurting her feelings. Still, I wasn't going to say no.

"I'm going to call a travel agent right now. Do you want smoking or nonsmoking?"

"I don't smoke."

"No, I know. But the fun people fly in the smoking section, so you might want to be with them."

"Okay." I felt odd, like I wasn't in my body. I was about to get on a plane and meet my dad in person after years of wondering about him, one session of praying for him, and then six weeks of regular phone calls. It seemed like I was imagining it all.

"Can Raquel drive you to the airport or should I order a car service?"

"I don't even know what a car service is."

"An airport limousine," my dad said.

"No, don't waste money on that. I'm sure Raquel will drive me. We don't have a good parking spot right now, so it's no big deal to move the car."

"Ah, excellent," my dad said. "You know we've got parking in Los Angeles. More cars than San Francisco and plenty of parking!"

**My father was** right about the fun people. I walked down the aisle of the People Express plane, past the nonsmokers silently putting on and adjusting their seat belts, to the smokers, half of whom were standing and chatting. I paused in front of a guy tapping open a pack of Camels.

He nudged his head in the direction of the empty seat. "You here?"

I looked at my ticket. "Yeah. I guess I'm next to the window."

He stood, stepped aside, and then put out his arm in the *after you* sign. I scooted in and sat. The window beside me had duct tape around it. Was the glass actually being held in place by the tape? When we took off, would the tape loosen and would I be sucked out the window? I stared at the window frame and then I looked down at my body. No way I'd squeeze through.

"Cigarette?" The guy standing in the aisle leaned toward me and held out the pack. I couldn't help but stare at the camel graphic, which a boy in high school English class had once shown me was drawn to look exactly like a penis. I never could see the penis, but I believed that it was there.

"No, thanks. Wait. Okay, yes!" Why not? I'd tried a cigarette once: a Marlboro, in the dressing room during *Mame* my junior year of high school. After one puff I was nauseous and my head felt spinny. Maybe the second time was easier? I took the Camel and stuck it in my mouth. Before my seatmate could light it, the flight attendant announced that we were to extinguish all cigarettes, take our seats, and fasten our seat belts. I was saved.

By the time we landed, I was so close to throwing up, I picked up the barf bag in the seat-back pouch and shoved it into my purse. It wasn't only the cigarettes I'd tried, it was the short flight that bumped the whole way as if we were bowling down clouds made of wood.

I walked off the plane and searched for a man who resembled me but had broader shoulders and was over six feet tall. I didn't recognize myself in any faces but suddenly sensed someone nearby staring at me. I met his gaze and, I swear, he looked exactly like the Berber Coffee guy: thick, windswept hair and shoulders that made it appear as if there were a wooden beam shoved across his shirt. His head was large. Even larger than Howard's, but it matched his neck.

"Dad?"

He leaned in and hugged me. It felt both awkward and familiar.

"Zippy!" he said in that rocky voice that I suddenly realized I'd known for years.

"Dad." I lowered my voice to a whisper. "Are you the Berber Coffee guy?"

"Yeah." He smiled and shrugged in a casual *What can you do?* way.

"Why didn't you tell me? Why did you say you were in advertising?" I felt a twisting disorientation. Suddenly all our conversations made more sense—I'd known that motorcycle grumble, but I'd never placed it in the right spot—even as I watched him on TV each night.

"Oh, Zippy. I'm sorry I lied. I didn't know what you or your mom were like and I was warned by my lawyer to get to know you first. Then after we'd talked once, I forgot about it. I mean, it's not like I sit around and think, *I am the Berber Coffee guy*." He shrugged; his giant shoulders rose and then fell like a brick wall.

"Holy moly. This is so weird." I wanted to call Raquel right then and tell her that her years-long crush *was my dad*! And I wanted to call Miss Lena, too! I'd tell her to throw away the first paper doll I made of my dad and to write on the back of the Berber Coffee guy paper doll, *I AM ZIPPY'S DAD!*

We stood there staring at each other. When he smiled, I did too. He had my exact smile. Or rather, I had *his*. A big, sideways, rectangular smile: the teeth of a marionette or a dummy on a lap. Also, my dad's eyes were the same tiger's-eye brown as mine. Why hadn't I (or anyone else) noticed how closely my features matched the Berber Coffee guy's? Was it so inconceivable that it was beyond our imagination?

Unlike me, my father's cheeks were so sculpted, they created shadows on his face. And he smelled spicy and clean. His clothing was impeccable: a bright white polo shirt. Ironed jeans, a snakeskin belt that matched the snakeskin boots he wore. I sensed people around us staring at him, whispering, pointing.

My seatmate came out of the men's room, paused, and stared at us. He tilted his head to try to figure out (I assumed) if I was standing with the Berber Coffee guy. Finally he said, "Bye, Zippy!"

"Bye! Thanks for the cigs!" I said, and he gave an *I see the Berber Coffee guy* thumbs-up before walking away.

"See," my dad said, "the fun people."

"Yeah, he was nice. But I feel like barfing from all the smoking."

"I thought you didn't smoke?"

"I don't. But the fun people like to share and I didn't want to be a party pooper."

"Let's get you some food." My dad took my arm and we headed toward the parking garage. He walked quickly. I kept up, glancing at him every other step as the conversation easily rolled along. Were those my lips? Yeah, they were my lips. My mother had a pouty mouth, like a cherub on a Victorian Valentine card. But my father, like me, had a wide, full mouth.

Once we were in his car, a sporty red convertible, my father said, "You're so charming. Now why do you think you've never had a date?"

"Oh . . . uh—" The Berber Coffee guy thought I was charming! "Well . . . boys aren't interested in me."

My dad flashed his head toward me and then back to the road. "I don't believe it! Are you shy with them? Talk about the moon! Talk about the Sea of Tranquility!"

"You're the only person I know who's also interested in that stuff," I said.

"Listen, you shouldn't feel obliged to discuss your love life with me. But I hope we'll be close enough eventually that you will share that kind of stuff too. And I don't want to pry into your private business, but if I can add a little fatherly advice, I'd like to say that when you do get around to having a boyfriend, promise me you'll use a condom."

I felt a rush of embarrassment. Surely the Berber Coffee guy had been dating since he was five, or fifteen, at least . . . I mean, he'd had a one-night stand with my mother when he was nineteen. Condom advice seemed misaimed at me; it was something *he* should have received long ago. "Yes," I finally said. "I promise."

My dad reached his arm out and quickly rubbed my shoulder again. "What about In-N-Out?"

I thought we were still talking about sex. Was there less of a chance of getting pregnant if the guy only dipped in and then out? "Uh . . . does that work?"

"What work?"

"Oh, wait, what are you saying?"

"Do you want to go to In-N-Out Burger?"

Relief! "I don't know what that is, but it sounds good." My face burned bright. I hoped he didn't guess at what I had thought he'd said.

We rolled into the drive-through. I was too nervous to look at the menu, so I ordered the same as my dad (burger, fries, and a chocolate shake). While we were waiting for the food, my father pushed a button on the dashboard and the top of the car went down.

"So the smell doesn't get trapped in here," he said.

"My mom's car permanently smells like french fries," I said.

My dad grinned. "Then we never would have made it as a couple!"

"If I ever drop something and have to search the floor of my mom's car," I said, "I always find a preserved, perfectly formed McDonald's fry. I once had an idea that there should be a McDonald's Fry Museum. Everyone in the world could donate their lost fries and they'd be displayed—you know, pinned like butterflies—in plexiglass cases with the likely date the fry had been ordered, what was ordered with it, the exact place it had been ordered, and—" I shrugged, reddened. Had I said too much and revealed myself as a freak?

My dad was still smiling, not quite laughing. "I like how you think, Zippy! The Fry Museum." He reached an arm over and pinched my knee.

Once the greasy bag was in my dad's hand, he pulled the car into the parking lot and then turned off the engine. The sun was much brighter than it was in San Francisco—as if we all lived under an umbrella up there, and here the umbrella was gone. The buildings and cars around me looked so clear and sharp, it was like they'd been outlined by a thick pen.

"So other than Disneyland, this is your first time in Los Angeles, right?"

"Yup. We drove down once, slept at a Motel 6, and spent the day at Disney. I think Mom liked it better than me. But I liked that I'd skipped school that day and got to hang out with her." I unwrapped my burger and took a bite. A round slice of pickle slid out like a loose goldfish. I caught it and tucked it into my mouth. I didn't want to finish before my father finished, nor did I want to have food left after he was done. All this, including the talking, was feeling chaotically difficult.

My dad shoved three fingers of fries in his mouth. I hadn't yet swallowed my burger bite; still, I reached into my fry bag, grabbed three, and bit off the ends.

"I've been living here since I graduated from college," my dad said. "And I have to say, I kinda love it."

"It's so cool that you studied drama in college." When he'd given me that detail on the phone, it had seemed strange that a man who went into advertising had studied drama. Now it made sense.

"And it's so cool that you did musical theater in high school," my dad said.

"Well, I usually worked on costumes, or did crew." I hurriedly shoved the rest of the three-fry hold in my mouth.

"That's still *doing* musical theater," my dad said. "I guess you got the gene from me."

We didn't talk on the freeway. It was too noisy with the top down and the wind blowing my hair around. This was okay, as it gave me time to think. All I could think was about how my life might have been different if I'd had a relationship with my father. He went to college! He was a professional actor! He did things I'd only dreamed of, like going to New York City and seeing a musical. Maybe, had I known him, I would have been able to do those things too.

My father pulled the car into a driveway next to a big Spanish-style house.

"So that's Richard Simmons's house?" I whispered, and pointed across the street.

"Yup. If he weren't out of town, I'd have made plans for you to meet him," my dad said, and then I followed him to the wrought-iron gate that opened to a front courtyard.

"Pretty," I said as he unlocked the gate. The courtyard was paved with Spanish tiles and a palm tree grew in the center. Flowers were planted around the palm.

"Look," my dad said, and he squatted down and rotated his giant pointer finger in a spiral over the head of a rose.

"Perfect," I said.

It seemed odd that my father had a house like this and my mother had a one-bedroom apartment with a swollen bathroom door that wouldn't shut. I wished I could snap my fingers and even up things between them.

"I've been here almost nine years now," my father said. "Jerome and I bought it together."

"Who's Jerome?" I worried that he'd told me about Jerome and I'd forgotten. What I'd learned so far was this: my father wasn't married, had no other children and only one sibling, a brother named George who lived in Utah. His parents still lived in the Bay Area, and my father, the Berber Coffee guy, was the first man in his family since his great-great-grandfather *not* to become a lawyer. For that, he was an outcast.

"Jerome's the person who inspired me to find you." My dad lifted his fist and gave me an affectionate bop on the chin. There was something sweet and funny about it.

The door was unlocked (I guess the gate was enough!); my father opened it and then waited for me to enter first. He followed behind and then called out from the echoey tiled entrance hall, "HELLO?"

The house looked even more grand once inside. The living room had a fireplace so big I could stand in it, and a shiny black grand piano on top of which were silver-framed photos. The dining room had a table that looked like it could seat fourteen people and a wrought-iron chandelier I could ride as a swing.

"Do you have big dinner parties?" I asked.

"Yeah . . . uh . . . we used to. Jerome loves cooking, so we'd throw huge parties with four or five courses and lots of drinking. Oh, Zippy, I'd love for you to meet everyone and I'd love to show you off at a party!" My dad wrapped his arms around me and gave me another hug. I didn't know how to respond, so I stood there, my arms pinned against my sides like a rolled spool of yarn. It didn't feel like a stranger, but it also didn't feel like when my mom hugged me. Finally my dad pulled away. "How's Howard doing? Did he get his claw yet?"

"Mom calls it a hook. It's been paid for and should arrive in a few weeks. But he can't even learn how to use it until his nub is fully healed and that could take a long, long time since he keeps getting infections."

My dad let out a low *holy moly, losing your fingers* kind of whistle.

"Yeah, the finger thing's a bummer," I said. "But he's pretty, uh, he's pretty adaptable. My guess is he'll have fun with his hook-hand when it's finally operating, and he'll never look back and miss his fingers."

"That's a guy with a great attitude," my dad said.

"He seems to approach life differently than most people. He has a huge head and he's proud of it."

"You mean, like an ego? A big ego?"

"No. Size-wise. Sniper's dream."

My father broke apart laughing. "Me too!" He pointed at his enormous head. "Sniper's dream!" He couldn't stop laughing.

"I didn't make up that joke," I said. "Howard did."

"Sounds like a great guy. Let's find Jerome. HELLO?!" My father took my hand and walked me through the dining room and then into the kitchen, which was the size of the entire first floor of my mother's apartment. French doors led out to the backyard. In the center of that yard was a long, rectangular pool surrounded by red Mexican tile. A thin bronzed man lay face up on a cushioned wooden lawn chair.

My father opened the door. "Jerome!"

The man in the chair sat up. I could see the shape of his anatomy: his ribs bowing out like the body of a ship, clavicles like drumsticks, a jaw like a hinge covered in a thin layer of skin.

"Hello, hello!" the man, Jerome, said, and he slipped on a glowing white T-shirt and slowly got off the chair.

I followed my father to Jerome. My dad put his hand on my waist. "This is Zippy."

"Oh, Zippy!" Jerome hugged me and rocked me back and forth like I was a baby who needed soothing. "Zippy, Zippy, Zippy, Zippy. I can't tell you how happy I am to see you here!"

I tried to adjust my face so I wouldn't look like what I felt, which was awkward, shy, confused. Was Jerome a roommate? Why would he and my dad buy a house together? Was it like Ernie and Bert—forever friends?

"I was just telling Zippy about our dinner parties," my dad said.

"Until this year, we threw the most fabulous dinner parties," Jerome said. "Here, sit. Let's talk." Then he looked up at my dad and said, "Darling, do we have lemonade or something for our sweet Zippy?"

I looked at my dad, then back to Jerome, then back to my dad, who was entering the house to get us drinks. And then I dropped onto the wooden lounge chair beside Jerome, who was lowering himself back into position. Was my dad gay? I'd imagined him as many different things. But because he'd had a one-night stand with my mother, and now it turned out that he was *the Berber Coffee guy (!!)*, the idea of him being gay seemed impossible.

"You're very, very pretty!" Jerome said.

"I, uh—" *Gay gay gay-de-da-gay gay gay.* I needed the question answered. "I'm not so pretty, but I've lost some weight since I moved in with Raquel, my roommate."

"Darling!" Jerome said. "Stop. You *are* pretty! Look at you!"

I said, "I agree I have nice hair, but people have always called me *fat,* so I've never felt pretty."

"First of all, you're not fat. But who cares if you are! Fat means you're alive! I like big women!"

"You do?" I saw my opening. "You mean, you like to date them?"

"Oh, honey, I'm as gay as Liberace! Unlike your gay father, who—obviously—has enjoyed the gifts of women over the years, I've never even French-kissed a woman."

I felt like my head was filling with pancake batter. My thoughts were thick and unclear. My *father*, the Berber Coffee guy, was someone who'd had sex with my mother, produced me, and now, after nineteen years, was introducing me to a man who was likely his boyfriend, with whom he'd bought a house?

"Has my dad always been gay?" I finally asked.

"Well, yes. But he has those *horrible* parents, who would disown him if they knew, so he's not out to many people. Even his agent doesn't know he's gay. No one wants to cast a gay man in anything. Especially the advertisers."

"It's funny to think that the Berber Coffee guy—who every woman I know wants to marry—is gay." Did having a gay father make me . . . gay *inclined*? Was I gay and didn't know it yet? Was that why I'd never had a boyfriend? But I'd never had a crush on a woman, so didn't that make me *not gay*?

"He wouldn't be the Berber Coffee guy if people knew he was gay. The Berber people *adore* the fact that your father is an international sex symbol!" Jerome gave a little hoot. "Women all over the world are in love with him! You know the ads play in Asia, Europe, and South America—so even when we travel, swarms of women recognize him. Berber forwards him loads of fan mail."

"I had no idea that people sent fan mail to actors in commercials."

"Not many. The iconic ones, like your dad and maybe the Old Spice guy. Do you know how many naked pictures he's received? Guess!"

"Naked pictures . . . like Playboy Bunnies?"

"No!" Jerome laughed uproariously. His body rocked and shook. "They're everyday women. Housewives! Secretaries! Actresses! Bankers! *Women who watch television!* They see him in the ad, take off their clothes, take naked photos of themselves that they send to him. I don't know how they do it; maybe they do that thing where you put the camera on a timer and then you run in front of it."

"Where do you think they get them developed?" The only thing worse than taking a naked photo, in my imagination, was getting one developed!

"Oh, darling, who knows," Jerome said. "Probably the one-hour drive-through. But the part that kills me is that they're imagining him staring at their photo, maybe thinking about making love to them, when in fact he barely glances at the photos because he wants *moi*!" Jerome gave a long, howly hoot that seemed to take the wind out of him.

My dad returned with a tray containing three glasses of lemonade and a plate of white cookies with big sugar crystals.

"Voilà!" my dad said, and he set the tray on a little table between my chair and Jerome's before sitting himself on the end of Jerome's chair.

"Zippy was about to tell me about her exciting life in the City by the Bay!" Jerome said, as if that were what we'd been talking about all along.

"Well, I guess it's sort of exciting now . . . uh, Dad, you're gay!" How odd that I was both comfortable enough to mention that he was gay *and* call him *Dad*! Was it biology that rushed us to a greater level of comfort than what we should have had?

"Yes, honey, I'm gay." He shrugged and said, "There are a lot of us in Hollywood. We're all hiding out."

I was content to sit by the pool and chat with my dad and Jerome all afternoon. They both spoke quickly and told excellent stories about the people they knew or adventures they'd had. Each story pointed to how odd and entertaining the world was, how fascinating it was simply to be alive. There was the boot that fell off a balcony in Positano, Italy, nearly killing a man on the sidewalk who ended up taking them to dinner at his mother's house. There was the woman from Peru at the Great Wall of China who collapsed with fatigue but didn't want to return to her bus, so my dad and Jerome carried her all around the wall on their broad shoulders and strong backs. And there was their celebrity neighbor, the talk show host Clark Dickerson, who often passed out drunk on his or any of the other neighbors' front lawns after parking his car anywhere, including in the middle of the road. My father had frequently gone out and carried him into his own home until the night his wife, looking at Clark draped across my father's shoulder, said, "For chrissakes, leave him where he flang himself!"

"Is that even a word?" I asked. "*Flang*?"

"Nope!" Jerome said. "That's why we like to say it so much!"

"Fling, flung, flang!" my father said, and we all laughed.

Around six, my father brought me into the kitchen to meet a woman named Rosa, who was making dinner. My dad introduced me as his daughter. Rosa gasped. She put down the spoon she held, wiped her hands on her apron, and then grabbed me and kissed me on the forehead. She spoke quickly in Spanish as she kissed me again, and my father said something to her in Spanish.

"She's so happy to meet you," my dad said. "We've been talking about you for weeks."

"You have?" How odd that strangers knew about me, in some sense, and talked about me.

"Let me show you some of the family," my dad said, and he led me out of the kitchen and then to the grand curved staircase, which was like the Spanish-style version of the staircase in *Gone with the Wind.* Along the wall, all the way up, were elaborately framed portraits that looked at least a hundred years old.

"Are these my dead relatives?" I asked.

"They sure are." We paused and my dad glanced at a looming woman who had a nose like a potato and a mouth like a button; she dominated the midpoint of the stairway. "That's your great-great-great-grandmother Margaret Bucks. As far as I know she was a nasty old loon."

"And part of that loon is in me?!"

"There are better people," my dad said. "Let me introduce you to your great-grandparents, Everett and Consuella Bucks." We went up a few more steps and stopped in front of a majestic-looking couple. He was standing, she was in a chair. Both looked out from the dusty greenish-gray background; it seemed a smile would have been impossible. Still, they looked happy, and she bore a strong resemblance to both my father and me.

"Wow," I said. "That's so strange. Some dead person, whose name I'd never heard until now, is biologically connected to me and looks a lot like me."

"They're *both* in you, but damn if you didn't get her face exactly." My dad and I stared at Consuella. The spiderweb cracking of the glossy paint made her look as if she were behind a sheet of glass. My dad took my arm and led me to the top of the stairs.

"So, you and Jerome have been discussing me for weeks?" I asked.

"Jerome brought you up a few months ago. He convinced me that my life, and his, would be better if I had a relationship with you. It didn't take long to find you once I set my mind to it. I'm still friends with some people who are friends with people who knew where I could find your mom." My father leaned against the black banister that created a fence between himself and a death-fall to the tiled landing.

"Did you remember my mom's name?"

"Of course I did!" my dad said. "We made a baby together!"

"She forgot your name," I said.

"Well, she was probably traumatized. I mean, she had a fling with some frat boy she met at a jazz club and ended up pregnant." We walked a few feet to where there was an overstuffed white sofa. In the hall! I'd never been in a hall so wide and open that you could place a sofa in it. My father sat. I sat beside him. We both looked out over the banister to the massive paned window that revealed a tumultuous sea of grape-green leaves.

"Funny. I always imagined it as a disco club."

"It was the sixties. Disco hadn't been invented yet."

"And you liked my mom then even though she was a girl?"

"At the time, I was trying to be straight. And she was so much fun—she had a wonderful laugh."

"Would you have started dating her if she hadn't gotten pregnant?"

"Probably. But it was finals week. I was studying. I didn't call her for more than a month and when I did, she told me she was pregnant. I was so confused and scared that I told my parents. And—" My dad shook his head.

"And?" I asked.

"My grandfather was brought in; my uncle was consulted. I guess today they'd call it an intervention," my dad said.

"Would it have been a problem if you'd impregnated *any* girl? Or was it that my mom was a French Canadian with no family or education?" I was feeling a little defensive of my mother. She didn't choose her childhood circumstances; she was born into them and did the best she could in spite of them.

"*Any* girl would have been a problem. But had it been a girl from a family they'd known, a marriage might have been arranged."

"That's intense."

"Yeah, invasive. And I was very immature, sheltered, and terrified, so I did as the family demanded and never contacted your mother again." My dad gave a frowning smile. "I feel terrible about it now. I mean, to imagine what I lost in not knowing you or fathering you . . . I'm ashamed."

My father's words triggered a surge of pride for my mother. For not having left town or put me up for adoption. For standing up against the shame she must have felt as a single mother. "My mother's family stopped talking to her after I was born," I said. "I knew it was because of me, but she acted like it was *good riddance* and she'd rather have me than them."

"She's obviously a very strong woman. Far stronger than I ever was."

"Yeah, she can survive anything." I thought about how easily my mother had given up her car to pay for Howard's hook, how she did whatever it took to care for the few things that really mattered to her (me and Howard).

"I bet you're that strong too," my dad said.

I looked up at my father and had the strangest sensation of actually becoming stronger right then.

**We met up** with Jerome downstairs in the dining room. The table had four differently sized silver candelabras, each holding lit candles. I'd never had dinner at home with a candle—let alone twenty. It seemed exotic, extravagant. My father and I were on one side of the table and Jerome was on the other.

Then Jerome moved his place setting across the table so he,

also, was sitting beside me, and said, "I want to sit next to Zippy too!"

My father shook his head in a charmed-but-fed-up way.

When my dad and Jerome each put their thick white napkin on their lap, I did the same. Rosa came in and out, putting plates on the table: a roasted chicken, risotto with asparagus (I didn't even know what risotto was, but Rosa announced each thing as she set it down), and artichoke, which I'd ordered once in a restaurant with my mom and Howard but hadn't eaten. It had confused me at the time and I was too embarrassed to ask how to eat it. My mom and Howard didn't know either, so we let it sit there on the table like a half-bloomed green flower. Rosa also put down a big green salad with radishes and nuts and cheese in it. I'd had lettuce. I'd had nuts. I'd had cheese. I'd even had a radish once. But I'd never had them together. Each new thing I tasted startled my brain as much as my mouth, especially the artichoke, which my father said was being served partly because I'd appreciate the Fibonacci pattern of the leaves (I followed my father and Jerome: rip off a leaf, dip it in one of the tiny bowls of melted butter, and then scrape off the buttery "meat" with my teeth).

After dinner, Rosa brought in three terra-cotta bowls of crème brûlée (something I'd had many times because my mother made it using a recipe handed down to her by her French Canadian grandmother). Once Rosa left, Jerome looked at the crème brûlée and groaned.

My father glanced over at him, as did I.

"Try to have a little," my dad said to Jerome.

"I'll try," Jerome said. He stabbed his spoon into the hard amber shell, breaking it into shardy lightning bolts.

I punched my spoon through the center and then took a bite. It was so good. Creamy and smooth with the sharp sweetness of the shell cutting in.

My father wasn't eating. He was watching Jerome, who had put his spoon on the table and dropped his head. Did this mean I couldn't continue eating?

"Dessert brings out strong feelings," my dad said to me.

"What kind of strong feelings?" I asked uncertainly.

"Oh boy," Jerome said, and he started to cry, or whimper, more, with tears streaming down his face.

My dad leaned behind me, reached his arm across my back and onto Jerome's shoulder. He rubbed it back and forth.

I really, really wanted to eat that crème brûlée, but there was no graceful way to do it with my father's arm grazing my back as he rubbed Jerome's shoulder. I leaned forward (closer to the very thing I wanted to devour) so as to be out of the way.

"I'm sorry, baby. I'm so sorry," my dad said, as he continued to rub Jerome's shoulder.

I finally looked away from the crème brûlée and to my dad. A tear ran down his face too. This was a version of my father that I hadn't gotten to know through our phone calls. He had seemed so logical, smart, interested in things large (galaxies, the moon) and small (atoms, cells). But now he was crying over crème brûlée! It seemed far too weird to even report to Raquel!

"Is dessert always this dramatic?" I asked, and my dad and Jerome stopped crying and laughed a little.

"Eat!" Jerome said, and he blew his nose into his napkin.

My dad sighed and then sat up and broke the crust on his crème brûlée. I took this as a sign that I could eat mine, even though Jerome wasn't touching his, so I scooped out another spoonful. I swirled the crème part in my mouth while my tongue flicked over the hard, sugary brûlée.

"I used to look more like your dad," Jerome said, "but I've lost fifty pounds."

"Fifty-five," my dad said, and he took another bite.

"You lost *fifty-five* pounds?!" I said. "That's a dream come true for me. Well, maybe not fifty-five. But twenty pounds would be great. How'd you do it? And why?"

"I have AIDS."

As soon as Jerome said those words, I felt like I was back at school, onstage, and the scene had suddenly cut to black. There was a *before* and an *after*. I was now suspended in the darkness of *after*.

I thought back over the afternoon. Jerome had hugged me; I was in his home! Were these my last healthy minutes on Earth?!

"Don't—" I looked at my dad. "Don't you have it too?" I was seated *between them*! Was this safe?! Could I get up and move across the table without demolishing this new relationship?! Wouldn't I happily demolish the relationship if the act of moving across the table would save my life?!

My dad shook his head, and then Jerome said, "Miraculously, he didn't get it."

I wanted to say *get it yet*! For all I knew, my father and I had both contracted it today! What if a droplet of spit left Jerome's mouth when we were talking and landed in my mouth, and I now had it?! Was my decision to leave I. Magnin and apron up at the Hardware Depot a hasty one?! If I only had months left, I didn't want to spend them sawing wood, the crumbs of which ended up in my eyelashes. I'd rather spend my final working days at I. Magnin while being ignored by most of the fifth-floor salesgirls, being loathed by some of the complaint-card-filling-out customers, and being loved by Miss Lena, who was happy to play paper dolls with me all afternoon.

"It's contagious, but not like most people think." My dad took another bite of his crème brûlée, and as much as I wanted to shovel more into my mouth, I felt mildly shocked that he could eat while Jerome was . . . dying! My father said, "The *only* way to get it is through blood or semen directly introduced into an open wound. You can't get it from kissing. Unless your mouth is bleeding and the person you kiss is also bleeding in his mouth. I've had many talks with many doctors about transmission. Even if you used Jerome's toothbrush, you wouldn't get it."

I looked at my dad carefully; our identical eyes locked and I could feel my heart slowing and my breathing becoming more steady. Everything I read in the newspaper said, more or less, what my father had said. But no one I knew seemed to believe that; people talked about AIDS as if you could become infected simply by looking at someone. I remembered my father's odd advice to use a condom. He was trying to protect me from AIDS, not pregnancy.

"So . . ." I couldn't finish my sentence for fear I'd hurt Jerome's feelings. But my father seemed to read my mind. He knew I was asking if I didn't have to worry about the contact I'd already had.

"I'll always keep you safe," my dad said.

"Okay." I believed him. "Jerome—" My voice caught and scratched. "I'm so very sorry."

Even though I lived in the geographic center of the AIDS crisis, the closest I'd come to the virus so far was through knowing about Pablo's "best friend," and I wasn't even a hundred percent certain he actually had AIDS. I hung out at Blue Light on Union Street and not at Kimos on Polk Street, or I-Beam, where Pablo had danced as if it were the end of something. Selfishly forgetting about AIDS most of the time had been easy enough.

Until now. At that dinner table.

**We took Jerome's** Saab to the airport, which my father drove, since we couldn't all fit in the convertible.

At the gate, Jerome hugged me goodbye first (I should admit, I turned my head away from his). Next, my dad hugged me. He didn't let go for a long, long time.

When he released me at last, he said, "It's so amazing to finally know you. I've been thinking about you your whole life."

"Have you really?" I asked.

"Yeah, I honestly, truly have," my dad said, and he hugged me one last time.

**I looked out** the window and barely moved during the hour flight home. There was so much to go over in my mind. I had a dad, and *he was the Berber Coffee guy*. He was also gay (!). And "married," in a sense, to a man who had AIDS. I still had been raised by my mom in the apartment above the liquor store. My mother was still married to half-his-fingers Howard. I still had left I. Magnin to help my mother and Howard with their medical bills. And I still worked as a woodcutter at the Hardware Depot. In the end, I decided that the background of my life had changed drastically while the foreground remained the same.

Everything felt exciting, tragically sad, and out of sync.

# Chapter 12

**Raquel picked me** up from the airport. I wanted to tell her immediately that my dad was the Berber Coffee guy, but I wasn't sure how to give that news while also working in the fact that my dad was gay and his boyfriend had AIDS.

"So?" Raquel said as we pulled out of the parking lot.

I couldn't stop myself from smiling as I told her about the day in general: what the house looked like; that my dad had a woman, Rosa, who cooked; how the pool looked like an ad for a boutique hotel ripped out of *Architectural Digest*.

Raquel said, "So, your dad is kind, generous, and rich."

"Yeah. But he's not in advertising like he'd said."

"What do you mean *not in advertising like he'd said*? Did he lie?"

"He did, but he had a good . . . or an okay-ish reason to lie." I'd decided, as the conversation progressed, that I'd give the story bit-by-bit, starting with the most explosive news.

"What was his reason and what does he do?" Raquel looked over at me then back at the road.

"He was advised by his lawyer not to say what he does for a living until he knew for sure that my mother and I wouldn't try to glom onto him and take his estate, or steal his money, or ask him to pay our medical bills or something . . . Not that he wouldn't pay our medical bills—he was *that* nice."

"Is he a drug lord or a billionaire or something?"

"Nope. Raquel, he's—" I stopped and stared at her until she stared back for a second.

"The drum is rolling, Zippy. What is he?"

"He's the Berber Coffee guy."

"No." Raquel said it flatly, as if I'd asked her to slow down or speed up.

"Yes."

"NO! Seriously? *Your father* is THE Berber Coffee guy?!"

"Yes. I swear."

"NO WAY!" Raquel pulled the car over and cranked up the emergency brake. She stared at me, open mouth, wild eyes, her hands apart like she was about to catch a beach ball.

"Way." I could feel my smile taking over my face.

"ZIPPY! What the *H-E*-double toothpicks?! I mean, seriously?! YOUR DAD IS THE BERBER COFFEE GUY! YOUR NUT-BALL MOTHER, WHO IS NOW WITH Q-TIP-HANDED HOWARD, HAD SEX WITH THE BERBER COFFEE GUY!"

"Yup." I was laughing.

"I WANT TO HAVE SEX WITH THE BERBER COFFEE GUY!"

"Ugh, Raquel! Think about what you're saying! It's my dad!"

She laughed and then she gingerly pulled back onto the road. "Wow. This is the coolest thing that's ever happened to us. My best friend is the daughter of the Berber Coffee guy. And my best friend's mother *had sex* with the Berber Coffee guy!"

The fact that she said I was her best friend made me flush with joy. "You'll meet him soon enough," I said. "We can go down there together. There was plenty of room in the house."

"I can't believe your mother never recognized him on TV. I mean, the guy is unforgettable!"

"Well, he was young. It was dark. They were both drunk."

"Can you imagine having sex with the Berber Coffee guy and being too drunk to remember it?"

"What I remember right now is that he's *my dad,* so . . . it's sort of nauseating and icky to think of him having sex at all."

Raquel laughed. "We have to celebrate that you met your Berber Coffee dad! Blue Light?"

"Sure."

"I'm buying! This is the most exciting day of my life!"

"It's not, but I love that you're saying that." I was excited, happy, but nervous. We were officially *best friends* so there was no question I was going to tell her about Jerome. And AIDS. The virus seemed like a heavy, not-fun secret to dump on someone.

When we got to Union Street, we each tapped Air Freshener Jesus and then sang the prayer. I tried to harmonize but couldn't quite find the notes. Jerome and AIDS were weighing on me. After twenty-five minutes, when we were about to give up and go home, a spot opened a couple doors away from Blue Light.

"HOSANNA!" Raquel said. "Air Freshener Jesus always pulls through!"

The bar was oddly calm; it lacked the electric-sexual energy that usually pulsed between bodies. The band was taking a break and so music played over the sound system. Even that was low-energy.

Raquel and I climbed onto the high stools. She ordered two whiskey sours without asking me what I wanted. I took a sip and then jerked back my head.

"Whoa. That's strong."

Raquel tasted her own drink and then picked up my drink and sipped. "Nope. That's how they taste."

"Okay." I took another sip.

"To meeting your totally hot Berber Coffee dad!" Raquel said, and she raised her drink.

"To my dad." I clinked glasses with her and then felt a strange discomfort, like my organs would burst out of my body if I didn't soon get out the whole story. "There's something else I have to tell you about my dad. But it's a secret. You can't tell a soul."

Raquel took a sip of her drink but held the glass against her mouth, like a baby's pacifier. Her eyes popped out in a *tell me quick* way.

"My dad's gay and he lives with his boyfriend, Jerome." I took a too-huge gulp. Drano burning down my throat.

Raquel slammed her glass on the bar. "NO! WOW! HONESTLY? SERIOUSLY?! NO!"

"I swear."

Raquel hugged me. "That is hilarious but so, so cool!"

I laughed with relief. "Yeah, it's—"

"Wait!" Raquel picked up her drink and took another sip. "Does your mom know he's gay? Was he always gay? OH MY GOD, THE BERBER COFFEE GUY IS GAY!" Raquel was screaming, though no one was close enough to hear.

I grabbed her forearm and pulled her toward me. "SHHH! I was serious about this being a secret! You can't tell *a soul*!"

"This is San Francisco! Half the population is gay!"

I leaned in close to her ear and said, firmly, "The people in Hollywood won't hire him if they know he's gay."

"Now *that* sucks!" Raquel pulled away from my grip, chugged her drink, and then placed the empty glass on the bar toward the bartender, whose back was to us.

"It totally sucks," I said.

Raquel hiccupped and then took a sip of my drink. She leaned in close to me and half whispered, "People would go absolutely crazy if they knew the sexiest and most handsome man in America was gay."

"Yeah, they would . . ." I nervously took a sip of my drink. "Also. Jerome, his boyfriend, has—"

Raquel looked at me intensely. Her brow furrowed like folded cake batter. She took a long, cool sip from my whiskey sour.

"Jerome has AIDS."

Raquel almost choked. She banged the glass down so hard, the drink sloshed out. "Stop! You're joking now."

"No. It's so sad."

She looked at my drink on the counter. Then she looked at me and said, "Oh my God, I've been sipping from your glass! What if you got it from Jerome?!"

My stomach dropped. I felt deflated. "Raquel," I said.

"Seriously. Did you taste food off his fork? Like, how much did you interact?" She pushed the drink toward me with the back of her hand.

"My dad shares a bed with him and he doesn't have it. They've consulted with all the experts and you can't get it from spit or tears. I didn't get it. We didn't share blood."

"And you didn't take in his semen."

"Yeah. I figured that one didn't need to be pointed out."

"No, sorry, *oh my God,* I didn't mean it like that. I was listing in my mind the ways you can *actually* get it. I'm so sorry. But I mean, AIDS is the worst thing that could happen to someone—like *a hundred percent* of the people die."

"Yes. It's very scary, and it's sad that Jerome has it. But I didn't get it from him, Raquel. I went over all this with my dad."

Raquel scooted her barstool back a bit. "I'm sorry. Will you be hurt if I call my doctor on Monday to check the *very* latest news about transmission?"

"Yeah, call your doctor." I did feel hurt. But I should have forgiven her right away. After all, I'd had those very same, if not worse, thoughts.

"Okay. I'm sorry again. I mean, I'm sorry your dad's boyfriend has AIDS. That's awful and scary and sad."

"It is." I felt sad for my dad and Jerome and for every single person in the world who had AIDS.

Raquel said, "I don't think you should tell anyone. You know. I mean, people are freaking out. You could lose your job or something."

Losing my job at the Hardware Depot was not on my list of worries. "Raquel, remember, we can't tell people my dad is gay because of the Berber Coffee job, so . . ."

"Yeah, right. Sorry. I'm so anxious about those sips! You know they've been firing gay men who have AIDS. Like, no one wants to work closely with them."

"That's terrible." I stared down at my glass. I didn't want the drink and I didn't want to be in Blue Light.

Neither of us spoke. The band started up again. It didn't make me want to move my body or sing. It made me want to hide someplace dark and small, like under a stairwell.

**When we got** home, Raquel dropped onto the couch and clicked on the TV.

I sat on the other end of the couch and stared at the TV without following what was happening.

"Are you going to tell your mom he's gay?" Raquel asked.

"I dunno . . . It might make her feel good to know that my dad didn't reject her for some other woman. But Howard can never keep a secret and she can't seem to keep anything from Howard. Once they've each had a drink, it's like they've uncapped their brains and anyone who wants to poke around is welcome."

"Yeah." Raquel's face was aimed at the TV, but I didn't think she was watching.

"At least they don't have AIDS, so there's no reason to shun them." As soon as I said that, I wished I could un-say it. My words made me feel mean and small-minded.

Raquel shrugged. I couldn't take the silence between us, so I got up and went to bed.

On Sunday, when I woke up, Raquel was gone. A note on the counter said she was spending the day with Paul.

I called my mother and forced excitement in my voice when I asked if she wanted me to come over to tell her about my dad. I wanted to give her the Berber Coffee guy news in person.

"Oh, honey, I've gotta clean and rebind Howard's nub today. It's not a good time."

"It takes all day?"

"Sweetheart, it's a busy day."

I stared at the phone after we hung up. Even though I now had a dad, I'd never felt lonelier.

**Raquel didn't come** home that night. By Monday morning, I was eager to get to the Depot and see human eyes. I saw loads of them but didn't see my mother's until I met up with her in the employee lounge where we took our two p.m. lunch break together.

"So?" my mother said. "What was he like in person?"

"He was great. You'd like him." I handed my mother the lunch bag I'd packed for the two of us. You'd think that now that we were face-to-face, I'd blurt out that he was the Berber Coffee guy. But something held me back. I guess I worried that his status as the most handsome man in America (Asia and Europe and South America, too!) would make him even more threatening to her sense of safety with me.

"This is lunch?" My mother dangled a baggie filled with sliced apples close to her face as if she were reading small print. Also in the lunch bag were cheddar cubes, Cornnuts, and a box of raisins.

"Yeah. Sorry." With Raquel MIA, I could barely focus on packing a lunch.

"Did your dad have a nice house?"

"It was beautiful. Will you go down there with me next time I visit?"

My mother shrugged and ripped open the Cornnuts. "Did you wear your I. Magnin clothes when you visited him?"

So far I'd shown up to every shift at the Hardware Depot in either a skirt and blouse or my Sgt. Pepper dress. Today I was wearing the pencil skirt, blouse, and the well-shined pumps. "No, I wore jeans."

"So you only go *fancy* for work?"

"Mom, are you mad at me?"

"I'm teasing you!" She faked a smile and shoved an apple slice into her mouth.

"Okay, well, whatever. But listen, my dad's not exactly the advertising executive he had led me to believe." It seemed I'd better get this news over with so we could move on and resume our normal relationship.

My mother gave a fake laugh that sounded like the word *HA*. "What? Is he one of those guys who stands on scaffolding and mops up billboards so it's *not truly* but sort of working in advertising?"

I liked the image. "Mom, this is going to sound insane, especially because you don't even remember what my dad looks like, but he's the Berber Coffee guy."

Mom fisted a pile of Cornnuts into her mouth. "That'd be as funny as him being a billboard mopper."

"I'm serious."

Regina from the kitchen department sat near us. She opened an enormous lunch pail that reminded me of the one Fred Flintstone carries. When she pulled out a giant chicken leg, it seemed highly appropriate "I like your outfit," she said to me, and then she bit into the leg.

"Zippy met her dad last Saturday for the first time." My mother tossed in another handful of Cornnuts. "She's trying to tell me he's the Berber Coffee guy."

Regina pulled the leg away from her mouth and tilted her head. "You do look a lot like the Berber Coffee guy," she said.

"Everyone always said she looked like me," my mother said.

"Nah." Regina took another bite, chewed, swallowed, and then said, "If I had to put money on it, I'd bet she was the kid of the Berber Coffee guy before I'd say she was yours."

My mother leaned forward and examined me. "You're kidding, right?"

A smile burst across my face. "I'm not kidding, Mom. My dad is the Berber Coffee guy."

My mother was silent. She looked stunned. And then she sat up straight and said, "I can't believe I made a baby with the Berber Coffee guy!"

Regina was now holding a chicken breast. I wanted to peer into her pail and see how much meat it held. "The Berber Coffee guy is *honestly* your dad?"

"Yeah." I ate a handful of Cornnuts, trying to play it cool.

"Marie," Regina said. "How could you have made love with the Berber Coffee guy and not known it?!"

"It was nineteen years ago!" my mom said. "He wasn't the Berber Coffee guy then! And he disappeared from our lives until now!"

"Nineteen years isn't much. I've had these shoes for nineteen years." Regina kicked out a flat-bottomed, lace-tied shoe that looked like it was made of rubber.

"He was only nineteen or twenty then. A kid!" My mother was smiling real big; she looked like she was on the verge of laughing.

"Okay, so? What was it like?" Regina ripped off a strip of breast with her teeth and leaned over her pail.

"I remember we laughed a lot," my mother said. "And I remember that he was cute!"

A woman named Francis who worked in electric came in and sat beside Regina. She was holding a bag of Frito-Lay potato chips.

"You'll never guess what," Regina said to Francis.

"What?" Francis opened the bag by pulling apart the two sides.

"Marie made love to the Berber Coffee guy."

"Seriously?! You cheated on Howard?! Where'd you meet the Berber Coffee guy?!"

"It was nineteen years ago, before Howard!" my mother said.

Francis stared at my mother and then stared at me. "Is he your dad, 'cause you look like him," she said, and then she put a fistful of chips into her mouth.

"That's what I said!" Regina pumped a chicken-holding fist in the air.

My mother grinned. Maybe there was something there to be proud of. Maybe she liked being the mother of the daughter of the Berber Coffee guy.

**"Hey, Mom," I** said when we were walking back to our stations.

"Yup?" My mom turned and looked at me. She hadn't stopped smiling since Regina and Francis had made such a fuss over her having made love to my father.

"I'm going to tell you a secret, but you can't even tell Howard, because he's on painkillers all the time and he blurts out any old thing."

"You think I can't keep a secret?"

"Yeah, you haven't been so good at secrets in the past. But this is one you *truly* must keep."

"Fine. What?" My mother crossed her arms and turned to face me. We were in the tile aisle with slanted shelves displaying everything from fake marble made of painted clay to Italian marble as shiny and reflective as the walls of the I. Magnin elevator.

"My dad is gay, but no one can know or he'll lose his job. And he has a boyfriend named Jerome who has AIDS."

My mother was silent for a minute, as if her brain had to translate what I'd said into a more comprehensible language. Then she said, "And your dad doesn't have AIDS?"

"No, he didn't get it."

My mother put out her arms and pulled me in for a hug. "I'm sorry, sweetie. I'm sorry your dad has to deal with that. That's worse than having a husband who cut off his own fingers."

"Yeah, it really is."

My mom pulled away from the hug and said in a half whisper, "It's so funny to think that the Berber Coffee guy is gay."

"Right?"

"Probably not the only gay man I ever had sex with—"

"I don't need to know about that, Mom."

"But AIDS . . ." My mother shook her head and exhaled.

"Worse than losing fingers," I said.

"Are you going to move down there and help your dad take care of him?" The worry lines in the center of my mother's brow made the number 11.

"No . . . I don't think so."

We walked a little farther down the aisle, in silence. Before we each veered off to our own area, my mother grabbed my hand.

"Hey, honey—"

"Yeah?"

"No matter what happens with your dad and his boyfriend, no matter how hard or intense it might get, I've always got you, okay? AIDS is some heavy stuff for a nineteen-year-old girl to deal with, so don't try to go it alone." My mom squeezed my hand once.

"Thanks, Mom," I said. "You're a really good mom. I mean, I'm glad I never had to wonder who you were or where you were."

"I'm right here," she said. "I'm never leaving."

I felt as safe and loved as I imagined Raquel did with the phone calls from her dad, or Sorority Girl with the credit card from hers. Never leaving counted for a lot.

**That day after** work, I went into my room, got into bed, and pulled the curtains shut. The good news, the bad news, and the weirdness with Raquel was making me wobbly. I was cutting wood at the Hardware Depot, wearing clothes like an I. Magnin girl, the child of someone who lived above a liquor store with a Q-tip-handed man, and the child of the Berber Coffee guy. I felt like a Picasso painting that had been pushed even further out of alignment.

The front door to the apartment opened and shut. Raquel called out my name.

"Here," I said, but I didn't shout and she couldn't have heard me.

"ZIPPY?"

I heard Raquel's footfalls as she went to the kitchen and played the messages on the answering machine. I could tell from the grumbly hum that one message was from my dad.

"Zippy! Where are you?!" Raquel knocked and then opened my door in one motion.

"Hey," I said.

"Are you sick?"

"You mean do I have AIDS?" I wanted to cry.

Raquel dropped her head to one side. "I talked to my doctor. He said there was no way you could have gotten it and that I should go home and apologize."

"What did you say to that?"

"I said okay."

"Oh."

Raquel took a running start and then leapt onto my bed, pulled down the covers, and got in beside me. "I'm sorry."

I rolled away from her at first. Then, I realized that I wanted nothing more than this to be over, so I rolled back and said, "Thanks."

"C'mon." Raquel sat up and pulled down the bedspread. "I'm taking us out to dinner. 'Cause we do it RIGHT on eating days!"

"Chapter . . . thirteen?"

"Exactly. Chapter thirteen: 'Doing It Right on Eating Days.'"

# Chapter 13

**The following Thursday,** Raquel and I were, along with most of America, watching *The Cosby Show*. The Day-Timers were on the coffee table. We were waiting until *Cosby* was over to start writing.

"Hasn't he worn that Howard University sweatshirt before?" I reached into my hair and pulled out a curled shaving of wood. I was so used to sawdust that I could no longer smell it, though I could always feel it. Whenever Raquel visited me in my bedroom, where she liked to lie on my bed, she would brush off my pillow to eliminate the wood dust that had fallen from my hair.

"I think he wears that one often." Raquel moved her feet from the coffee table to my lap. Her head was on one end cushion. She played with the red plastic heart dangling from a chain around her neck. Paul had given it to her and she didn't like it—she'd wanted pearls—but she wore it anyway.

"How great would it be to have a dad like that?"

"Uh, Zippy. You have the Berber Coffee guy for a dad. I think that's better than Cosby."

"Yeah, you're right. I guess I want a husband like him."

Raquel looked over at me. "I don't know . . . The sweaters are awful."

"Yeah, the sweaters are bad. But he's funny, he's interested in his kids, he helps everyone out. He's faithful to his wife."

"Who knows what the real Cosby is like?" Raquel said. "For all we know he's some perv who's hitting on Lisa Bonet when the cameras stop rolling."

"No way!" I said. "Bill Cosby would *never* be a perv!"

Raquel gave a knowing shrug. The phone rang and we both turned our heads and looked at it on the kitchen counter.

"Paul?" I asked. He often worked late and usually called Raquel around this time.

Raquel hoisted herself off the couch and went to the phone. She answered with her breathy Marilyn-like hello. And then she pulled away the receiver, held it against her chest so the caller couldn't hear, and whisper-yelled, "It's some woman-man for you. Old smoker rasp."

It was Miss Dani. "Zip!" she said.

"Hey!" I glanced at the clock. It was eight thirty. The store closed at nine p.m. on Thursdays. Miss Dani was probably hiding in her office waiting for the register count-out.

"Can you come in and see me tomorrow?"

"Sure. Can I come on my lunch break from Hardware Depot?"

"Absolutely."

"Are you going to try to convince me to come back?!" I asked before I could stop myself. My face instantly flushed.

"The position's gone. Miss Kitty put her niece in your place. Some snot-nosed girl from Encino who graduated from Stanford. She thinks that a degree in . . . marketing or something absurd like that makes her heir to Kitty's position."

"Ooooh, Miss Yolanda must despise her!"

"She does. Even Miss Lena hides out in the fitting rooms to get away from her."

"Wow . . . so is the purpose of my visit to say hello?"

"Nah, I want to talk to you about a couple things, including those dumbass complaint cards that weren't written by customers after all. I'll tell you about it when I see you tomorrow," Miss Dani said, and she rushed off the phone.

When I returned to Raquel on the couch and *Cosby* on the TV, I felt light and feathery. It was wonderful to know that the complaints had been fabricated and I hadn't actually failed at selling dresses.

"Who do you think wrote them?" Raquel asked, when there was a commercial break.

"Ugh, I'm not sure. But it's awful to think that someone dislikes me *that* much."

"Don't think about it until you see Miss Dani," Raquel said, and she readjusted her body so her feet were on my lap again.

**The next day** I wore my pencil skirt and a soft cashmere sweater Raquel's mother had given her. It was baby blue and Raquel, who looked stunning in everything, claimed she didn't look good in baby blue. I'd never owned cashmere and couldn't help but stroke my sides whenever my hands were free.

At lunchtime, I darted into the employee lounge to tell my mother I wouldn't be joining her.

"Zippy, wait'll you see what I brought!" My mother dropped onto the soiled couch and opened a brown grocery bag. It was her day to bring lunch.

"I've got to run an errand," I said. "Save it for me and I'll eat it tomorrow." Raquel was seeing Paul the next day. That meant we both could eat.

"But it won't last until tomorrow! Howard made it. He sliced up these giant dill pickles and then laid them across cream cheese and mustard on bagels."

I paused as my brain ran through that image: Howard with his giant Q-tip hand opening bagels with a serrated knife, fileting pickles, spreading on cream cheese, and then adding mustard. "I dunno, Mom. Not quite my thing."

"He was so proud of this creation! I took a bite already, and I hafta tell you, the man is right. It's a tasty combo!"

"I've got to run out, Mom. Give it to someone else. I'll see you at the end of the day." I waved and left before my mother could say another word.

The number 11 bus was pulling away the second I got to the stop. I ran after it for half a block, but it was hard to move quickly in my pumps. As I was walking to the next bus stop, the cable car approached. I looked for the easy opening and then climbed on as it slowed. Before it turned toward the water, I hopped off and walked the next few blocks to I. Magnin.

It was strange to enter through the shoppers' entrance. There was no time to chat with anyone, so I kept my head down and quickly skirted between crowds of customers while avoiding the eyes of Mimi in particular, who I could see was busy putting makeup on a woman who looked so puckered and angry, I wasn't sure how much of a difference could be made. (I'd had that same thought often as I watched women with "done" hair adjust their "do" in the mirrors at I. Magnin. The difference between their before and after looks was imperceptible, making the act of fixing their hair utterly pointless.)

When I got off the elevator, I bowed my head again, as I didn't want to be seen by the Fifth-Floor Dresses ladies. I could hear Miss Yolanda down her fitting room corridor yelling at a customer. A floater in Miss Liaskis's area caught my eye (Miss Liaskis always had Friday off). And I felt one of the Braughns (I didn't look up to see if it was L or R) staring at me. There was a shield of customers between me and Miss Lena, Miss Lee, and Miss Karen.

I knocked on Miss Dani's office door.

"Yup!" Miss Dani yelled from the other side.

I opened the door and went in.

"Zip!" She stood and gave me a hug. "Have a seat."

I moved a pile of knit dresses off the wooden school chair and onto the shelf behind Miss Dani so I could sit.

"How is everything here?" I asked.

"The same. Good and bad. Do you miss it?"

"Tons," I said. "So much."

"Ah, we all miss you," Miss Dani said.

After an awkward silence I said, "So, you wanted to discuss the complaint cards?"

"Oh, that." Miss Dani waved her hand. "Do you care?"

"Isn't that why you called me in?"

"Not exactly. But you should know that because of what happened to you, the store canceled the complaint card program. A lot of crazy, jealous women were writing up mean things about people they didn't like."

"How did you figure it out?"

"I looked up your sales on the computer. You weren't selling the stuff they were complaining about on the days you got the complaints. And a couple complaints were dated for days you weren't even here. It was all bull-malarkey."

"Bull-malarkey." The word alone made me miss Miss Dani. "And the person who created that bull-malarkey . . ." I opened my palms like I was waiting for a platter.

"Oh. The Braughns."

"Really?!" It felt like a man-sized fist had just landed hard in my stomach. "That's so awful. Wow, I guess *Canadians* are even better at being clandestinely malicious."

Miss Dani did an airy snort. "Yeah. Someone heard them talking in the lunchroom and eventually the story made it to me. I'm certain they did it, but unless we fingerprint the cards, there's no hard evidence, so . . ." Miss Dani shrugged.

"So they'll be working here forever."

Miss Dani nodded. Then she sat up straighter and said, "Hey, Zip. Do you know which line sells the most on this floor?"

"Yeah. The Donna Karan."

"Do you know what percentage knits were up from last year?"

"Well, yeah," I said. "Because remember that I was surprised you were marking them down when they seemed to be selling so well. You told me then that they were up eighteen percent."

"What line do you think won't be around in five years?"

"These are fun questions," I said. I liked thinking about this stuff. "My guess is the Jessica McClintock won't last the way other designers do. It's too singular—nothing changes except the print on the fabric. It's like a Reese's Peanut Butter Cup. You get the exact same thing no matter what year it is."

Miss Dani smiled so hard, her head rocked back. She rolled closer to her desk and quickly scribbled something on a Post-it note. She ripped off the note and handed it to me. "Go to the tenth floor right now. I'm calling up there and telling them you're on your way."

"Is this about the Braughns?"

"No. You have an interview to be a buyer in training."

I looked down at the Post-it note. It had the name Melody Clarkson written on it. "What do you mean?"

"You'd train to be a buyer. You start out as an assistant; it's grunt work, but in about two or three years you'd be buying, traveling—the whole shebang."

"No! Yeah?! Really?!" I knew my teeth were showing and my smile was taking over half my face.

"Would you like that?"

"Of course! I'd love it! I mean, who would ever think of *me* as a buyer?" I was smiling, but it was a lip quiver away from crying.

"I think anyone who saw how you worked in this store would think of you as a buyer. Even though you were rotating two outfits—"

"Three. And then four."

"Okay, three and then four. But you know what, Zip?"

"No, what?" I was still beaming.

"They were three perfect outfits. They were the exact right things to wear. You nailed it."

"Did I?"

"Yeah. And you can nail it again. Go upstairs and get that job. If you want it."

"Okay! I will. I want it. I'm choosing it!" I stood and Miss Dani stood too. She hugged me and I hugged her back so hard, I embarrassed myself.

**Miss Yolanda caught** me as I was waiting for the elevator. "You back?"

"No. I mean, I wish I were." I hadn't stopped smiling since I'd left Miss Dani's office.

Miss Yolanda looked at me closely, as if she were suspicious of my joy. "It was those Braughns, you know." She nodded toward their station, where I could see Miss Braughn R standing at the register, staring into space.

"Yeah, I heard." How strange that I now didn't care. The complaint cards felt so far in the past that they were inconsequential.

"The new girl is torturing them. She thinks they should be friends because they look *faaaancy* and New Girl thinks she's fancy too." Miss Yolanda moved the candy ball to the other cheek. "It's like watching a dog lick a stone thinking it will eventually respond."

"Funny." I looked past the Braughns toward Miss Lena's station. I missed her. I knew I should see her, but I had to get upstairs and then I had to get back to work. I made a vow right then that I would visit her soon.

The elevator doors opened, and Miss Yolanda glanced at the *up* triangle as I stepped in. She tilted her head, as if she were trying to figure out where I was going. Then, by the look in her eyes, I had a feeling she knew exactly where I was going. After all, there was nothing about the goings-on in the store that eluded her.

"See ya!" I said before the doors shut.

"Bonne chance," she said, and I swear I detected a thin smile.

**Melody Clarkson had** dark brown hair that looked like silk and a face that was a perfect circle. She wore a white suit and had on so many gold chains, I wasn't sure if there was a blouse beneath the suit jacket. The time with her went so quickly, I felt airy and disoriented when I finally stood. We had talked about dresses, sales, the San Francisco Giants (she was a fan and had a ball cap on her desk), and the twins who regularly shopped in the store.

"Do you have another hour?" she asked. "I want you to talk to Paige right now."

"Sure!" I hadn't realized I'd been there an hour until she'd used the word *another*. And I had no idea who Paige was.

"Great. Hold on a sec." Melody picked up her phone and then said, "I've got Zippy here and I think you should talk to her now, if possible." She said a couple of *uh-huh*s and then hung up and said, "She's waiting for you."

"Excellent! Who is she?" My knees were shaky, but I knew I wouldn't fall.

"Paige Allouche. The merchandise manager. The boss of all the buyers."

"Oh wow. Yes, I'd love to talk to her!" I wondered who Melody Clarkson was exactly if Paige was the boss of the buyers.

"Two doors over. She looks like me. People get us mixed up." She smiled and shrugged.

"Do you mind if I make a phone call first? I have another job now and I want to make sure I'm covered."

"Of course! Dial nine to get an outside number. I'm going to grab myself some lunch and leave you be." Melody waved her hand toward the phone and left.

I went to the side of the desk and pushed nine with a quivering finger. And then I stared at the phone until I decided who I'd call.

Howard answered on the first ring.

"Hey," I said.

"Ah, milady calls in the middle of thy workday!" Howard said.

"Howard, I need you to go to the Depot and cover for me."

"Ah, but mine fingerless hand doth not do what the Lord intended it to do!" I imagined him punching the air with his giant Q-tip nub.

"It doth, Howard. You made a sandwich today. You carved pickles and bagels. Most people with all their fingers can't cut a bagel as well as you."

"Mi lovely lady! I no longer am employed thusly!"

"Howard, I'm making a choice here. I'm choosing to not go back today. I'm choosing to have you replace me, as I replaced you."

There was silence for a minute. And then he dropped the Elizabethan accent and said, "I was about to meet my friends at the Buena Vista."

"I need a career. You and my mother need money. The Buena Vista will be there after work. I'm at an interview now."

More silence and then: "Where?"

I didn't want to tell him. To say it might curse it or make it disappear. "Howard, I promise you, I've never wanted anything more than this job I'm about to interview for. Please go cover for me."

"Ah fine! As milady wishes!"

"Great. Thank you, Howard." I hung up and then called Jeff at the Hardware Depot to apologize for being gone so long and to tell him Howard would be replacing me from then on out.

"Thank God," Jeff said.

"I guess I wasn't your ideal woodcutter."

"Nope," Jeff said. "Even one-handed Howard will be an improvement over you."

Before I left Melody Clarkson's office, I paused at the gold-framed mirror near the door. My hair looked fine: no sawdust or wood shavings. My face was clean and smooth. My eyes were bright. And my father's smile was taking up the lower third of my face like a lipped harmonica with teeth.

**Paige Allouche was** a little cooler and more detached than Melody Clarkson. She did, however, talk with me for ninety minutes. When we finally stood up, she stuck out her hand and said, "You'll be hearing from someone soon. Monday or Tuesday at the latest."

It took me a second to find my voice. "I hope I'll be seeing you again."

Paige Allouche nodded and thanked me again for my time.

**On my way** out, the elevator stopped on Designer Dresses and Miss Meredith got on. She looked at me. "Hello," she said. "Fifth?"

"No," I said, flustered. "First floor. Front door."

"Okey-dokey," she said, and she pushed the button and down we went.

# Chapter 14

**Raquel and Paul** were making out on the couch when I entered the apartment. They both bolted upright and mumbled simultaneously as they straightened their disheveled clothes.

"You're home so early," I said.

"It's Friday," Raquel said, "and . . . I don't know. I thought, I work sixty or seventy hours a week; maybe I should say to hell with it all and go home."

"She needs to live a little!" Paul said in that charming Irish accent.

Raquel scooted over and I dropped onto the couch beside them.

"What?" Raquel said.

"What what?"

"Your face. What's going on? Did you quit the Depot?"

"I did." Now I grinned.

"Damn! Good for you! Did you find a new job?"

"I interviewed for one today."

"Where?!" Raquel sat up straighter. She grabbed my thigh.

"I. Magnin. I interviewed to be a buyer in training. And I was at the interview so long that I called the Hardware Depot in the middle of it and quit."

Raquel did a silent scream. She jumped up and then hugged me. Next, she rushed into the kitchen and soon returned with an open bottle of wine and three glasses.

"To you being the chooser!" Raquel said, and we all toasted.

"But . . ." Paul paused. "They have to choose her, right?"

"Well, yeah, but . . ." Raquel punched Paul in the arm and said, "Don't ruin it!! Zippy, grasshopper," she then said to me. "I'm really serious about what I have to say: you've interviewed to be a *BUYER* at I. Magnin! You can do anything."

"Buyer in training," I said to Raquel.

"Buyer in training," Raquel said. "Now you need to call Just John."

"Yeah!" Paul said. "Call!" The two of them started clapping on beat and chanting, *CALL CALL CALL CALL!*

I took three gulps of wine and then put down the glass and said, "I'm going to do it!" I was feeling bold and full of *something,* though I'm not sure what I would have called that *something. Life*? *Hope*? Maybe it was power. Maybe I had found the power of feeling like I belonged somewhere. The power of having good friends, the power of having a family, the power of not being alone in the world.

I did an exaggerated model's walk to my room to get my Day-Timer. When I returned, I went to the kitchen counter and opened the Day-Timer to the page where I had saved the cocktail napkin with Just John's information.

I picked up the receiver on the phone and then carefully dialed. "It's long-distance, but I don't care!"

"I'll pay. You don't even have a job. YET!" Raquel shouted from the couch.

"I'll pay!" Paul said.

"I'll pay!" I said when a voice both familiar and strange answered the phone. "OH! Is this Just John?"

"Zippy?"

"Yeah, it's me!"

"I can't believe you called!"

"Why not?"

"I dunno. I thought I was only a passing face. Some guy you made out with."

"Was I only a passing face?"

"No. I've been thinking about you ever since. That was a good kiss."

My body felt like a tuning fork that was vibrating after being struck. "Yeah, it was."

"Maybe we should do it again," Just John said.

"Okay. Uh . . ." If I asked him to come to San Francisco, would that be too bold?

"I'll be totally free in a week. I'm a senior at Ann Arbor. But I'm going to law school at Boalt next year. That's why I was in San Francisco when we met. I was visiting the schools who said they'd have a dumbass like me."

"Oh. Wow! My roommate is a lawyer."

"And you?"

"I . . . uh . . . well, I just interviewed for a job I desperately want. But I don't want to jinx it and say anything about it."

"Okay," Just John said. "I won't jinx it by asking questions."

"And I quit my job at a hardware store today. I was cutting wood."

"You were cutting wood? Like, in the lumber department?"

I wondered if I'd blown it. "Yeah . . . uh . . . I mean—"

"Amazing!" Just John said. "I would have bought wood, then asked you to cut it, bought more, asked you to cut it again, and then stored it all in my garage only to have an excuse to observe you operating a power tool."

I wondered if he could sense my face-engulfing smile. "Do you have a garage?"

"No, I live in an apartment. But in the fantasy where you cut wood for me, I have a garage."

"In your fantasy where I cut wood for you," I said, "I don't work at the hardware store and I never operate a miter saw, a jigsaw, a band saw—"

"A chain saw?" Just John asked.

"No saws!" I said, and then I glanced over at Raquel and Paul on the couch and felt guilty for staying on a long-distance call for so long.

"When I visit you next week," Just John said, "we'll make *saw* the verboten word."

"Deal," I said.

"Deal," he said.

"Hey, what's your middle name?" I asked.

"It's a ridiculous middle name."

"More ridiculous than *Just* as a first name?"

He laughed. "No, equally. It's Regis."

"Regis," I repeated. "That's not awful."

"What's yours?"

"Jane."

"Zippy Jane. I love that. But I especially love the Zippy part."

"You're kind." I was glad he couldn't see me blushing.

"No, you're kind."

I didn't know how to respond, so I tried to wrap it up. "Well, I should go. So, uh, I'll be seeing you soon, Mr. Just John Regis . . . Something or Other."

"Reilly. Just John Regis Reilly." There was something airy about his voice that let me know he was smiling. "And you are Zippy Jane Something or Other."

"Zippy Jane Tremblay."

"So, Zippy Jane Tremblay, what days are you free next week?"

"Let me look in my Day-Timer." I flipped to the calendar and glanced at next week. "Looks like all of them."

"Excellent. You'll probably be working during the day at that new job I can't jinx, so keep your nights open."

"Done." I wrote *BOOKED* on my Day-Timer, as if he could see it.

"I'll call you as soon as I know my exact schedule."

"Okay. Cool!" Ugh. *Cool* sounded like the most uncool thing to say.

"Yeah, cool," Just John Regis Reilly said. And it sounded really cool.

**The following Tuesday,** I dressed in the Sgt. Pepper dress and took the bus to I. Magnin. I entered through the customer door and dashed straight to the escalators, avoiding Mimi and anyone else who might want to chat. I wanted to get upstairs to see Miss Lena; I'd visit Mimi on my way out.

The fifth floor was like a bowling alley. Miss Lee and Miss Karen looked at me as I stepped off. I waved; Miss Lee waved back and Miss Karen nodded. Miss Liaskis was actually helping a customer, Miss Braughn L was playing statue, and Miss Yolanda was off the floor—probably back in the dressing rooms with one or two customers. The new girl was standing at the register looking as bored as someone who was waiting in a very, very long line. She tilted her head as I approached.

"Can I, like, help you?" she asked in Valley Girl upspeak.

"Is Miss Lena around?"

She shrugged and rolled her eyes. "She's, like, on her break and you're, like, the second person who's come by looking for her? I can help you? Like—"

"I'll wait for her." I wandered the area and examined the new dresses that had come in since I'd left. There were some green jersey knits, to the knee, that probably wouldn't move. They were too librarian-looking, too old-fashioned. But the wrap dress with the blue-and-green peacock swirl, well, that was very 1985!

I was looking at the price when I heard Miss Lena say, "OH! Jesus has blessed us today!" She rushed to me and we hugged. Then she hooked her arm in mine and we walked to the register counter so she could stash her purse.

"Uh, like, I'll take my break now?" the new girl said.

"Go ahead, dear, take your time," Miss Lena said. "This is Miss Zippy, who used to work here!"

"Whatever," the girl said, and she walked away.

Miss Lena was pursing her lips, trying not to laugh, as was I. "Her heart's not in it," Miss Lena said. "Now, you have to tell me everything about the hardware store, and have you been talking to your father? Oh, and we must play now before Miss Pammy gets back!" Miss Lena opened the drawer and pulled out all the paper dolls. She shuffled through them, found Jesus, and set him up on the register keyboard. Then, as usual, she randomly dealt out a few to each of us and lined up the remainder along the counter so we could pull them in when needed.

"I wore my I. Magnin outfits every day while I cut wood." I put my palms up and did a little curtsy as if to show off my dress.

Miss Lena grinned, and then she picked up the Dad doll and said, "My daughter, my dear! Don't you have to wear an apron or coveralls at the Hardware Depot?"

I shook my head. "Wait!" I said. "Let's use the Berber Coffee guy for my dad. I met my dad and . . ." I picked up the proper doll and handed it to Miss Lena.

"You met him!" Miss Lena clapped and jumped up. "Jesus blessed you with a father you now know in person!"

"Yeah, he was nice."

"Did he look like the Berber Coffee guy?"

"He did. But I want to tell you the details about that later. Okay?" It seemed like it might be a longer conversation, something to discuss over lunch.

"Okay," Miss Lena said, holding the Berber Coffee guy. She spoke in the grumbly voice she remembered from my father calling on the phone. "Now tell me about the woodcutting job."

I reached into Miss Lena's pile of dolls, picked up myself, and said, "Dad! I wore the Hardware Depot apron *over* my dress and my skirt. People thought I was being snobby, but I wasn't doing it to be snobby. I was doing it because I like these clothes."

Miss Lena teeter-walked the Berber Coffee guy doll toward me. "Oh, daughter! Miss Lena and all of the customers have missed you since you've been gone. But I bet you've made the people at the Hardware Depot very happy!"

I walked the Me doll closer to Berber Dad doll and said, "Dad, I wasn't very good at cutting wood. I don't think I made them happy at all. I think I often made them mad or frustrated."

Miss Lena picked up the Miss Yolanda doll and said in her choppy French accent, "Heck yeah, they were probably FURIOUS that you never changed your outfit!"

We both laughed and then I, the Me doll, said, "But I feel like I'm exactly the person I *want to be* when I'm in my I. Magnin clothes. It makes me happy to wear them."

Miss Lena bounced the Miss Yolanda doll up and down and said, "I don't like happy people! And you know who likes happy people even less?!" She paused and stared at me, the real live me, before bouncing the doll again and saying in Miss Yolanda's voice, "Those stuck-up Braughn sisters!"

I put down my doll and looked at Miss Lena. "You heard that the Braughns wrote all those awful things about me, right?"

Miss Lena said, "Yes, everyone knows. That was truly mean. Even Miss Yolanda talks about how cruel they were. I pray for them now. I pray that they become better people."

I picked up the Miss Dani doll and walked her toward the Miss Yolanda doll, which was still in Miss Lena's hand. "Have you heard the latest news about Zip?"

Miss Lena said in Miss Yolanda's voice, "What news?! If there's news, announce it quickly! I don't have time for these meetings!"

I jumped the Miss Dani doll up and down on the counter and said, "Meeting! Meeting now! Meeting!"

Miss Lena and I grabbed all the dolls of the women on Fifth-Floor Dresses and arranged them in a semicircle around Miss Dani. "So—"

"Dahling, I don't have time for this," Miss Lena said in the Eva Gabor voice as she lifted the Miss Braughn L doll.

"But I want to tell you—" I said in Miss Dani's voice with the Miss Dani doll.

"Hurry up! I need another candy ball!" Miss Lena said in Miss Yolanda's voice.

I laughed and wiped my eyes. Then I said in Miss Dani's voice, "It's very important you know—"

Miss Lena picked up the Miss Karen doll and said, "Hmph," then she picked up the Miss Lee doll and said, "Speak!" Next she picked up the Miss Liaskis doll and said in a teary, crying voice, "Please let Miss Dani say what she has to say! I want to go home to Mr. Liaskis, whom I love so much and who loves me in the color red!"

I jumped the Miss Dani doll up and down and said, "Miss Zippy interviewed to be a buyer in training here, and guess what?"

Miss Lena's eyes widened. She picked up the Miss Lena doll and said in her own voice, "What? Tell us what happened?"

I bumped the Miss Dani doll to the Miss Lena doll and said, "Okay, so, here's what happened: Zip got the job. They called her this morning and she starts next Monday. She'll be upstairs, on the tenth floor."

Miss Lena placed the doll on the counter. She picked up my hands and her eyes teared up. "Oh, Zippy! You got a job as a buyer in training?"

I nodded and my eyes teared up too. Miss Lena took me in her arms and held me. "I am so very proud of you."

And then I cried. Only a little. It was so nice to be where I wanted to be. It was like I'd spent my life as a puzzle piece sliding around a huge table with a mishmash of other loose pieces. Maybe I'd even been lost on the floor for a while, kicked into the kitchen and then kicked back again. And now, finally, I'd been picked up—or maybe I'd picked myself up—and I snapped into the exact right place. It felt . . . perfect.

Miss Lena looked up and down the sales floor and then whispered, "I think we need to pray." She swiped the dolls into the supply drawer and then took my hand and led me back to the first and largest fitting room. Miss Lena slipped off her shoes and went to her knees. I kicked off my pumps and then knelt beside her.

"Okay." My palms were pressed together. "Do you think God knew all along that I should be training to be a buyer and that's why I got the job on the sales floor?"

"No, dear. I think you knew all along."

"Really?" I dropped my hands.

"Really."

"Wow." I took a deep breath and lifted my hands again, but my head felt too fuzzy to pray.

Miss Lena and I looked at each other in the mirror, and then she said, "Maybe today instead of praying, we listen."

"To?"

"To God. Let's just close our eyes and listen." Miss Lena's eyes were shut before she'd even finished the sentence.

I watched her for a moment and then I placed my chin onto the blade of my joined fingertips. All I could hear was a roaring static in my brain.

"This is hard," I whispered.

"Breathe and listen."

"Okay. But . . . Miss Lena. I always breathe. That's something I don't have to work on. It's the listening that's hard."

Miss Lena turned her face toward me. "I know, dear. It can be difficult to find your own thoughts when so many people fill you up with their advice and opinions."

I nodded. "Yeah, I get a lot of advice, don't I?"

"It's nice they're trying to help. But, Zippy, sometimes it's best to listen only to yourself. That's how you hear what God is saying."

"So, if I listen to myself—"

"You'll know everything." Miss Lena smiled and then she shut her eyes and bowed her head again.

I pucker-squeezed my face and then relaxed it. In my mind I repeated the word *listen* over and over again. Soon, I could sense something happening deep inside me, like passages were expanding and creating more room. It felt like my lungs were spreading and I was breathing through my skin. I watched the word *listen* drift out of my body. *Listen, listen, listen, listen, list* . . .

I listened. And in the center of that great big hole of silence was me: my feelings and desires—all of it so close I could cup it in my palms.

# Acknowledgments

My heart is full of gratitude for everyone at Mariner Books and HarperCollins. Special thanks to Eliza Rosenberry, who worked so brilliantly on my last book; to Maya Horn, who never fails to deal with a request; and to the behind-the-scenes people: Kelsey Manning, Lisa Glover, Kaitlin Severini, and Elsie Lyons; to the smart, always-working sales team that covers the entire US; and, most of all, to Katherine Nintzel, whose genius touch is like magic on my words. My agent, Gail Hochman, is my fairy godmother and I will always be grateful to her. Bruce Vinocour at CAA makes big things happen and I will always be grateful to him as well. SONY 3000 Pictures has been generously supportive of my work; I'd like to thank Elizabeth Gabler and Erin Siminoff in particular. Enormous thanks to Kim Allouche, Michele Barr, Fran Brennan, Jane DeLury, Lindsay Fleming, Liz Hazen, Boo Lunt, Danny Rosenblatt, Deborah Solomon, Claire Stancer, Tracy Walder, and Tracy Wallace for endless support, advice, and friendship. My family is the greatest fan club a writer could have. Thank you to Bonnie Blau, Sheridan Blau, Cheryl Hogue-Smith, Becca Summers, Satchel Summers, Shiloh Summers, Hannah Downy, Joshua Blau, Alex Suarez, Sonia Blau Siegal, Maddie Tavis, Ilan Rountree, Ella Grossbach, and Zack Kupferberg. I love you all.

Last thing, thank you to I. Magnin, San Francisco, for hiring me a long time ago to work in the Petite Dresses department when I had never bought anything from the store. Thank you to the lifetime salesladies who tolerated me on the floor.

# About the Author

Jessica Anya Blau was born in Boston and raised in Southern California. Her novels have been translated into many different languages and have been featured on the *Today* show, *Good Morning America,* CNN, and NPR, and in *Cosmo, Vanity Fair, Bust, Time Out,* Oprah's Summer Reads, and other national publications. Jessica's short stories and essays have been published in numerous magazines, journals, and anthologies. In addition to writing novels, Jessica works as a ghostwriter, a screenwriter, and a writing professor. She lives in New York.

ABOUT

# MARINER BOOKS

MARINER BOOKS traces its beginnings to 1832 when William Ticknor cofounded the Old Corner Bookstore in Boston, from which he would run the legendary firm Ticknor and Fields, publisher of Ralph Waldo Emerson, Harriet Beecher Stowe, Nathaniel Hawthorne, and Henry David Thoreau. Following Ticknor's death, Henry Oscar Houghton acquired Ticknor and Fields and, in 1880, formed Houghton Mifflin, which later merged with venerable Harcourt Publishing to form Houghton Mifflin Harcourt. HarperCollins purchased HMH's trade publishing business in 2021 and reestablished their storied lists and editorial team under the name Mariner Books.

Uniting the legacies of Houghton Mifflin, Harcourt Brace, and Ticknor and Fields, Mariner Books continues one of the great traditions in American bookselling. Our imprints have introduced an incomparable roster of enduring classics, including Hawthorne's *The Scarlet Letter,* Thoreau's *Walden,* Willa Cather's *O Pioneers!,* Virginia Woolf's *To the Lighthouse,* W.E.B. Du Bois's *Black Reconstruction,* J.R.R. Tolkien's *The Lord of the Rings,* Carson McCullers's *The Heart Is a Lonely Hunter,* Ann Petry's *The Narrows,* George Orwell's *Animal Farm* and *Nineteen Eighty-Four,* Rachel Carson's *Silent Spring,* Margaret Walker's *Jubilee,* Italo Calvino's *Invisible Cities,* Alice Walker's *The Color Purple,* Margaret Atwood's *The Handmaid's Tale,* Tim O'Brien's *The Things They Carried,* Philip Roth's *The Plot Against America,* Jhumpa Lahiri's *Interpreter of Maladies,* and many others. Today Mariner Books remains proudly committed to the craft of fine publishing established nearly two centuries ago at the Old Corner Bookstore.